The Wayward Sisters

KATE HODGES

HODDER &
STOUGHTON

First published in Great Britain in 2023 by Hodder & Stoughton
An Hachette UK company

1

Copyright © Kate Hodges 2023

A CIP catalogue record for this title is available from the British Library

Hardback ISBN 978 1 529 37152 9
Trade Paperback ISBN 978 1 529 37153 6
eBook ISBN 978 1 529 37155 0

Typeset in Plantin Light by Manipal Technologies Limited

Printed and bound in Great Britain by Clays Ltd, Elcograf S.p.A.

Hodder & Stoughton policy is to use papers that are natural, renewable and recyclable products and made from wood grown in sustainable forests. The logging and manufacturing processes are expected to conform to the environmental regulations of the country of origin.

Hodder & Stoughton Ltd
Carmelite House
50 Victoria Embankment
London EC4Y 0DZ

www.hodder.co.uk

For Mum and Sarah.

'By the pricking of my thumbs, something wicked this way comes.'
William Shakespeare, *Macbeth*

Prologue

1761

At 3.01 a.m., on the sixth day of June, 1761, Nancy Lockaby watched the night sky buckle and the stars above her head slowly start to wheel. As she watched through her telescope, her breath stopped. The stars were *dancing*. It was happening, just as predicted. *Oh, please, let them continue*, she thought, transfixed. Against the lens, her eye narrowed.

As her vision swam with reflections of those tiny white lights, her mind raced. This is what she had waited for, had longed all this time to see. Yet those long hours, years of observation, measurements and calculation had ill-prepared her for this magnificent sight.

Head tilted firmly over the telescope, her left hand scribbled notes. Tonight, her habitually neat script was more of a scrawl, but surely in the circumstances, that was forgivable. At least now the figures were committed to paper. The information she had so needed, now entrusted to pen and ink. She pushed back her bright-red curls, and continued to peer through the instrument, the fingers of her right hand on the brass focus dial.

Behind her, even at this dark hour, London glowed. Yet up here, on top of the Greenwich Observatory, a whisper of a breeze leavened the night's sticky heat. This was the spot she loved most in the world. At thirteen, she'd been thrilled to discover the red-bricked building's balustraded roof and, ten years later, still felt a tingle of excitement every time she climbed the stone steps that led to this secret place above the city.

Tonight, the studies and libraries beneath her feet were alive with bluster and busy preparation for the evening's other, long-predicted important astronomical event. But here on the roof, in the still, silent night, she felt as if she were among the dancing stars.

The points of light were moving a little faster now. They seemed to disappear into the breach in the firmament, only to bob back again, balancing on the edge of the vortex, as if that part of the sky was twisting round on itself.

'As if it were truly a Fold,' she murmured. *A Fold.* The words seemed to hang, silvering in the air. She had read them countless times, written in her mother's butterfly script, dotted across the pages of the notebook tucked away safely in the bag at her feet. A notebook bound in buttery emerald leather, outlining mama's observations, thoughts, calculations and predictions, its delicate, flowing lettering left with gaps ready to be filled on the night of the transit of Venus. Tonight.

Eye still fixed to the telescope, Nancy's fingers fumbled across the trestle table next to her, alighting on her sextant. Her hands trembled as she prised it open, glints of moonlight highlighting the words etched in flowing letters on its delicate gold curves: *To my dearest daughter, Keep your eyes heaven-bound.* Swiftly, she moved her eye from the larger telescope to this smaller instrument mounted on a filigree frame, then expertly adjusted its small mirror, sliding the arm that pivoted from its spindle. She reached for her pen, already dipped in ink and wrote a series of numbers and letters.

Coordinates safely scribbled down, she allowed herself to let out the breath she'd been holding. She was giddy; the sight of this wrinkle in the sky was, in equal parts, glorious and petrifying, as if everything she had learned about the heavens had both been turned upside-down and confirmed. There was not a description of any astral phenomenon that came close to matching that which shimmered and flowed before her, so this *must* be the movement in the heavens forecast by her mother.

The stars continued to whirl and spin. Faster, faster. There was something at the whorl's centre, a brightness, peeping through what looked like a tear in the sky. She shook her head in bewilderment and adjusted the focus of the telescope, but no matter how hard she willed it to sharpen further, the view was as clear as it could ever get.

Without warning, the tear seemed to open, to part like a wound in the instant before blood starts to flow. Then lights, shining. Beams across the sky, almost solid in their brightness. Gold, yellow fingers spilling into the heavens. She tore her gaze from the telescope, her hand over her mouth. The beams were, remarkably, faintly visible to the naked eye. For a brief moment she considered running down to Dr Maskliss, sat below in the Octagon Room.

However, something kept her from crying out. Out here, under the night sky, in the still, warm summer air, this crystalline moment was hers alone. Perfect. Spots of pink appeared on her pale cheeks, and again, she put her eye to the telescope. It was terrifyingly beautiful. She drank in the sight.

Then a change. A faltering. She rubbed her eyes as the rays faded, and slowly the hole sealed itself shut.

Even as her eyes searched more keenly, the spinning-top sky appeared to slow, its brightness fade. Her fingers gripped her telescope harder, willing the spectacle to continue, but the stars' formerly wild gavotte was now almost imperceptible. She frowned as the sky gave one last shiver, before stopping dead, as if nothing out of the ordinary had occurred. The constellations were back in place, steady, unblinking. Sagittarius forever drawing back his bow, Taurus frozen mid-leap. Nancy waited, eye to the glass, not breathing, for another few minutes, but the Fold had gone.

Hands trembling, she glanced at her watch, then laid down the sextant, wide eyes back on the heavens. Beneath her purple-and-yellow-bodiced dress, her heart pounded like a drum. She allowed herself to imagine for one brief moment a stack of papers, neatly bound. A treatise, her name printed – *printed!* – on the cover. A vision of her standing behind a lectern at the Royal Society, the crowd murmuring in anticipation at her debut talk about this incredible new phenomenon. *At a mere twenty-three! A prodigy? Why thank you, sirs!* Shaking herself sternly, she steadied her long-fingered hands before swiftly recording the time, date and position of the phenomenon. A glance at the stair that led down to the Octagon Room. She must tell Doctor Maskliss, although she suspected already his likely response.

★

Another glance at her watch. The transit was almost upon them. Hurriedly, she packed up her things and made her way to the stair. An anticipatory shiver ran through her and she took a last glance at the sky above.

It felt as if every stargazer across the globe had spent the last 45 years in preparation for the next few precious hours. Even as a small child, her parents had told her the story, until it became as familiar as a nursery rhyme: how, in 1716, Edmond Halley had suggested that man might use the planets as a gigantic calculation machine, and determine, once and for all, how far the Earth lay from the Sun.

Mama had been so excited. 'Truly, Nancy, we are blessed. This is a golden time to be an astronomer – our time on Earth coinciding with two transits in quick succession. Two! Venus will travel in front of the Sun in 1761 and eight years after that, in 1769. And we shall see them both. Chart them together. It's a queer pattern, Nancy, but scrutinise the mathematics and it makes perfect sense.' How she missed her mother's fervour. Tonight, the absence of her parents had been the cloud on the horizon. They had not witnessed even one of the transits.

It was cooler inside the building, and her face glowed damply in the light of her little lantern. She hurried her way down the flight of stairs and pushed open a heavy wooden door.

A hot, whisky-scented fug hit her. The room was loud with raised voices. Candles cast their orange glow, sending flickering shadows and silhouettes up the wood-panelled walls. She took in the familiar sight. The eight-sided room was easily as tall as four men, clad to half its height in light wood panels. Elaborate cornicing snaked in the gloom of the ceiling edges. Six of the room's sides were windowed, the huge casements bare, designed that the occupants might look out unhindered into the heavens. Three grand clocks were set into the panelling on the wall behind her, and at the centre of the room sat the long telescope, over which three men in white wigs and brown frock coats fussed.

Dr Maskliss was sitting at a table, charts in front of him, talking earnestly to another man. He glanced at Nancy, and then looked back to his companion. Nancy put down her notes with a bang. 'Dr Maskliss! My mother was right! I've seen it. I've seen the Fold!'

The grey-ringleted man creased his brow and held up his hands. 'Miss Lockaby, please. What are you talking about? This is not the time.' He turned to the man next to him, 'Dr Ferguson, this is Benjamin and Elizabeth's daughter, Nancy Lockaby. She is an... an *enthusiastic* scholar and one of our computers at the observatory.'

Nancy nodded briefly at the beetle-browed man sitting next to Maskliss, but could not hold back. 'It was the most incredible sight! My mother's theory was right after all. It happened. The sky, the stars, they were whirling, folding in on themselves, flowing in one area of the sky.' She pulled the piece of paper from her pocket and smoothed it out on the table in front of him. 'Here!'

The Doctor peered downwards at the scribbles on the creased paper in front of him, and shook his head, 'Coordinates. To the north. High in the sky.' He harumphed. 'These are no more than numbers on a piece of paper, I'm afraid, Miss Lockaby. They tell us no more. This is not evidence.' It was a fair observation. Coordinates alone, Nancy knew, proved very little without corroboration.

'It… it was unlike anything I've seen before. The stars themselves were moving…' Nancy cursed her scattered mind. Ordinarily, her description would have been clear, her account precise.

'Moving?' he repeated.

Nancy took a deep breath. 'I was ready, at the time my mother described – the start of the transit being visible from Earth. And she was correct. The sky, it started moving, like a whirlpool. As if it were liquid. This was unlike anything I've seen, unlike *anyone* has seen.' She indicated the stern portraits of the previous Astronomers Royal – Flamsteed, Halley – that loomed watchfully above them. 'I have documented the location precisely.' She thumped the piece of paper. 'Please. Take a look at my notes.'

Maskliss eyed her slowly over his spectacles, then turned to Dr Ferguson with a wry expression. 'Miss Lockaby has been a near-permanent fixture at the observatory since she was a child. The Astronomer Royal, Mr Bradley, has always maintained that she is blessed with extraordinary talent. Yet I–'

He looked rather coldly at the red-haired, damp-faced figure who pointedly remained standing in front of him. 'I am sorry, Miss Lockaby. This— this Fold in the sky that you insist on searching for, it simply cannot exist. Could you perhaps have mistaken, say, the aurora, for something more?'

Here was the response she had expected. 'No. As you know, I am perfectly familiar with the appearance of the northern lights. This was beyond, deep into the stars.'

A trace of contempt entered his stare. As was her habit, Nancy looked away from his gaze. 'Your eyes then? Perhaps you are tired. I cannot believe you give your mother's childhood theories the slightest credence. Surely you know that she was persuaded that this *Fold* was a goose chase. She gave it up! There was, as you must recognise, no evidence. And we are both fully aware that astronomy is all about finding evidence.'

Frustratingly, he was right. Nonetheless, Nancy bristled.

Maskliss turned back towards Dr Ferguson, his flow of speech unbroken. 'There can be no time-wasting on such an important night. We will soon need to have our wits about us.' He winked at his companion.

Dr Ferguson turned to look evenly at Nancy, his head tilted to one side. 'Perhaps we should hear the girl out. At least look at the evidence? Maskliss?'

His companion snorted. 'You are getting soft, Ferguson! The transit is nearly upon us. The girl's eyes have deceived her.'

Much as she was tempted to grab Dr Maskliss and proclaim loudly that she knew what she had seen and it must be documented or the astronomical world would be the poorer for it, she resisted. After all, he was right: soon the sun would rise, the transit would be visible, and work must start.

Dr Maskliss nudged Ferguson and muttered under his breath, 'I'm yet to be convinced that women and telescopes are the most productive combination.' The other man half-smiled politely.

Nancy's face began to set in fury, but she quickly composed herself. Past experience had taught her not to rise to her superior's dismissive words, bait that tended to be thrown when there were other fellows to impress. The man often seemed to forget his title was 'Assistant to the Astronomer Royal', not 'Astronomer Royal'. That title still officially belonged to her very dear Mr Bradley, or James, as she knew him.

Maskliss rose and raised his voice. 'Five minutes until sunrise! We must focus and prepare ourselves. All ready?'

Nancy bit her lip. The sun was about to rise, and the world of natural philosophy was taking a deep, anticipatory breath. She took out her pen and papers, sighed, then alongside every man in the room, she held her smoked glass to her eye and looked out of the tall windows. Edging its way over an orange horizon was a fiery glow. The transit was about to reveal itself to London.

Chapter One

Eight years later

For the last few hours, Nancy had sat with her eyes half-closed and the carriage curtains drawn, too tired even to drink in the views of frozen waterfalls and mountains thick with snow. Opposite, Cora was asleep, a few loose strands of black hair peeking from beneath her white maid's cap. More than a week spent sitting on horsehair seats and trying to sleep in unfamiliar coaching-house beds had left their bodies aching and optimism dented. More pressing than any physical discomfort, however, was the disquiet rising in Nancy's stomach.

A shiver. Her breath snaked into the air. Outside, in the darkening afternoon, the thinnest sliver of new moon hung brightly in the sky. The appearance of this old friend gave her heart, and despite her misgivings, she smiled. Soon the stars would come out, thick in their thousands. They would be clearer here, away from the smoky skies of London. And perhaps her thoughts might have similar clarity, where she could no longer hear the muttered chorus of barbed comments. Her fingers drummed on the wooden sill. Yes, this was a place of discovery.

The carriage hissed over the compacted snow. A sign, still visible in the dusk, told her Inverness lay only three miles away. They had made much better time than expected, and would arrive at their destination a full day ahead of schedule.

She reached into her bag, pulled out a gold watch and flipped it open. Less than half an hour by her estimation. As she put the timepiece back, her fingers brushed against a crumpled letter, which she took out and smoothed open. The carriage light spilled in, allowing her to read, although she knew the words almost by heart.

Blackthistle, Inverness
Saturday, 11th February 1769

Miss Lockaby,
I write to offer you the position of Astronomy Research Fellow, to assist in my studies at Blackthistle House, Inverness. Your diligent approach and depth of knowledge, evident in our communication thus far, is most impressive, and I am certain that your work and research at the Observatory will be useful and illuminating for us both. As outlined in my previous letters, I feel there is a degree of overlap between literature and science. Indeed, that the edges of all disciplines are more pliant than many men would have us believe. I am convinced that, with our respective research, you and I have much to offer each other and that our work will not only provide rich intellectual stimulation but also bear ripe fruit. I apologise for my obscurity as to my precise purpose, but I am in no mind to risk my precious theories landing in the hands of a mailman and thence my rivals.

That you are a woman works only in your favour. The scholarly world serves ladies most poorly, and I am of the firm belief that the female mind is not only capable of equalling that of the male, but that the fairer sex tackles intellectual and practical challenges in a manner often superior to, and with more flexibility than, their more orthodox male counterparts. I am keen to learn of all that may be discovered in the skies, by whomever should discover it.

*As described in my initial approach, this is a live-in
position of twelve months' duration, and my staff will be
at your disposal. My housekeeper, Mrs McLoone, has
been in my service for many years, is of the highest moral
standing and most capable. Your expenses will be covered,
in addition to a yearly stipend of £100, and you will be
free to continue with your own studies; I shall require you
only for an hour or two each evening.
I shall expect you on the twelfth day of March.
Yours,
Caleb Malles*

That the letter's sparse lines did not reveal a great deal of the
nature of the work she was to undertake was a little frustrating, but also thrilling. The first few letters Mr Malles had sent
were similarly bare-boned: an unsolicited enquiry wondering
if she might be interested in a research position in Scotland,
followed by a few short missives asking more about her work
at the Observatory and her personal situation.

Initially, there appeared no reason for Caleb Malles to
appoint a research fellow. Nancy took most scientific journals,
yet his name was not familiar. Regardless, he had appeared
willing to pay a handsome sum to someone – a woman
even – with whom he'd only communicated by letter. Before
accepting the invitation, Nancy had determined to find out
more about her mysterious patron-in-waiting.

Her enquiries had led her to the parlour of Charlotte
Lennox, literature scholar and writer of the notorious
Shakespear Illustrated, who had come highly recommended
by a fellow Bluestocking.

'The mysterious Caleb Malles!' Charlotte had exclaimed
over cups of chocolate and rout cakes. 'His work is seminal.
His analysis of Shakespeare was reaching towards something
incredible.' She popped an entire tiny cake between her lips.

'His family are from Inverness, I believe. Wealthy, apparently, but no-one really knows much of him. He studied in London and still keeps a house down here as far as I know. From what I've seen of his work, he has the most extraordinary mind. But I've heard nothing of him for a good number of years. No papers published, no lectures, not an appearance in the society pages. I've not seen him at a London theatre or in town for as long as I can remember. It's almost as if he's vanished. I'd be fascinated to know about his affairs.'

It made no sense. There seemed no reason for a Shakespeare scholar to have approached an astronomer with no interest in literature, and yet Mr Malles was offering her a year's fellow-ship. Charlotte's gleaming, hungry eyes confirmed to Nancy that it would be unwise to tell her that her employer had made his home in Inverness. She smiled. 'Please, tell me more about your conversations with Mr Malles. I'm fascinated.'

However, Charlotte gave little more away. On leaving she touched Nancy's arm lightly. 'Tell me. Are you really going to go alone to Mr Malles' house?' Something about Charlotte's look reaffirmed Nancy's suspicions that any information she gave would soon be bobbing around in the gossip that eddied around the capital, so she merely smiled politely as she took her leave.

*

Nancy was aware that, like Charlotte, many of her peers took a dim view of her trip to the most northerly tip of Scotland. Naturally, the Bluestockings were encouraging, buoyed that a scholar had gone out of his way to search out a female collab-orator, while even some of the natural philosophy crowd with whom she occasionally mixed told her that they understood why she would be travelling alone to Inverness to study.

However, the potentially scandalous situation of an unmarried woman journeying to study with a man who lived alone had created quite the sensation, and news of the trip spread beyond the ivory towers. The Sackville sisters had whispered pointedly behind their hands at a fundraiser she had been obliged to attend at Ranelagh Gardens. However, they made a habit of lazy prattle and it only justified further her dislike of gossip-greased social events. Since she was a child, she had hated the clanging hum of chatter and the nagging feeling that she would never correctly understand the unwritten rules of etiquette.

Cora assured her that the party invitations that landed on the front porch of Crooms in the weeks before Christmas made excellent kindling for the fire. 'Living in blissful ignorance' felt much healthier, she told her maid. There was, however, no escaping the whisperings that came from the rest of her staff. The night before her departure, descending the stairs of Crooms, she overheard two figures talking in the doorway that led to the drawing room.

'It ain't seemly,' she'd heard her housekeeper tut. 'Two ladies on their own travelling all that way. And to stay with a man they've never even clapped eyes on.'

Cheeks aflame, Nancy had been sure to click her heels extra hard on the floorboards as she walked across the hall until the talking stopped abruptly.

The words had cut deep, but the staff could hardly be expected to understand that which compelled Nancy northwards. The patronising smiles that danced on the faces of her Observatory colleagues when she dared to challenge an established theory. The waspish asides that greeted her daily. Her mother had once muttered to her, with a roll of her eyes, 'A female observer must work twice as hard, our calculations must be twice as accurate, and we are expected to do it all with a silent smile and in impeccably white gloves.' Over the thirteen years since her parents' accident, those words had resonated more and more.

On occasion she even doubted her own abilities, wordlessly passing her calculations to a junior colleague to check before submission, or second-guessing Maskliss' likely response. She cursed her insecurity. But again and again, that whisper of self-doubt would rise.

Her journey to Scotland would put distance between those in the knot-tight world of natural philosophy in London who sought to still her hand, and also take her to a place where she might have the space to work unhindered by convention. Mr Malles' brief correspondence had given her heart that here was a man who might celebrate her abilities rather than dismiss her research. And so she had hushed her misgivings as to the exact nature of the study upon which she would be embarking. Nevertheless, she worried. Leaving her place at the Observatory was not without risk and she fretted that, should her trip to Scotland end in ignominious fashion, she would find it impossible to find further employment in the field. Yet her conviction that the Fold was a prize worth pursuing buoyed her.

★

She still wondered how Mr Malles might have heard of her work. Her name had not been attached to any published papers and most of the mathematicians at the observatory would have preferred her hidden in the cupboard among the inkwells and broken lenses. He had sidestepped the question in their correspondence, so she had determined to ask him at the earliest possible opportunity.

The carriage lurched again, the driver cursing under his breath before shouting, 'This is Inverness, ladies!' Nancy was jerked from her thoughts and craned her head out of the window.

Already they were among the turfed roofs and chimneys on the outskirts of the town, lit surreally by the snow. Through their casements she glimpsed glowing firesides and felt a pang of longing; hopefully they would soon be warming their feet in front of a hearth. A striped cat was running alongside the carriage. She heard it hiss.

As the coach rolled through a darkened market square, Nancy's fingers drummed harder, her nails rat-tat-tatting on the sill. Although her parents had been dead almost fourteen years, and she'd faced many challenges alone, she'd always done so from the security of Crooms.

Opposite her, Cora murmured in her sleep. Her maid was only a few years older than her, but had been in her service since Nancy was ten. Yet Cora would be in Scotland only a short time, as her parents had been stricken with smallpox. They lived a mile or two from Greenwich, in Deptford, and Nancy had assured them their daughter would be away from them for no more than a month. A letter had been hastily sent to Mr Malles, who had sent a short reply assuring Nancy that Scotland had no shortage of suitable ladies' maids, and Isobel, a girl in service at Blackthistle, would step in to assist.

Privately, she despaired at the prospect of her time ahead without her beloved maid. In the years following her parents' death, Cora had become indispensable and was now not merely a maid, but – to the disapproval of the rest of Nancy's staff – a dear companion, her constant Northern Star. That friend with the sly, knowing smile, who was the only soul aware of how that tangle of hair at the nape of Nancy's neck might be teased out with the handle of a long comb.

She remembered the nervous look Cora had given her as she had folded her clothes and packed them in a trunk.

'Ma'am, I am a little concerned. This Mr Malles… you ain't even set eyes on him, yet we're to stay at his house. And what of the troubles in Scotland? Even the ring of our voices might put us in a tight spot. The Scots are meant to be awful wild.'

Nancy had spoken gently. 'I understand your concern, Cora. I consider you a friend. And you have been more helpful than you could imagine these last few years. But please, trust me. I have been assured that Inverness is a friendly town, and it's a journey I have to make. My work is, I fear, considered laughable by my colleagues in London, but in Scotland, I think there might be more chance of my being taken seriously. At the very least, I can work uninterrupted on my theories ahead of the transit in June. Cora tilted her head to one side. 'I thought you would be working hard with this Mr Malles?'

Nancy nodded, 'Of course I shall be, but Mr Malles has assured me I will have ample time to focus on my own studies, as well as assisting him, which will be tremendously thrilling too. I can see you're worried, but I assure you, it will be safe. We are only visiting the north of our own kingdom after all, not the other side of the world.' Cora had flushed and shrunk back a little.

However, even as Nancy had rolled her maps, doubts had surfaced and she was painfully aware that Cora's fears might not be unfounded. She knew little of her new benefactor, and was only hazily aware of his area of research. There was no guarantee of the kind of work she might be asked to do, or what Mr Malles expected of her. His letters spoke of an open mind and ground-breaking research, yet of those she had seen no evidence bar the handful of missives he had sent. More generally, the Jacobite Rising was still fresh in the memories of the Scottish people, and she'd heard the most horrible stories of crofters and shepherds being driven from their farms like sheep.

Cora would be with her in Scotland for less than a week. Nancy had swallowed, and run her finger along the little leather-and-brass telescope given to her by her father, its familiar lines giving her some comfort.

A sharp blast of cold air through the carriage window brought her back to Inverness. The coach driver shouted down to his passengers: 'Not far now, ladies.' Her body ached. Perhaps she ought to have kept up the running of her father's well-padded coach, but she had sold the damaged vehicle after her parents' accident and instead relied on hired transport. Cora opened her eyes, her forehead crinkled in confusion.

'We're nearly there,' said Nancy. 'But a few minutes away now, I think. Best make yourself ready.'

*

A bump. They were crossing a bridge, the dark surface of a river swelling beneath, glinting like polished Whitby jet. In the darkness, two spots of light grew closer. Lanterns.

The lanterns pooled light around tall, wrought-iron gates set in a high wall. As they approached and slowed, Nancy gasped. There, maybe ten feet away, lit on the edge of the lanterns' orangey-red glow, stood three women, eyes wide and unblinking, fixed on her.

They locked gazes. A strange whine hummed in Nancy's ears. The youngest woman had fair hair, tangled like sheep's wool on a sharp rock, her face pale and unlined, a black gap where one tooth should be. Around her neck hung a ragged necklace of bleached animal bones.

The next woman was older, with dark skin. She had an orange-and-green-patterned scarf tied around her head, and large gold earrings that swayed gently.

The third's cadaverous face was cracked like parched summer earth, her thin grey hair greased against a yellowing scalp.

As the carriage drew to a halt, the women shrank back into the shadows of the trees. The whine stopped abruptly.

Curious townsfolk. News of her imminent arrival had obviously caused a stir. Nancy felt a queer prickling dread in her hands, down her back. She was tired. It had been a very long journey.

She looked back. The darkness of the copse revealed no sign of the women. She was so tired that it was entirely possible she had imagined them.

'Miss?' Cora was travelling in the rear-facing seat so had not seen the trio, but there was no reason to worry her.

Nancy kept her voice level. 'It is nothing, Cora.'

The driver opened the gates, then hopped back up to his seat. 'Giddy yip!' The carriage wheels crackled over an icy, gravelled path.

Against the canopy of bright stars rose the silhouette of a building: Blackthistle House. More imposing than its name suggested, it was almost a castle. A steep roof was forested with chimneys, while a round turret stood at one end of the building.

As they neared the house, something flickered. What appeared to be trapped lightning, flashing in one of the windows in the turret. Nancy felt her skin prickle. The shade seemed unnatural; colder than candlelight, it was the bone-bleached colour of the moon and shone unevenly against the casement. A thin shadow was silhouetted in front of the curious light. As she watched, a figure raised its arms heavenward, outline shaking against the glare, twitching as if it were possessed. The light flashed more intensely, then it was gone, leaving the window black and unblinking. Nancy rubbed her eyes. The long days of relentless travel were indeed taking their toll. Her heart pounded. This was not the welcome she had expected. But, again, there was no need to worry Cora. She could be easily spooked.

'Here we are. Habitable enough,' Nancy whispered to Cora.

The carriage drew to a halt in front of an arched doorway. The horse whinnied nervously and shifted its hooves even as the driver tugged at it to stand still. He peered down into the carriage and said, rather flatly, 'Blackthistle House, ladies.'

He jumped down from his seat onto the drive, pulled open the carriage door and offered his hand to Nancy. She smiled wearily as she climbed down. She glanced upwards, and dropped her bag to the ground, hand in mouth. The stars! Never before had she seen them shine so luxuriantly, so plentifully. Here were her skies! Any questions she might have been asking herself about the unsettling women and strange light at the window evaporated into the chill of the night air.

'Ma'am, if you don't mind. I must make haste. My inn will be near to closing.' The driver spoke quickly, then crunched across the icy drive and pulled the bell cord next to the huge front door. It opened almost immediately. Light spilled into the dark and the shape of a woman peered out. 'Miss Lockaby?' Nancy tore her gaze from the heavens. This must be the housekeeper, Mrs McLoone. Her voice was sharp, and Nancy felt obliged to make apologies. 'Yes. We are earlier than I imagined we might be. I'm sorry.'

The woman's face was younger than her voice suggested, yet her hair was greying and scraped back into a bun. She wore a dress the colour of boiled mutton. Nancy suddenly felt conscious of her own scarlet boots, her unruly mop of red hair escaping from beneath her cap, and deep-blue cloak scattered with glittering, gold-thread stars. Even in London, her choice of brightly coloured clothes had drawn attention. Here, they seemed to shout even more loudly.

'No matter,' the woman replied, although her tone suggested that it did matter very much. 'Come in.'

The driver took down their trunks and bags and left them on the step, then jumped back onto the carriage and clattered hastily away. He was due to return to take Cora back to London towards the end of the week.

They stepped into a large, stone-floored hall, panelled in dark wood. A few candles struggled in vain to light the room, but Nancy could make out a wide staircase, rising into the gloom. On her right a huge stone fireplace sat bare and cold, and next to it a clock in a long case. Above its face was a painted dial that, at this moment, showed a severe-looking moon. Nancy glanced upwards. Several portraits looked down at her sternly, but much of the walls remained unadorned, patchworked with rectangles and squares – the dark ghosts of paintings no longer in place. The austere darkness made a stark contrast to Crooms' bright, blush-pink entrance hall. Embarrassed, she realised she'd expected blankets and hides rather than this hard stone and unvarnished wood. Oh, what a pampered pug she was, used to the swagged salons of the city.

The woman dipped a short curtsey, her face unreadable. 'Mrs McLoone, ma'am. You'll have had a long journey, Miss Lockaby, Miss…?'

'This is Miss Black. My companion.'

Cora dipped her head. The gesture was not returned by Mrs McLoone, whose icy countenance looked never to have been fractured by a smile. Nancy raised an eyebrow at her maid.

'We have had quite the ride, yes.'

Mrs McLoone opened a door and indicated with her hand that they should enter. 'You'll both be hungry.' She disappeared down the corridor.

This room was smaller and less glacial. A few grey-pink ashes glowed in the grate. The walls were lined with bookcases, leaning into each other as if in their cups. Three plain chairs were pulled up to a stripped-wood table, a stub of candle lighting the scene. Nancy sat on one and leaned on the table on her elbow. Cora nervously pulled out the chair opposite.

She hissed, 'She doesn't seem very welcomin', ma'am.'

'Let us give her a chance, Cora,' replied Nancy brightly. 'The Scottish have a reputation for reserve.'

A few short minutes later, McLoone came into the room. She carried a plate bearing a few slices of bread, some chunks of cheese and two waxy apples, while a dish held two, hard-looking pats of butter.

'Thank you, Mrs McLoone. Tell me, if you will. On our arrival there was a *welcoming committee* outside. Some women from nearby, perhaps?'

'I'm sure I don't know what you're talking about.' The woman turned abruptly and left the room.

Nancy almost called the woman back to reprimand her for her rudeness, but thought better of it. Not now. That eerie light and shadow had made her jittery. She was exhausted from the long journey and very hungry. She buttered her bread with a shaking hand. Supper would comfort her.

'This is a simple but good supper, Cora. Just as we needed.' She smiled as brightly as she could, ignoring her companion's questioning look.

A chill curled around her ankles. She heard a rustle and looked around the room. A green vase of dried plants sat on a wooden bookcase, translucent, moon-shaped honesty, spiky rosemary, some time-browned sage blown gently by a draught. The case's shelves were packed with leather-bound books, gold letters shining on their spines.

Nancy stood up, walked to the shelves and peered at the books.

Coriolanus, Hamlet, Othello. Familiar names, although she suddenly wished they were more familiar. Since his invitation, she had fretted that Mr Malles might assume she had a working knowledge of Shakespeare's work. Periodically, her eyes had lingered fretfully on the eight, black books that sat on the shelves of the library at Crooms, with their gold-embossed leaf that promised *The Works of Shakespeare: In Eight Volumes.* Yet she had not even taken them down, fearing that reading them would only deepen the mystery that surrounded the nature of her employment.

She had watched a production of *Hamlet* at a theatre by the Thames with her parents, ten or so summers before, but she had been more transfixed by the hubbub of the audience than the lines declaimed by the players on stage. However, the words that she had been able to hear had had a certain charm. Relishing the memory, she pulled down *A Midsummer Night's Dream.* Despite being bound in leather, it felt icy to the touch.

Someone coughed behind her. She started and pushed the book back onto the shelf.

'Will you be needing anything else?' asked Mrs McLoone impassively.

She turned and looked at the housekeeper. 'Is Mr Malles at home?'

The woman pursed her lips. 'He is. But he will not be disturbed tonight. We were, after all, expecting you tomorrow afternoon.'

'I see,' said Nancy. 'I trust I shall make his acquaintance soon enough then.'

'That you will.' The woman gave a tight smile. 'I'll show you both to your room.'

She turned and left. With a shake of the head, Nancy followed, Cora behind her.

Mrs McLoone held a candle that sent flickers across the panelled walls of the dark corridors. The house was colder than any Nancy had visited, and her breath trailed into the frosty air. She felt exhausted to the marrow, wanting nothing more than to be asleep. At last, Mrs McLoone held open a door. A room. A lamp. A curtained bed, on which lay her bag, and another mattress on a truckle beside it. Nancy and Cora stepped inside.

'Thank you, Mrs McLoone. Good night.'

The woman nodded and left wordlessly, clicking the door shut behind her.

'Ma'am...' Cora stood behind her, her fingers moving quickly to unpin her mistress's cap and let down her hair. Nancy barely noticed the maid unbuttoning her dress and removing the thick folds of material. Gently, Cora helped her pull on a nightdress, and sat her in the bed, the coverlet drawn up to her waist.

'Please, pass me my bag, Cora,' Nancy said sleepily.

She undid the clasps, took out a large piece of paper, unfolded it and laid it over her knees, as she did nightly. This was a chart she knew by heart, but could look at over and again. The thick parchment was scattered with hundreds of stars embossed in shining gold leaf, between them planets and moons, trajectories trailing. Laced between these representations, in the tiniest, most orderly hand, were calculations, numbers, Xs and Ys and square roots taking up every inch of the firmament's space. Her mother's familiar writing.

Furrowing her brow, she traced her finger around a small space on the chart. The inscriptions here were faded through continual touch. She bent more closely to the paper. Written in the ghostly hand was a single sentence: *Keep searching beyond.* Smelling the paper, she caught the faintest scent of violets, the perfume that had trailed in clouds behind her mother.

She laid the paper on the bedside table. Cora was already snoring softly on the low bed next to hers. Nancy blew out the candle, lay back and closed her eyes. The faces of the women outside the gates danced before her, their hair wild as wind-tossed twigs, brown ragged dresses like leaves, skinny, angled branches for arms. Despite her dreadful tiredness, Nancy was still awake as the big clock downstairs struck a dolorous three, Outside, the trees rattled in the wind.

Chapter Two

For a moment, the strange brightness of the morning light confused Nancy. She turned sleepily as Cora pulled open the curtains, revealing an unfamiliar landscape. Distant low, purplish hills, swathes of piney forests, white fields and fences crusted heavily in white snow. Another layer had fallen and the ochre sky promised more. Still, the view was a calm sigh after the fiercely rugged roar of the mountains.

She watched through half-open eyes as Cora busied round the room. She had not slept well – the women had stalked her dreams. She was nervous enough meeting Mr Malles for the first time, without this kind of distraction. She stretched.

'Mornin', ma'am!' Nancy's eyes snapped open at Cora's familiar, cheery greeting. 'Time to hop out!' She waved a little silver hairbrush. 'Look what I found in the cabinet drawer! Looks softer than the one I use. Let's try it an' see later.' Nancy smiled. Cora was always keen to find new ways to help her untamed hair lie a little straighter and to look, as the maid liked to put it, 'more seemly'.

The two breakfasted together, sitting at the same stripped-wood table at which they had eaten the night before. Mrs McLoone was no more talkative, but informed Nancy that Mr Malles would see her at eleven. 'He's out,' she had said shortly. The housekeeper's taciturn manner was beginning to grate, and for a moment Nancy wished herself back in London. Then she glanced out of the windows at the wide horizon, and remembered how it had bristled thickly with points of light; stars she hadn't a hope of spotting back in Greenwich. 'Our breakfast view is a little more spectacular than in dull old Crooms, is it not?' she said to Cora.

A walk would keep her from thoughts of her meeting with Mr Malles, but her maid wasn't keen to venture outside. 'It seems awful cold, ma'am. And I need to speak to this Isobel and tell her about your needs.' Cora was far more particular about her mistress's arrangements than had ever been required, and Nancy pictured her schooling the unfortunate Isobel in the finest detail: how her dress should be laced and the exact shade of brown she preferred her toast.

Exploring felt like an opportunity to fix her bearings and perhaps find a choice stargazing spot. Nancy pulled on her boots and cloak then stepped into the morning's dazzle.

It had stopped snowing, but the cold bit more deeply here than in London, so she congratulated herself that she'd had the foresight to wear her warmest woollen stockings.

She turned and shaded her eyes against the sun. In the daylight Blackthistle appeared smaller, greyer, the roof patchy with yellow lichen. It had, for the most part, three storeys, with walls that loomed disapprovingly high. Some of its crenellations had started to crumble, leaving gaps like a broken smile, and the odd pane of window glass was cracked. It felt like a house in mid-sigh. It would not be likely she would need to brave parties here. Over in the turret, the mysterious glowing window was dark and unprepossessing. The light had surely been just a bright lantern. She had been so tired.

Once out of the gates and onto the road, Nancy looked over the bridge towards the town, where low houses clustered around what looked like the ruins of a castle and a stern, square-towered church. For a moment, she considered how she might introduce herself, should she encounter anyone on a walk into town. She had brushed off London's disapproval, but would the people of the Highlands be even more judgemental about a spinster staying under the roof of a man she barely knew? She might call herself Mr Malles's assistant, perhaps. Colleague? Employee? Having not yet set eyes on the man, she felt uncertain as to how he might want to describe her. Or if the people who lived in Inverness would expect such an introduction.

Her cousin had written to tell her that the Scots were wildhaired and savage, but the carriage driver had confessed over a cup of hot chocolate to her and Cora that he found the citizens of Inverness puritanical and purse-lipped.

'Puritanical?' Nancy had looked at him in surprise. 'I heard that the people of Scotland were never happier than when they were drunk and fighting.'

The carriage driver had laughed loudly. 'Not the kind of folk that will pay a carriage driver to take them from Aberdeen to Edinburgh, ma'am.'

Regardless, she did not feel inclined to brave the eyes of the townspeople just yet, and that stargazing spot wasn't going to give itself up without a hunt, so she set off in the opposite direction, towards the countryside.

Nancy padded along the road. The air was thick with the peculiarly intense quiet that only a blanket of snow could bring. She passed two smoke-plumed cottages, then the road softened into wide fields. A fox trotted alongside her for a minute or two, red fur outlined against the snowy backdrop, and Nancy wondered idly if she might see a wolf while she was here. She'd heard they still lurked in this part of the world and smiled at the prospect.

The landscape layered like scenery at a theatre. In the distance lay sleeping-giant mountains, dark against unnaturally yellow skies. Nearer, the pines lined up like an army of ten thousand soldiers, and closer still sat a small hillock, topped with a scrub of gorse. She would walk to that point and then turn back, as it was surely too cold to go too much further.

Her steps became purposeful; she was of the mind that walking not only improved one's health, but also provided an opportunity for deliberation. It had been years since she had been in such luxuriant isolation; her walks in Greenwich Park or to the river front had invariably been punctured by meetings with neighbours and dimly remembered acquaintances with whom she was obliged to make small talk. Here it was just her, the skies and the odd flutter of a partridge.

The richness of the sharp, clean air made her feel almost giddy. Already it felt as if her mind was becoming more fertile, with green shoots of new theories. If only she could be as sure about her appointment later that morning. That Mr Malles had not greeted her last night was a little worrisome. Surely any decent man should – at the very least – have introduced himself to an unmarried lady guest.

In the fitful depths of the night, she had imagined Mr Malles must have some darker motive for inviting her to Blackthistle. In the bright winter sun, she chided herself for her ungracious thoughts. Perhaps students of literature were a little more forgiving and credited female thinkers with expertise more readily than men of natural philosophy.

Snow started to swirl from the whitening sky, flakes settling on her navy cloak. The mountains had disappeared from view. Within seconds, the pines also vanished. She pulled her cloak tight against the sudden chill and continued in the bleached silence, ignoring her jitters.

The snow became heavier, and her steps more effortful, icy flakes stinging her face. It was but a few steps to the hillock, she was sure, yet reaching it seemed to take forever.

The muffled quiet was pierced by a harsh squawk, and Nancy looked upwards, hands shielding her eyes from the white. Above her circled the outlines of three birds, dark against the sky. Crows? She stopped and stared upwards at the trio, their wings spread wide like bony fingers. Nancy shook her head. She knew they posed no threat, yet felt a faint rising alarm in her throat.

The black silhouettes spiralled closer and she tilted her head back, mesmerised. They became a little more sinister with every movement, their cawing growing louder and louder. Nancy felt rooted to the spot, her unease growing. Logic told her that these creatures channelled no emotion, brooked no argument, yet they seemed to be eyeing her with intent.

Lower and lower they circled, until their wings almost brushed the top of her head. Nancy wanted to run but found herself frozen with fear. There was something about their tattered shapes, their cruel beaks, and the gleam in their black-marble eyes that brought to mind the women she'd seen standing at the gates of Blackthistle the night before.

Her hood fell back from her head, the birds' ragged cries raging in her ears. Their heavy, flapping wings beat closer, sending tattered black gusts across her face. She dropped to her knees and screamed, shutting her eyes as one tugged at her blue-and-yellow-striped ribbon, pulling it loose, while the others cackled.

A shout echoed through the snow, followed by a loud whinny. The birds scattered immediately, cawing regretfully as they soared back into the sky. Nancy opened her eyes to see a tall black horse rearing against the white snowstorm, a rider on its back.

'For goodness' sake, get up!'

She scrambled to her feet, cheeks reddening, hair loose, struggling to control the panicked gasps still shaking her chest. The voice was deep, with a Scottish burr. He shouted, 'What in God's name are you doing out alone? This weather is fierce.'

One hand at her mouth, the other half-raised, she squinted hard at the man. He was dressed head to toe in black, with shiny knee-high boots, tight breeches and a thick greatcoat. Like a farmer, he wore no wig; his unruly dark curls were tied back, but some strands had escaped. Consternation flashed across his angular, pale face. Nancy was discomfited by the reproach in his voice.

'I am fine, thank you, sir.' Her knees still felt as if they might buckle in shock.

'You seem anything but fine,' he retorted, although he now seemed calmer. 'And with good reason. Those birds looked half-crazed. Who knows what might have happened had I not chanced upon you.'

Continuing into the storm had been a grave mistake, yet the condescension in the man's tone sounded uncomfortably close to that of Dr Maskliss. Nancy's face grew pink, just as it had countless times in the Observatory. 'Thank you, sir, for your assistance.' She spoke as witheringly as she could muster. 'I am perfectly capable of defending myself against a few birds.' She hoped he might not hear the tremble in her voice.

He appeared not to notice her agitation. 'What on earth did you do to disturb those creatures?' He patted his horse and smiled more kindly. 'Come, let me take you to your home.'

Nancy shook her head vehemently. 'Thank you, but no. I will see myself back.' She brushed snow from her skirts and pulled up her hood. The man surveyed her coolly with indigo eyes.

'Very well. The storm looks to be easing, but take care, madam. It can get dangerous quickly here.' He dipped his head, nudged his heels against his horse and galloped away.

Nancy bowed her head. The weather was appalling, and she had foolishly let herself get lost in reverie rather than notice the gathering storm. In London, she could be in the warm in five minutes, but the wilds of the Highlands were, she could see now, less forgiving. She had been shaken. Not just by the actions of the three crows – although their cries were still hoarse in her ears – but by her encounter. The man's withering look had stung most forcefully; the same withering look that Dr Maskliss had reserved for those moments when conversation strayed to her convictions about the Fold.

Perhaps she should have turned back when the weather started to worsen. Yet that was surely her decision to make, regardless of the consequences. Her hair hung over her shoulders, her ribbon gone, presumably with the crows. She huffed and patted down her dress, exhaled loudly, then trudged her way back crossly through the snow to Blackthistle House.

Chapter Three

Mrs McLoone had looked disparagingly at her sodden boots, but said nothing as she took them away to dry in front of the kitchen fire. Once in her room, Cora helped her pull on a pair of satin shoes the colour of blackbird eggs, then ran a comb through her hair, aghast as Nancy told her of the morning's events.

'Attacked by crows? Oh, ma'am. This place feels like it's on the edge of the world. Your hair! Where is your ribbon? And what did you see last night? The welcoming committee? I heard what you said to that McLoone woman.'

'Just a few local women, Cora. Curious to see what a moral-free London lady looks like, I'm sure.'

Cora rolled her eyes, 'If you say so, ma'am. But really, are you sure you should stay?' Her voice dropped to a whisper. 'I worry what will become of you when I'm gone. And it's not just outside, it's in here too. This house has something sad about it. Like the frost has got in and it won't never melt.'

'I'm sure I can make it a little jollier. It's what happens when a man preoccupied with study lives alone.' Nancy forced a brightness into her voice.

Cora pursed her lips. 'Feels as if the chill won't be chased by a few embroidered cushions, ma'am.'

'Oh, Cora. Don't be a nincompoop. It's just very different from London. Colder at the very least.' She indicated her necklace and Cora fastened it around her neck. 'Thank you, I'll take care of the rest.' A look passed between them and the maid recognised that her mistress wanted to be alone. She bobbed a curtsey then left the room.

Nancy peered into her looking glass, licked her finger and smoothed her eyebrows. Moss-green eyes stared back, set in a face that Nancy had once declared with a sigh was, 'rounder than the full moon'. She was not, as many men had chosen to remind her, conventionally beautiful, yet she rather liked her gap-toothed grin and nose that wrinkled when she smiled.

It was almost eleven. Suddenly she felt a vast distance from Greenwich, from Crooms House, the rest of her staff, her archives. She leaned back in her chair, eyes shut. Still now she sometimes felt the need to steel herself before a meeting, to pull on the armour forged from years of facing her fears alone.

Appropriately for a mathematician, she was very much the sum of her parents. Mama's talents had been nurtured from a tender age by a sharp tutor, who had polished Elizabeth Bradley's prodigious affinity with the planets. In time, Mama's uncle, James Bradley, the Astronomer Royal, had secured her a place as a junior at the Observatory. At eighteen, he had introduced her to Papa, Benjamin Lockaby, who had constructed the powerful, eight-foot transit telescope that still took pride of place in the Octagon Room. Inevitably, the pair fell in love, and within weeks the star-obsessed lovers were married. Alongside James, Elizabeth and Benjamin formed an alliance both academic and alchemic, bound tightly, consumed gleefully in work at the Observatory. In time, their daughter Nancy, with her particular talent for methodical research, had joined them.

At only seventeen, the deaths of her parents had almost destroyed her. However, the fortune amassed by her grandfather had been a rock of security. She had clung thankfully to that as her astronomical obsession continued to burn brightly, a guiding light through the tumult of grief. The planets, the stars, the moons were steadfast friends who anchored and comforted her.

Uncle James became just 'James' and continued her tuition at the Observatory, a place to retreat into the order and predictability offered by hard numbers, and when Nancy was twenty-one he had officially employed her as an assistant.

Moreover, James also provided tender advice and expertise in running a household. Without him, she was sure she would have had to give up Crooms House, which stood just down the hill at the north tip of Greenwich, and perhaps even have been compelled to shrug on the double shackles of marriage and motherhood. His death, the year after the 1761 transit, had left Nancy almost as devastated as she had been at the loss of her parents.

Dr Maskliss had taken over from James as Astronomer Royal. Nancy had done her best to keep her relationship with her new employer and tutor cordial, but he barely cared to conceal his disdain for women who spent time hunched over figures or peering through a sextant rather than raising children or smiling on the arm of their husband.

Others in the employ of the Observatory muttered that she should be grateful that Dr Maskliss had deferred to his predecessor's wishes and continued her education. Her parents' generous bequest had, she thought grimly, possibly been conducive to his acceptance.

However, she had always assisted her tutor with a fierce diligence, quietly turning his telescope towards areas of the sky she thought might prove fruitful, correcting his calculations without comment, acutely aware that her depth of knowledge and technical prowess was contributing to countless new discoveries.

Yet any sense of achievement was dulled by that which she could never accomplish. There were only so many times she might smile at the publication of papers with a blank space where her credit should have been. Papers that should have trumpeted her discovery of the Fold.

The day she had realised the extent of her mother's mathematical prowess remained etched on her mind as precisely as the engravings on her telescope.

A drizzly afternoon, rain coursing down the windows of Crooms. The fifth day of May 1759. She remembered it with precision as it was almost exactly three years after the deaths of her parents. Searching for a misplaced Newton in the gloom, she'd felt something soft on the top of a shelf and pulled down a dusty notebook, bound in emerald leather. It was written in a familiar hand. That precise, tiny script that looked as if it had been written with a single feather barb, unmistakably her mother's.

> *Bradley's Illusion and the Fold: The Transit and the Rotating Stars. Elizabeth Bradley, 1734*

The Fold. The words meant nothing. Her heart paused. There was her mother's maiden name. Used in an academic context, it looked stark and unfamiliar, yet with understated intent. 1734. Elizabeth would have been sixteen; she was already working at the Observatory but had not yet met Benjamin.

Once, when side by side, peering through telescopes, Nancy had asked her mother why she had never studied at a school, and the reason her name was missing on the final papers published by her father and Mr Bradley. Her mother had explained, with a trace of resentment, that 'The best most women might hope for is to cloak their discoveries in their companions' work. There will be more to tell when you are older.' Nancy had grown older, yet her mother had not, so she had never heard more.

However, these papers showed most clearly that the young Elizabeth had not always resigned herself to anonymity. This

looked to be a complete thesis, albeit unpublished and handwritten by a sixteen-year-old. *Bradley's Illusion and the Fold.*
Slowly, Nancy turned the page, hands shaking with anticipation. The words had faded in places but she could still make
many of them out. Her mother had, in an old stack of papers at
the Observatory, uncovered a French astronomer's account of
the 1639 transit of Venus. The name Louis del Sol had meant
nothing to her.

> *Louis del Sol's account is most fascinating: he tells of a*
> *rend in the sky, an anomaly that lay in the north at the*
> *time of the transit, where the stars disappeared and swam*
> *'like little eels'. I presumed it was fantastical, yet thought*
> *scrutinising it might be a worthwhile assignment.*

Reading it was like having her mother back with her, whispering in her ear.

Nancy was well aware of her mother's prodigious talent,
but the clarity and intensity of the notation and observation
in the thesis was breathtaking. Even as a young girl Mama had
possessed the numeric articulation needed to document her
hypotheses with precision. Her mother had taken the basics
of Newton's Theory of Gravity – that familiar friend of an
equation was at the centre of the first page – and Roemer's
work on the speed of light, and had somehow melded them
together, binding them in space, distance and time to produce
the most complex of suppositions; that large objects in the
cosmos might create distortions, rips in not just space, but
time too.

There were sketches of skies, crimped and crinkled, bent
in on themselves, holes joined by tunnels. The map that
Nancy read each night was folded into the book. And a
prediction, scratched away on the centre page, trailing off,
almost half-lost.

*If my calculations are right, this particular Fold will
appear on the night of the transit in 1761, between 2 and
4 a.m. The exact coordinates, however, I cannot yet tell.
They will come.*

For two years Nancy had pored over the notebook, made her
own notes, attempted to narrow down where she should focus
her telescope. On the day of the transit, Nancy had climbed a
ladder and pulled her mother's notebook from the shelves of
Crooms' round library room, her fingers tracing a couple of
sparse lines of text. Two sentences she'd read over and over.

*I am certain that the Fold, this swirl of stars, this portal
to who knows where, is real. And so, this anomaly might
appear at the transit... in the north.*

Of course, she had to be there, at the Observatory, searching
on that night in 1761, and had made the joyous confirma-
tion that her mother – and del Sol – had been right. That
there had been, *was* a nebulous area in the northern sky
that inhaled and exhaled that which surrounded it. That
phenomenon now both consumed and fuelled her passion.
It was confounding; the Fold had been there as plain as a
pie on a plate, yet others had seemed unable, unwilling to
see it.

There was something deeper that continued to gnaw at
her; a feeling that perhaps her mother had known more of
that shifting, transient space in the sky than was in her notes,
and that she had been on the edges of uncovering more of
its secrets. But, as all good astronomers maintained, evidence
was everything.

Witnessing the Fold from atop the Observatory had fired
in her a seething determination. Defying Dr Maskliss' rejection, she had worked alone, late through the nights, into the

mornings, piecing together the theories strung through her mother's secret thesis. And writing, calculating, theorising until she had gathered enough evidence for *On an Anomaly: The Fold* – a work that combined her mother's theories with her own research. A work that Maskliss had insisted she recalled and destroyed.

He had spoken with ice in his voice. 'Miss Lockaby, you have, I suppose, proved yourself to be a good lady astronomer, and the speed of your calculations equals that of some men. But this obsession, this fool's errand, is undermining your hard work. This paper shows no credible evidence for this *Fold* you insist you saw. None! It is all hypothesis. The little evidence you have was seen only by your eyes. No-one has verified it. Not one person. Surely you can see as well as I that it is poppycock. So, for the sake of the Observatory's reputation, this paper cannot be seen!'

The memory of withdrawing her treatise still raged harshly. Having to request *On an Anomaly: The Fold* be returned from the press only a few short days before its publication last year had been a humiliating experience, and she had burned all bar two copies – Maskliss had the only other still in existence – in a bitter little blaze on the back lawn of Crooms House. Years and years of research, calculations and supposition had been poured into those pages. Both her years and, even more wretchedly, her mother's. However, Maskliss' explicit threats of the withdrawal of her research position at the Observatory had left her with little choice.

Yet, her investigations continued privately in the drawing room of Crooms House, workings hidden even from those closest to her. Measurements taken surreptitiously at the Observatory, scribbled secretly into tiny notebooks and transferred laboriously to her papers at home. She'd toil even as the sun reached its zenith, then draw heavy curtains that she might sleep in the afternoons.

There were doubts. The Fold seemed to thumb its nose at scientific reason, making its existence frustratingly difficult to prove.

The next transit was in June, less than three months hence. This was her final chance, her only opportunity to prove her mother's theories. Should she decide to stay here, she would have her large new reflector telescope sent up by ship from London. Her meticulous notes and the coordinates she had scribbled at the last transit would be her ammunition this time around. Everything was in place. She knew from her calculations that this time, the Fold was due to open at precisely the same time the transit itself took place.

Scotland was, she knew, not the best place from which to view the transit itself, but her mother's notes and her own research suggested that the Fold would be visible from any spot on Earth. Here she might be left in peace to document and capture her quarry. This time she would be more prepared to take the measurements and detail she would need to prove its existence once and for all.

Her mother had once whispered some advice, out of the hearing of even her husband: 'Try not to capitulate, Nancy. I have yielded, let some theories float into the ether, just to keep the peace. I hope that you'll never know the indignity, the agony of acquiescing in that manner.'

Nancy sat up and looked once more into the mirror. The eyes that had once sparkled with enthusiasm at the prospect of naming new stars were dull. The fine lines that led from them traced creases borne of frustration.

Mr Malles's offer had felt like an outstretched hand, offering to pull her from the dark place in which she had found herself. This might, finally, mean the slate was wiped clean, and that there would be a fresh chance of recognition.

If she were researching alone, yet in parallel with a well-regarded scholar outside of the astronomical sphere, she reasoned, her work stood more chance of being acknowledged. She might even find encouragement in her study of the Fold.

At the very least this employment – whatever it might entail and no matter how queer its genesis, or how appalling the living arrangements might seem to society – would finally allow her the luxury of time away from the hothouse of competition and subtle oppression that was the Observatory, and a chance to study deeply without distraction or resentment. This, perhaps, would be her chance to finally write 'Miss Nancy Lockaby' or even 'Dr Nancy Lockaby' into those blank spaces on the documents announcing a major new discovery.

A knock at the door jolted her. She glanced at the plain wooden clock that sat on the mantle. It was five minutes to eleven.

The waspish face of Mrs McLoone peered into the room. The woman whispered, 'Ma'am, would you come with me to the study, please?'

Chapter Four

Nancy tucked her folder of charts and manuscripts tightly under her arm, then followed the woman down the corridor. A dour bun of grey hair peeped out from under the housekeeper's headscarf.

Blackthistle's corridors were almost as dark in the daytime as at night, narrow and refusing to follow straight lines. Unlike the warm-wooded floors of Crooms, their echoing flagstones were damp and uneven underfoot.

Downstairs, McLoone motioned her through a door. The furniture was more like that of a London drawing room, though nowhere near as colourful. Staring out of the window bleached white with light reflected from the snow was the silhouette of a man, one hand at the top of his nose. His outline was instantly familiar and, as he turned, Nancy saw it was the stranger from earlier in the day. That supercilious soul was Mr Malles. She felt a hot flush spread down her neck.

The man's recoil told her that the recognition was mutual. However, he recovered his composure near-instantly, forcing a thin-lipped smile. He shook his head. 'Miss Lockaby,' he said a little stiffly. 'I see you found your way back safely.' So this, then, was her employer.

'Mr Malles? Today has been rather unusual.' The words sounded less bold said aloud than in her head. 'I don't make a habit of getting into such situations.'

He looked at her impassively. 'Miss Lockaby, I may have been a little brusque, but my main concern was your welfare.

As I remarked earlier, it can get dangerous very quickly in these parts.'

It would be necessary, she realised, to show a little humility in order to make reparation. Perhaps she shouldn't have strayed so far from the house in such weather, and he *had* offered help, even if his tone had been harsh.

'Anyway, we shall start afresh. Welcome to Blackthistle.' He spoke brightly, and Nancy relaxed her hands enough that her nails stopped digging into her palms; her composure, she hoped, smoothly regained.

He continued. 'Tell me, how is London? I keep a place there. Durham House, in Spitalfields. I haven't visited for a good ten years.' His voice faded a little.

'I know Spitalfields a little.' She thought of the Mathematical Society which gathered there. Small talk was not her forte, but for once she was grateful to slide into it, smoothing out any awkwardness. 'It's a most agreeable part of the city, and home to some remarkable minds. Minds that might be far more qualified to assist you than me. Were you not tempted to return to London in order to further your studies?'

He looked at her sharply. 'I must remain here. Miss Lockaby, I understand that the process of your engagement has been *unconventional.* You must be curious about what I require.' He moved closer to her. His black neckcloth was tied in a loose knot, revealing a silver locket sitting on his collarbone. Mr Malles caught her stare and his hand moved up to tuck the necklace away, before reaching onto a polished oak table and picking up a piece of paper. Nancy recognised it as her reply to his initial enquiry.

He held it to the light. 'So, you consider yourself an accomplished astronomer, Miss Lockaby?'

Nancy looked him in the eye. 'I do, Mr Malles. I have studied for many years under two Astronomers Royal and my parents,

Elizabeth and Benjamin Lockaby.' Her voice quavered almost imperceptibly at their mention. Nancy was aware that her father's reputation often preceded her, yet Mr Malles looked blank.

'My father was an astronomer and astronomical instrument-maker. Even the King thought him the finest scientific craftsman of recent years,' she said, navigating through her thoughts. 'He, my mother and Mr Bradley – the former Astronomer Royal – taught me about the universe,' she continued briskly. 'As I said, I have studied under two Astronomers Royal in Greenwich, and specialise in mathematics. My work is regarded as scrupulous, I am notoriously quick in my calculations and I pride myself on my presentation.'

Mr Malles regarded her. 'Accuracy and a fair hand are both considered very desirable qualities, in the world of natural philosophy, are they not?' he murmured. He tossed the letter back onto the tabletop.

Now was the time, thought Nancy.

'Mr Malles, might I ask how you heard of my work? After all, my name has never appeared on a paper, even as a footnote.'

He picked up an old black book, and flicked through it idly. 'I have been assured of your dedication and abilities.' Nancy could not suppress a grimace.

'By whom? When?'

Mr Malles rubbed his stubbled chin and continued. 'A friend to whom I made a promise of anonymity. I have been told also of your tendencies to venture into more *unconventional* territories.'

His face remained frustratingly unreadable. Who was the friend of whom Mr Malles spoke? No-one at the Observatory would have recommended her, unless, perhaps they wanted her away from London. Or were playing some kind of awful joke. She knew that now was not the time to demand this particular answer.

'I am, of course, keen to learn your friend's identity, but respect that they wish to remain unnamed.' She raised an eyebrow. 'However, please, I must know something. What is the nature of your work, and the studies we shall be undertaking? I assume Shakespeare will be centre-stage?'

For a moment Mr Malles's expression betrayed amusement, but it was almost immediately replaced with an intense stare. 'As I suggested in my letter, I not only require a fellow researcher but also an ally. Someone with a thirst to discover, to uncover. Like you, I am a student, and I will always remain a student.' He paused, before continuing more gently. 'But also like you, I think, I am more than an academic. I am searching, pursuing, something further.' His eyes glittered. 'My interests lie in the true power of the written word. In particular, those most brilliant of words written by Shakespeare.'

Bending towards her he said, almost in a whisper, 'Within his plays, harboured in his verse, I believe lies the universe. And so,' he swallowed, 'Just as I voyage into the spaces between those vowels and consonants into deeper meaning I need you to unshackle those iron-work constraints of mathematics and determine how far we might stretch logic and reason. I require the presence of a bold thinker by my side.' He smelled like the sun-warmed spices that stood in crates on the London Pool docksides.

She held his gaze, her throat tightening. Every stroke of each number of her work was founded upon evidence. To be asked so bluntly to consider making those hard boundaries fluid and put aside the principles upon which her work was built made her head throb. However, there was something beguiling about Mr Malles's manner. She spoke carefully.

'Mr Malles, those iron-work constraints are forged through slow graft and careful reckoning. Logic cannot, by its nature, be stretched.' The faintest trace of a smile played around her lips. 'Humour this mathematician and tell me in plain fashion our field of enquiry.'

Mr Malles looked gently amused, then started reciting:

'These earthly godfathers of heaven's lights

That give a name to every fixed star

Have no more profit of their shining nights

Than those that walk and wot not what they are.'

The words were unfamiliar, but must have sprung from Shakespeare's pen; her interviewer was making gentle fun at her expense. For a moment she faltered. She had travelled all these miles merely to be mocked once more. However, there was a serious undertow to Mr Malles's playful manner, as if he were testing her mettle, poking in jest, yet hoping that she might reveal something more. This was a different prospect to the one-dimensional derision she had endured in Greenwich. He had thrown down a gauntlet. She stood up and looked him in the eye.

'One should learn not only the names of the stars, Mr Malles, but also their paths and what the future holds for them. Only that way will we uncover their mysteries, for secrets lie in the spaces between that which we already know. Now, please, humour me, and spell out in the most elementary manner that which we shall be studying.'

Mr Malles gave an approving laugh. 'You match me, Miss Lockaby. I believe I have chosen precisely the right person.' Once more, his face became serious. 'Very well. I have a theory. Our greatest writer, Shakespeare, is perhaps more singular than believed so far. Not only is his work concerned with the fundaments of man's emotion and being, but that time and time again, he returns to the same theme; our relationship with the heavens.'

His eyes widened and he spoke with more urgency. 'There are hundreds of mentions of the stars in his plays. One of his most fascinating characters – Prospero – was surely derived from Mr John Dee, Queen Elizabeth's favourite natural philosopher. But of course, you will be more than familiar with the work of Mr Dee. Forgive me.'

Nancy gave a polite smile. John Dee had, of course, made great strides in the field of astronomy. Indeed three of his books lay in the chest that she had sent up from London, yet he had lost himself in the supernatural, the realms of the occult and that which he described as 'magic'; work that rested upon flimsy fantasies, obsidian mirrors and unsubstantiated half-truths. Astrology, rather than astronomy had snared him. Mr Malles could not have alighted upon a more inexpedient figure. Yet a light in his eyes warned her not to interrupt him just yet. She must find the purpose of her appointment.

Unaware of her disquiet, Mr Malles continued. 'You see, Miss Lockaby, Shakespeare too was wrestling with our position in the universe. He wanted to discover whether we are pulled this way and that by the influence of planets and constellations, or if each man determines his own circumstance, and that the stars hold no sway over our future or nature.'

That old, familiar argument. Even at Bluestocking meetings, Nancy would often be asked what bearing the stars held on the questioner's future. Surely from the moment Copernicus had been bold enough to make his theories public, every right-thinking scholar – even those who studied literature rather than the planets – had known that man must follow only that which was rooted fully in fact and reason, and cast aside any unprovable flights of fancy. If she had known that Mr Malles even contemplated this flim-flam, she might not have come to Scotland.

Malles glanced across at Nancy. Her lips were pursed, eyes narrowed in thought. 'I can see you will not hear of any notion that the stars exert an influence on this planet,' he said.

Nancy sighed. 'I am surprised there would exist even a query.'

Everything must be proved. Astrology was but astronomy made selfish, fate merely the discharge of responsibility. She had always been fond of Voltaire's description of astrology as being astronomy's crazed offspring, "The mad daughter of a wise mother." Yet for now, she would keep her counsel.

Surely, if she kept to her principles and advised Mr Malles accordingly, then her integrity would remain intact? The thought of a calm, remote space in which she might carry out her own research into the Fold was, after all, very appealing.

After a pause, she replied, 'I am willing to cast an eye over your hypotheses. After all, truth will only emerge through scrutiny.'

Mr Malles smiled thinly. 'And that, Miss Lockaby, is why my decision to bring you here was correct. Your steadfastness and diligence are what I require. I need you to teach me the fundaments of astronomy, from naming the stars to charting, calculating orbits and *coordinates* – is that what they're called? – so I might better understand what Shakespeare might have known… or not known. And when my flights of fancy threaten to carry me too far. I need your proven theories. And even your unproven theories! Let us have no boundaries, eh? I am willing to be convinced by you.'

It felt as if she'd waited countless years to hear those words. She breathed deeply. 'Then I hope that my truths bear out my convictions, Mr Malles.'

Mr Malles nodded. 'Already, I feel our intellectual union will bear the sweetest fruit.'

A wry smile played around Nancy's lips.

Mr Malles continued. 'I keep late hours. Our studies will commence daily at seven and I shall see you only for our work. Outwith those hours, Mrs McLoone will look after you. We start tonight.'

She was used to working evenings, and was relieved that Mr Malles had not suggested an earlier start. 'Thank you, Mr Malles. I appreciate the leap you have taken in employing me, and seek to assure that you will not regret your choice.'

'Tonight then, Miss Lockaby. We will meet in your study.' Mr Malles walked brusquely out of the room.

*

Nancy stared out of the window. The skies were now clear, the sun glittering on a snowy lawn. A phrase wisped into her mind, something her mother had murmured to her one night as they were industriously pen-scratching the infinitesimally small movements of the stars into charts: 'The veil between science and the unknown is thin, and we push it one way, allow it to flow back again now and then.'

Nancy tilted her face into the bright winter sun.

On the fence outside, unnoticed, sat the ragged silhouettes of three large crows.

Chapter Five

The sky was pinking as Mrs McLoone showed Nancy to her study, a small corner room on the first floor of the house. It was lined with shelves filled with books, belonging to Mr Malles, she supposed, a large table, her trunk and two writing desks. Nancy noted approvingly that the large windows on two aspects of the room faced both north and east; perfect for observing the stars. She had requested that when studying, her supper should be left on a tray for her, and it sat on the windowsill, covered by a hessian cloth. As she bent to unlock her trunk she noticed a small red ball almost hidden in the corner of the room, and picked it up, threw it in the air and caught it one-handed, then put it on the table.

The rest of the table was soon hidden under neat stacks of charts and thick books. Her small travel telescope stood on a spindly tripod at the window, and a series of wooden boxes lay neatly on the shelves. Nancy opened each one, checking her precious instruments had remained intact, greeting them like old friends. The dearest, she left until last, reverently opening a small battered box.

Inside, a narrow silver cylinder, topped with a golden globe – the Sun. She took it from the velvet-lined case, unfolding its spindly, right-angled arms. Each supported a tiny stone planet: jade for Mercury, Venus in ivory, a malachite Earth, Mars represented by garnet, Jupiter in polished coral, and Saturn threatening in onyx. Some of those spheres had filigree arms of their own, topped with delicate pearl moons, cleverly designed to be unfolded by a child's hands.

The cylinder fitted neatly into a mechanised base, the size of a dandelion clock. Nancy placed it on the table. As she turned a dainty key, the fingernail-sized cogs purred, and the planets started to rotate smoothly around the central globe, each tracking its own, pre-ordained orbit. The familiar ticking sound made Nancy smile, and she traced the engraving around the base, which read: *For our little stargazer. Mama and Papa.*

Her father had made this orrery when she was tiny, and his love was embedded into each perfectly spherical stone, every tiny-toothed wheel.

As ever, the orderliness soothed her. She watched the fingernail-small coloured planets wheel precisely around the miniature sun.

Her mother's academic abilities had always been more esoteric than those of her father. He crafted instruments with feather-barb precision, and his work was solid and reliable. Yet her mother's mind wheeled and birled, her hands plucking theories from East, West and beyond, binding them with threads pulled from deep in her own, magnificent, careening mind. However, that searing brilliance had, as Nancy had discovered, often put her at odds with the rest of the Observatory, and some of her theories had been too far-fetched for even her husband and Mr Bradley to indulge.

She'd watched her mother in the throes of academic reverie, her fingers skittering across charts and into the air. She too, in her early years of learning, had studied so hard that a trance-like state had descended upon her, and, on wakening, could barely remember how she might have calculated the figures inscribed on the page before her. Yet each equation always balanced. Nancy thought back to this morning's conversation. Mr Malles' propositions were, after all, merely that;

propositions. No matter how fanciful, they were still hypotheses ready to be disproved – or even proved – through research and the presentation of cold fact. Her mother would have surely leapt at the chance to reach across scholarly boundaries, and to weave new theories on the cusps of academic disciplines. This is what she had thrived on. Nancy remembered the giggle in Elizabeth's voice, 'Discoveries come more readily when your mind is joyful and open.'

The orrery slowed to a halt. Outside it was growing dark. Surely she should not dismiss her employer's theories when, despite being grounded in observation and diligence, the Fold still sat unproven and mocked.

At least she might afford Mr Malles the dignity of subjecting his suppositions to a degree of scrutiny. Giving him a basic schooling in the fundamentals of the universe would be easy enough; his mind seemed sharp and open. And, away from the demands of Dr Maskliss and the Observatory, she would have time to – perhaps – prove the science behind that impenetrable wrinkle in the sky. There were, after all, mere months until the next transit, and she must prepare for her only chance to prove her mother's theories correct.

She stood and sighed, then wandered over to her telescope, bent her eye to the glass and was soon lost watching the stars awaken.

Nancy started as her new colleague entered the room without a knock and let a heavy armful of books fall on the table. Nancy turned from her telescope just in time to see some of her maps flutter to the ground. She curled her lip, but Mr Malles ignored both the papers and her annoyance. He threw his coat on a chair, pushed up his shirt sleeves to the elbows, lit a lamp and grinned.

'Good evening, Miss Lockaby.' His eyes scanned the room, pausing briefly, Nancy noted, on her orrery, before his gaze returned to her. 'At last, we start. We have much work to do, and I am eager to begin.' His voice had the faintest tremble.

Her fellow scholar indicated the small table next to the door. 'I have my own study, but for now we will work together in here. This desk will be mine; the one by the window yours,' he said. 'When you are not needed, you are welcome to continue with any work you were undertaking in London. I will, however, have questions for you, which I expect to be answered in a timely fashion.'

'Naturally.' said Nancy.

'But first, the fundamentals. I know, of course, the very basest of principles, but no more than the names of planets and a few constellations. Would you start tonight to teach me more?'

Nancy nodded, the notion of being regarded as an equal, or more, by her research partner sent a thrill of nostalgia coursing through her veins. 'Of course. Let us start with planetary orbits.'

Mr Malles was a fast and enthusiastic learner. Nancy found herself working at a faster pace than she had expected, and her student's questions were well-timed and astute. That Mr Malles had a sound grasp of fairly advanced mathematics came somewhat as a surprise. When pressed he, somewhat bashfully, explained, 'My father may have had his failings, but he considered education priceless. After a childhood spent in the company of some of the best tutors in Scotland, he would have been furious if I had come away without knowing at least the basics of calculus.'

In less than an hour or two, she had covered the first principles of orbits, parabolas and parallax, and she stopped to take a sip of water. Mr Malles shot her a sharp look. 'I am not yet tired, please, if you can, go on.'

She smiled. She was still a little weary after her long journey. 'I think that is enough for tonight. I find that it's better to work

intensely for short periods then let the information dissemi-
nate a little.'

For the briefest instant, Mr Malles's eyes appeared to narrow
in frustration, but he gave a brusque nod. 'Very well. Thank
you, Miss Lockaby. That was an illuminating lesson. My head
will be full of numbers tonight. It's been a long time since I
thought in terms of equations rather than sentences. You are a
fine teacher.' His words fell like rain on a parched field. Nancy
turned away, stifling a flattered smile.

When she turned back, she saw that Mr Malles had picked
up a well-worn book. He started to flick through its pages a
little theatrically. Nancy took her cue. 'Might you tell me more
about your studies?'

Mr Malles held up his book with a wide smile. 'This, Miss
Lockaby, is, I believe, the pinnacle of Shakespeare's achieve-
ments.' For a moment his eyes glittered darkly. '*Macbeth*.
Most of my time now is devoted to this work of genius. I
have theories, but I require the help of someone well-versed
in the movement of the stars, the moon, to uncover its most
cryptic secrets. Tell me, Miss Lockaby, what do you know of
Shakespeare?'

She smiled, a little surprised that it had taken him this long
to ask. 'Not a great deal, Mr Malles. When I was in London I
enjoyed a trip to the theatre to see Mr Garrick's excellent performance, and Shakespeare's stories seem to capture something of
the human condition, but my knowledge is superficial at most.'

Malles's brow furrowed at these words. 'As you know, my
interest in Shakespeare is a little more *profound* than those who
seek only entertainment from his work.' He fixed Nancy with
that gaze once more. 'You must understand, Miss Lockaby,
that although I present myself as a student of Shakespeare, I
am searching beyond mere words. His works open me to those
experiences, those places, those people beyond the absolute,

beyond documentation, that exist on the outermost, furthest fringes of knowledge. Yet I must be sure that this knowledge is built on the firmest of foundations. Foundations that I hope you will build with me.'

Nancy's heart thudded. She could barely remember how it felt to be treated as an intellectual equal: the nodded respect, the assumption that yes, her opinions held value. She briefly thought of telling Mr Malles about her own, disparaged discovery. His words marked him as a man open to such things, perhaps more so than anyone she had met. However, she resisted. No matter how tempted she was to bring up the subject, that must wait until she could be more sure of his response.

Mr Malles coughed and looked down at Nancy's supper. 'I too will eat here. Now, I have work to continue, as do you. I will ask more when I need.' He sat down at his desk and started to read. The silence felt natural; the kind of easy quiet that often falls over those who study together. It felt almost like those nights at the Observatory before that companionable hush was replaced with the low hum of simmering resentment and arch whispers.

Nancy watched Mr Malles for a few seconds, his black, curling hair bent over the pages before she turned back to her work. The red ball she'd picked up earlier sat beside her papers, and as she read, she rolled it idly round the table under one hand. She glanced up. Mr Malles was staring at the toy.

'Miss Lockaby, if you could be so kind, I would like that.' There was a trace of a tremor in his voice, like the distant boom of thunder on a summer day. Nancy handed him the ball, and he took the plaything roughly without speaking, stuffing it into his pocket.

With a shrug of the shoulders, she unlaced a leather wrap to find a pen and set to the evening's measurements.

Chapter Six

The coach driver was due to take Cora on her journey back to London that morning, but she seemed reluctant to leave. It seemed she had not been heartened by her conversation with Isobel and, on meeting the new maid, Nancy had some sympathy with her point of view.

The girl seemed younger than her fifteen years. Eager as a puppy, her hands were barely calloused and her eyes still not downcast as those belonging to girls in service tended to be. Yet when Nancy had asked her if she might tease a little height into her curls, the girl had goggled in bewilderment, and blurted out, 'Surely a bunnet would not fit over such a thing?' before clapping a hand to her mouth and reddening. After some assurance from Nancy that she might speak freely to her, without fear of any conversation reaching the ears of the dour Mrs McLoone, she had proudly told her new mistress of her history with the Malleses.

She lived with her family in a small cottage on the outskirts of the estate. Her father was the estate's gardener and gamekeeper, and her mother had died four years past in childbirth, so the eleven-year-old Isobel had gone into service as a maid in her place.

Cora pulled the strings on her corset tight, so the garment hardened around Nancy's soft, pillowy waist, cinching it tightly. 'Isobel is but a child, ma'am. You will have to teach her everything, tell her all you need, show her what's what. It will be like having a baby trying look after you.'

Nancy tutted. 'She will learn fast I'm sure, Cora, and won't answer me back in such overfamiliar fashion.' She turned and winked at her friend, then put her hand on her shoulder. 'Thank you, Cora, for travelling all this way with me. I wish you could stay. However, I do understand how much your mother and father need you.' Her voice softened into nothing.

'Thank you, ma'am. I wish I might stay too.' She bit her lip.

'Well,' said Nancy brightly, 'we shall write. Those long hours I spent teaching you copperplate will not go to waste! Be sure to speak to that girl up at the observatory. Robin, was it not? She might provide us with news of what passes there.'

'Of course, ma'am. I will be sure to send lots of letters.'

Nancy grasped her hand, and squeezed it. 'Do not worry on my account, Cora. This is where I want to be, where I need to be.'

Cora squeezed Nancy's hand back, and hesitated before replying, 'Don't lose yourself in the stars, ma'am.'

An hour later, Nancy waved her off, the coach skidding a little on the ice. As she turned and went back into the house, she saw Mr Malles at the window of one of the rooms on the second floor, his eyes fixed on the skies, lost in thought.

★

Cora's departure was less painful than Nancy had imagined, and within a week, she had settled into a routine. The higgledy-piggledy flagstones of Blackthistle House began to feel familiar, if still icily cold, under her slippered feet, and she grew a little more used to the austere furnishings worn from years of elbows and polish. Isobel's nimble fingers swiftly became almost as fast at lacing Nancy's yellow-and-purple dress as Cora's had been, although Nancy missed the confidences she had been able to make in her old friend. There had been no more sign of the mysterious light that had so unnerved her on her arrival at Blackthistle, yet the place felt steeped in damp, chilly dolefulness. More disconcertingly, on two or three occasions, Nancy had snapped awake in the early hours, roused by what sounded like a tap on her window, a laugh, a clatter of wings. A ridiculous fancy, of course.

Working late into the night meant Nancy habitually rose late. She had attempted to engage Mrs McLoone in conversation over breakfast, but her words had fallen on flinty ground. Still, Nancy resolved to keep a cheery disposition when around the housekeeper, and continued to chit-chat to the woman, regardless of whether her words were met with anything approaching enthusiasm.

Days were spent researching or escaping the morose atmosphere of the house on walks into the countryside where she would watch eagles rise above mountains softened in drizzle. As the snows melted into sodden fields, and April crocuses peeked cautiously through the near-bare earth, she spent more and more time on the moors and fells. Her cheeks soon lost their London night pallor.

She supposed that most would be bored senseless by these solitary hours, but after years of being obliged to keep Crooms House running smoothly, in addition to applying herself to study, she rather relished this time spent alone with her thoughts and theories. While walking, her mind soared alongside those eagles coasting on their thermal currents, her trains of thought rising and falling undisturbed. On these wanderings, Nancy rarely saw another living soul, although on one occasion she fancied she saw the skinny, ragged figure of an old woman disappear into the trees and on another, the drift of laughter floated over the hills, with no apparent source. And each time the shadow of a crow passed in front of the Sun, she would pull her shawl tighter and turn for home.

Work became a comfortable routine, and Mr Malles's earnest attentiveness made for easy study sessions. Although her pupil remained somewhat serious and showed little of himself he would occasionally gently question her,

'Tell me, Miss Lockaby, what is the most remarkable sight you have yet seen? What spectacles have you enjoyed?'

Yet, despite his interest in her wider thoughts about the universe, she remained a little cautious, and had revealed to him little of what she was researching privately. She had never encountered the master of Blackthistle during daylight hours. There was the odd door bang, and she swore she had once heard his boots clicking along the corridor, but as a rule, she saw him only during their time together.

She familiarised herself with Inverness, attending church each Sunday. At first, she had noticed that some heads would turn as she wriggled into a pew, but her novelty swiftly faded and she sat almost unnoticed. Sometimes she would crane her neck, wondering if she might see the faces of the women who had stood at the gates of Blackthistle on her arrival, but, as far as she could ascertain, they were not church-goers.

Her spirits had never soared at prayers, and she felt no pull towards the words of the Bible; indeed, as she sat and gazed at the giant window set high in the wall behind the priest, her thoughts would dwell on her predecessors vilified by popes and cardinals for their heretical insistence that the universe did not revolve around the Earth. However, she supposed her attendance was expected, and so Nancy did her duty. She had never seen Mr Malles at a service.

After church, she had taken to exploring the town alone. The houses were coarsely built, stones poking out from roughly mortared walls and curious round windows that made those who peeped out look as if they were in the stocks. Bobbing through the narrow streets in her emerald-green gown, she was like a popinjay among pigeons. Both women and men dressed in thick, belted blankets – plaids and arisaids, Isobel called them – that they pulled over their heads to protect against the rainy gusts of wind that eddied around the corners of the town or whose folds snuggled tiny babies. Although they understood and spoke English, they conversed quietly together in soft, throaty Gaelic, into which, Nancy suspected, they shifted when they wanted to make comment on her. However, while no doubt curious as to her position in Blackthistle House, people were generally polite and the store-keepers helpful in ordering her paper and inks. Mr McBride, the beef-faced general-store owner became an acquaintance, and they would discuss the build-ing of the town's new church, and dispatches from London.

She would tear open the latest *Caledonian Mercury* and read it standing in McBride's store, searching for reports of James Cook's journey as he sailed HMS *Endeavour* across the globe to Tahiti to document this year's transit. His was the grandest, most expensive, of all the exploratory voyages. She allowed herself the odd jealous harrumph.

McBride let her sit and read in peace. 'What news from the other side of the world, lassie?' he would eventually ask. 'And have you found us a new planet yet?' His manner was amiable and his conversation erudite, so she started to look forward to their brief chats.

Although Isobel had yet to successfully tackle that annoying tangle of hair at the nape of her neck, she provided chatter when Nancy craved company. The girl had a curious nature, and Nancy had begun to teach her a little writing and mathe-matics, as she had taught Cora. She was a firm believer that if a person showed promise, they should be given opportunity, regardless of their station, and while Isobel was not as fast to grasp principles as dear Cora had been, she tried her very best, and slowly made headway learning her numbers. Together, they would steal minutes before luncheon, or scribble a few letters when the maid brought Nancy milk at night. Even if she made slow progress, the girl provided companionship, and Nancy grew to look forward to their tutorials.

This morning, Isobel was attempting to tame Nancy's hair, her mistress scowling as the comb caught in her thick red curls.

'Ouch.' Nancy indicated the little silver brush that she had found in the cabinet drawer. 'Perhaps you might try that brush, Isobel? Cora seemed to think it would work better.'

She stopped. The girl's lip was trembling, her eyes fixed on the brush, her hand moving slowly to her mouth.

'Ma'am, no. Not that one.'

Nancy wrinkled her brow quizzically. 'I'm sorry?'

'That shouldn't be here. I'll take it, if you don't mind.'

Isobel reached for the brush and put it into her pocket. Blinking and white-faced, she excused herself. Within seconds, she had left the room. Her fast footsteps echoed down the corridor. Nancy shook her head, at a loss at what had just happened. The brush looked in no way valuable, but it quite obviously had belonged to a lady of some means. A previous visitor perhaps.

Nancy was left confused. Slowly she finished combing her hair herself. That this house held secrets, there was no doubt, but she felt no closer to uncovering what they might be.

*

The design of her studies with Mr Malles allowed little opportunity for asking personal questions, and she had no desire to mix the private with the professional. On a few occasions, she had steeled her nerves to ask her colleague about his past, but the words had remained dry in her mouth. Theirs was, for now, very much an academic relationship. Relaxed certainly, but with conversation barely extending beyond facts and calculation.

In little more than a month, Mr Malles had progressed far more quickly than Nancy could have imagined. She had led him beyond the basics of astronomy and he could recognise most constellations, and already they had made deeper inroads into the dark arts of calculus. In another life, he might have made a sturdy computer for Dr Maskliss.

However, although many hours were dedicated to teaching, the pair also studied in parallel, usually in agreeable silence, his pen scritch-scratching, the occasional scrape of tripod feet across the uneven floor as Nancy moved her telescope.

Yet she wondered if there was something else, something specific in Shakespeare's work perhaps, that Mr Malles was circling, even if he might not yet know the exact nature of his quarry. Every so often, he would lift his head, fix Nancy with a quizzical look. 'Miss Lockaby, tell me, what do you know of eclipses? Might you tell me how many this country experienced during the eleventh century? Are all events in the sky as predictable?' Nancy would pull out her Flamsteed or Halley, and answer the query as speedily as she could.

She thrived, as she always had, on the warm feeling of being useful and Mr Malles's sincere encouragement as she alighted on what appeared to be a significant piece of information spurred her onwards.

Occasionally, out of nowhere, Mr Malles would read out loud, not in a conceited manner, but merely revelling in the rhythms and rhymes that drove Shakespeare's work. Through his recitals, she traced the story of Macbeth; the dramatic frissons of his meeting with the witches made the study fizzle with supernatural intent, while the machinations of his wife, and the bloody murder plot that followed had her eyeing the walls of the room, fearful that she might see them dripping in gore. She followed his journey from Thane of Glamis to Thane of Cawdor and finally King, breath held, the pen in her hand occasionally trembling at particularly thrilling passages, although she kept her excitement hidden from the narrator in front of her, her eyes firmly fixed on her work.

Mr Malles had a talent for imbuing words that had dried flat on the page with emotion and context. The scenes in Shakespeare's play took place around Inverness itself. She had walked the same streets that once echoed to the screams of Duncan, murdered by the treacherous Macbeth – the discovery of which sent a small shiver of delight down her spine.

Meanwhile the witches were said to have lived nearby in Brodie, while Forres, which was only a day's ride away, was where Duncan's castle was to be found. She began to relish the times he would push back his chair, and then begin a performance.

'Out, out, brief candle!
Life's but a walking shadow, a poor player,
That struts and frets his hour upon the stage,
And then is heard no more; it is a tale
Told by an idiot, full of sound and fury,
Signifying nothing.'

Full of sound and fury. The words took on an almost physical form, their bitterness and ravaged pain sharp in Nancy's ears. She continued to peer through her telescope, keeping her back to Mr Malles.

'From the play?' she asked.

'Of course.'

She turned to face him. 'What does it mean?'

'Macbeth has been told of his wife's death and is contemplating his bleak situation. He's lost, tormented.' Mr Malles spoke more quietly, his eyes closed. 'His wife was his world, and now his world is crumbling. And he is realising that life is a sham and has no more reason than the ramblings of a madman.'

His fingers reached for the locket around his neck, his face pale in the candlelight. The chill and gloom that pervaded Blackthistle seemed suddenly to have seeped into the study. Nancy thought of the house's austere furnishings, the fear in Isobel's eyes as she snatched away the silver hairbrush, the empty spaces where paintings had once hung. It felt as if an actor in this play was missing, lines left unspoken, that there were ghosts at the feast.

Mr Malles remained in the room only long enough that his swift exit retained a semblance of dignity. He left with a mutter: 'I'm sorry, Miss Lockaby, but I fear I am taking sick. A chill, perhaps.'

★

A week later, the incident lay near-forgotten. Perhaps as penance, Mr Malles had allowed Nancy a little more time for her studies. Tonight, he had given her two extra hours after nightfall before lessons started, time she was determined to use wisely. The transit was, after all, only weeks away, and, although she had made good headway, she had not yet readied all she needed in order to document the reappearance of the Fold.

Her preparations for this transit were more exacting and with far greater ambition than the last time Venus had swept across the Sun. This was, after all, the only chance she would have to prove and build upon her mother's theories. And if she could not persuade the great and the good of the scientific world of the existence of the Fold this time around, then, surely, she was no astronomer at all. Although the night was spring-warm, she shivered and pulled her shawl closer, sitting quietly, drawing the charts that might be filled less than two months hence, on the third day of June.

She glanced at the clock then folded away her papers. Mr Malles would soon be here. Tonight she was determined to teach him more of parallax. As she placed her papers safely into her trunk, she smiled. What better example of the use of the technique than the transit?

She sat down, picked up a pen and sketched a rough diagram, marking out Venus' progression between the Sun and Earth. As she worked, she hummed gently to herself.

'A song to welcome me, Miss Lockaby?' Nancy coloured, caught unawares.

'Mr Malles.'

Mr Malles was in the habit of dragging his chair to her desk, and sitting opposite, chin in hands, as she taught.

'Tonight, once more, we shall tackle parallax.' Her pupil nodded enthusiastically. For a few minutes they talked of the nature of the measurements needed to calculate distance.

'Of course, the best demonstration is the transit of Venus across the Sun. You are familiar, I am sure, with the event?'

Mr Malles dropped his pen. He fumbled as he picked it up.

'Mr Malles? You know of the significance of the transit, I am sure.'

His voice sounded over-measured. 'I am aware it is of importance to astronomers. However, when it happened last I was preoccupied with other matters. I know it's only a short while until it takes place again. Tell me more about it.' He gripped the pen and raised his eyebrows. 'Please.'

Nancy traced her fingers over her sketch.

'If we view Venus from different positions on Earth as the planet tracks in front of the Sun, we can use the principles of parallax to measure our distance from that great star.' Her eyes glowed as she recounted how, in 1716, Halley had issued a rallying call to the future Western astronomers and mathematicians of 1761, to leave their well-appointed observatories and travel to far-flung countries and measure, measure, measure.

Taking a new sheet of paper, she wrote a series of dates.

'As is usually the case with astronomical events, the pattern of Venus's transits is logical. But there's something queer about it.' She laughed. 'There's a pair of crossings, eight years apart – there was one in 1761 and will be another in June – then a wait of 121½ years, then another pair. Then another wait of 105½ years, then the pattern repeats.'

Mr Malles listened intently, his long fingers trailing over her diagram.

'What did you see, when you saw the transit?' he asked.

When Nancy was eight, Uncle James had taken her hand and described how it felt to watch a total solar eclipse. He had, he told her, seen two: one while studying at Oxford, and another when he first became an astronomer. He had spoken gravely, as if she were an adult. 'Gazing at the stars made me want to become an astronomer, but witnessing the eclipse led me to become a man of God. The strange still in the air minutes before – even the birds fell silent – the way the shadow of every leaf turned crescent-shaped before my eyes, that curtain of darkness sweeping inexorably over the hills and meadows, Nancy, it was as if the four horsemen themselves were galloping towards me! And when the rock of the moon passed in front of the sun, its outline ringed with a halo of flame, truly, my child, it was a sight that confirmed the hand of our Lord and filled me with the fear of hell. A sight that combined the divine and the profane!' She remembered vividly the spark in his eyes as he spoke.

When Nancy had witnessed the Fold, something fundamental within her had shifted. She might not have had the religious fervour of dear Uncle James, yet seeing the sky pouring and swirling in on itself had changed her perception of place, although she knew not if she had been anchored more firmly in her universe, or if her insignificance and impermanence had been magnified in the most dreadful way. More than anything, she wanted to confide in someone who might have the faintest understanding of the enormity of what she had seen. For one moment, she considered telling Mr Malles about it. Yet, there was something in the intensity of his gaze that stilled her.

She looked away. 'It was spectacular, Mr Malles. In that short night we learned much.' She muttered, almost beneath her breath, 'Some of us more than others.'

Briskly, she folded up the diagram. 'Enough for tonight, I think.'

'Thank you, Miss Lockaby. I think you are right. I am tired. Until tomorrow.' He stood, packed up his things swiftly and left the room without further farewell. A few papers fluttered to the floor.

Exhausted, Nancy opened the casement and leaned on the ledge, gazing aimlessly into the sky. Then, a flash. As she peered down the wall and into the turret on her right, she saw the same barred window she had been drawn to upon her arrival at Blackthistle. All at once, it again began flickering and crackling with bright light. Silver-birch-bark white. As before, the fierceness, the intensity of the glow filled her with a prickling hot dread. She stared at the otherworldly light she had seen on her arrival, that vision that she had thought a figment of her tired imagination. *Good heavens!* She felt the same acrid dread that had risen unbidden on seeing the women at the gates of Blackthistle, the same intense fear that had engulfed her as the crows attacked.

Her eyes started to water at the brightness, yet she felt compelled to stare towards the flashes. Then they were gone, extinguished. She sank back into the chair at her desk, exhausted and shaking. The fire in the grate had long faded and her breath laced the chill air. She sat staring out of the window into the skies, watching the clouds scudding across that bright, unforgiving, full moon.

Chapter Seven

Blackthistle House
Inverness
Scotland
7th April 1769

My dearest Cora
Thank you so much for your letters. I had feared that I might miss Greenwich, but you capture both its hubbub and serenity in such vital fashion that I feel I am still in my favourite spot, on its fringes. Your reassurances as to the smooth running of Crooms are also appreciated. I fear that William may neglect the arbour in my absence. Would you remind him that it needs pruning before spring starts in earnest?

My studies here continue. Mr Malles is a most agreeable colleague, although at times a little demanding. He is yet to join me for dinner and I see him only during our working hours. As you well know, I intended to use some of my time here to persevere with my studies, and have made good progress. I have been heartened by Mr Malles's open-minded approach to the new thus far, and might even perhaps be inclined to share some of my theories at some point soon, although I am not yet wholly sure.

However, I wish you were here that I might tell you more. Mr Malles has not spoken explicitly of his affairs, but it is becoming apparent that there is a sadness that hangs over Blackthistle. You know I am not one to whis-

per, but I have found no evidence of a woman having ever existed here. As you are aware, my experience of the world is limited through circumstance, but surely this is most queer. I know you will have thoughts regarding this matter, which I wish to hear by return. I miss having a companion in whom to confide.

As you might surmise, I have decided to stay. Would you package up in sheep fleece the brass eighteen-inch aperture reflector telescope that stands in my bedroom, and send it by ship? I will need it for the transit in June.

I send my very warmest regards to your parents and hope they are now in better health.

With fondness,

Nancy

The next morning a small parcel lay on the breakfast table. Isobel hopped from foot to foot in excitement. 'Open it, ma'am!'

Confused, Nancy unwrapped the package, gossamer-thin black paper fluttering to the floor. Inside lay a copy of *Macbeth* bound in the softest red leather, its edges gilded so freshly they reflected light beams around the room.

There was a note folded into the book in Mr Malles's looping handwriting.

Miss Nancy Lockaby,

I write in appreciation of your calm, guiding hand. Your patience and depth of knowledge inspire this awkward, slow-witted pupil daily.

With thanks, Caleb

Nancy paused at the unexpectedly effusive words – first names were now evidently acceptable. Her lips curled into an involuntary wide smile. She closed the book and held it up to the impatient Isobel.

'*Macbeth*,' she said.

Isobel replied, 'I know *Macbeth*. I think even the mice in this house's kitchen know of *Macbeth*. Is it from Mr Malles?' The present was unexpected, yet there was something endearing about Mr Malles's open thankfulness, even if he didn't feel able to express it to her directly. The warmth of being useful, a good teacher flooded through her. *Caleb*. It was surprisingly easy to call him by his Christian name.

That afternoon, she lay on her bed and reread a scene aloud. Hesitantly at first, but then with more confidence. It was one of the most gloriously dramatic parts of the book, set at a banquet held at Forres Castle. It was as if the ghosts of Macbeth and Lady Macbeth drifted into her room and whispered conspiratorially around her. A life spent in neat numbers had left her unprepared for the depth of emotion that literature might conjure.

The story transported her in the same way the stars lifted her into another world. For an afternoon, she walked among the kings and the thanes.

It will have blood, they say. Blood will have blood. She murmured that line aloud. 'Blood will have blood.' These events had taken place within sight of Blackthistle. Lady Macbeth would have stared into the Ness as she had done, Duncan would have gazed up at the same stars. Macbeth's footprints might still lay imprinted in the moors that ringed the town. It was becoming apparent why the book fascinated Caleb. The boundaries between the world conjured by Shakespeare and her own suddenly felt paper-thin. She shivered and closed the book, laying it on the bedside table.

Perhaps this more remote life was starting to fray the edges of her mind. She determined to seek out some company outside the house before too long.

★

It had been Isobel who had told her about the fair in Inverness – or 'the Snecky' as she called the town – that Monday, the first of May. ''Tis Beltane, ma'am. You'll not be wanting to miss that. The town will be full of it,' she whispered. ''Tis courtin' time. 'Tis time for the flames.' She had told Nancy of 'Belenus' and fire-making, and how it was to be the end of spring and the start of summer, and that Ma'am just must go for there were good things to eat, and music, and laddies, and reeling and the spring and, oh the laddies. Nancy had given her a wry smile and told her that she wasn't interested at all in the laddies and reeling, but that perhaps she was craving some company. So she agreed that they should attend the fair together. It would be more seemly to have a maid accompany her to town, after all.

Nancy thought of the procession that she'd watched snaking through Greenwich on the first day of May every year. Viewed from the privileged windows of Crooms, she'd always thought it a rather sweet affair, bringing blossom and colour to the greasy docks.

However, yesterday, she had overheard Mrs McLoone telling the baker's boy at the kitchen door that she had no intention of visiting the Beltane fair, muttering, 'If you ask me, for most 'tis just an excuse for rutting in the bushes.' Perhaps Inverness's version of the festival was a little more *elemental* than the picnic she was used to in Greenwich. But, she laughed, surely a woman who could brave a room full of waspish mathematicians, ready to pounce on the smallest error, was bold enough to venture into even the wildest party.

She needn't have worried. Inverness looked almost jolly in the late-afternoon spring sun. The bridge's parapets were studded with large bunches of green-leafed branches, tied with wide purple, yellow and red ribbons and below, the river was low and serene. On the banks of the river stood a huge pile of wood, being readied for a bonfire. The structure was taller than the houses surrounding it: planks of timber made up a rough frame, with logs and branches piled on top. Its edges were softened by trails of ivy and pine branches, but no amount of decoration served to make it look any less sinister. Looming over the town, its shape echoed that of the brooding, ruined castle that lay only a few streets away.

Nancy had picked out a sunset-orange dress trimmed in yellow, whose bright colours always made her smile broadly. Isobel wore her usual squirrel-grey pinafore. The two silhouettes contrasted; the girl twiggy and budding next to Nancy's solid, blossomed figure. Her maid may not have had the greatest mathematical brain, but she was easy company; her life in service had not yet been long enough to quash her spirit.

Above many of the town's doors were branches, thin-leaved and hung with white flowers, again tied with ribbons. Their cloying scent clouded the hot, heavy air. Rowan, perhaps. On the steps of some of the houses sat cups filled with beer, the warm, hoppy fumes mingling with the blossom's fragrance.

Laughter and music sang from every open window. Peeping through casements, Nancy saw girls dressed in long, white cotton dresses having flowers braided into their hair, and boys shining their shoe buckles. The town felt erumpent with anticipation.

The sound of violin music and laughter floated out of a tavern, followed shortly by two beefy men, grappling and rolling onto the pavement, locked in a brawl. Nancy calmly stepped around them while Isobel goggled.

'Ma'am, they're fair mauled! Did that not scare you?'

'I have seen far more shocking on the quayside at Greenwich,' said Nancy evenly.

On every street tumbled children. Many wore masks, butcher-floor animals made from scraps of fur and sun-bleached bone. They scampered around her, laughing.

The crowds were beginning to grow, shouting loud halloos to each other, carrying arches and hoops of flowers, jangling bells and flasks. The half-closed eyes and reddened faces of many she passed belied hours of heavy drinking.

People gathered around stalls selling warm bannocks and jugs of mead. Some of the men wore animal pelts, glassy-eyed heads still intact, whereas the women's dresses were hitched up and pulled down to reveal milky thighs and cleavage. The stony-faced minister from the Old High Church strode through the crowd, shaking his head.

The air was heavy with the smell of baked apples and smoke. They rounded a corner and reached the market square. The transformation from its usual sleepiness was breathtaking.

Dozens of stalls were set on the cobbles, each clustered with people. Smoked fish hung on ropes, sun-orange, while a man with a heavily lined face invited the two women to peer into his barrel of eels. Crofters sat chewing on their pipes, in front of greasy yellow sheep wool clouds. A tall pillar stood on a set of stone steps, about which merchants bartered their goods.

Isobel pointed at a huge, bluish lump of rock. 'Look, ma'am, this is the stone where the ladies rest their washing, the Clach-na-cudhin. We all ken it's proper old like.' Her eyes widened. '*Old ways* old.' Nancy peered at the rock, which had been decorated with tiny yellow flowers, then gave Isobel a few coins and sent her to queue for bannocks.

It was fascinating that the old religions seemed nearer the surface here. She remembered her father telling her how church-builders would pilfer little nuggets of detail from existing beliefs – a Green Man carving on a buttress here, a Sheela-na-gig there – in order to draw in the crowds who followed the ancient paths to the new places of worship. She supposed that if you scratched the veneer of any religion, you'd find layers of worship much older and more elemental beneath.

She began to look around the tables absent-mindedly. Directly across from the stone was a stall hung with silks in every hue, fluttering like flags in the spring breeze. As the scarves floated above her head, however, she felt a peculiar prickling sensation in her hands. She looked up sharply.

Through the flitter of silks, she saw the faces of three women – the women she had seen on her arrival at Blackthistle. By the stars! Her stomach lurched, and her vision flickered and faltered, as if she was looking through her telescope at the trio. The bustling market faded into the background, the hubbub of the crowd replaced by a high-pitched whine.

Swallowing she tried to recover herself and take a proper look at the women. They made an imposing sight. The youngest dressed in shades of mud and mountain, wore an apron dirty with grease. The next had a belt slung round her hips, hung with small velvet bags. Gold earrings shone bright against her soft, dark skin. The oldest woman's robes were so tattered their edges seemed to crumble into the air. She leaned on a thick stick topped with a silver crescent. They stood behind a nearby stall that was tucked into an arch at the side of the square

She stepped away from the scarves and silks, drawn almost in a daze towards the women's pitch. Their table was hung with spidery branches, decorated with ribbons and a few feathers. From the branches dangled little calico bags, drawn tightly with string. An old man glanced at the wares, shook his head, and hurried on. The young girl was in animated conversation with a customer, a nervous-looking young man, fluttering her eyelashes. She was showing him something in her hand. 'They is awful strong, so just ten will do you one night.' The eldest woman turned to Nancy, cracked a smile and beckoned, her knuckle joints gristled purple.

As she drew closer, Nancy could see each bag had a paper label: meadowsweet, mistletoe, blackthorn, yew, hemlock. The table was covered in larger packages, alongside bunches of dried herbs tied with colourful yarns, jars of dried mushrooms with pointed tops and long, thin stalks, and small wooden boxes, open to reveal ash-like powders, sticky waxes and seeds. The woman with the gold earrings, her hair wrapped in a scarf, smiled knowingly at Nancy, a gold tooth glinting.

The eldest wheedled in an undulating accent, 'Come, Child of the Moon. Come and take a look.'

Child of the Moon. How could they know about her interest in the planets? Curious, she moved cautiously towards the stall. A thick, sweet smell rose from the sun-warmed herbs. The woman with the scarf pointed out the labels on the herbs in a deep, rolling voice. Nancy recognised a French accent. 'Yarrow to heal, Peterwort to cheer, for protection. Perhaps miss would be interested in comfrey for safe travel?'

'I believe that a well-maintained coach is perfectly adequate in ensuring my safety,' she said, with a flinty half-smile.

The pedlar nodded. 'As you say, miss. Although there are more dangers when travelling than holes in the road. Even when you reach your destination, you might need to remain on guard.'

Nancy wrinkled her nose at this warning, a well-practised sales pitch of an accomplished saleswoman. However, she had a fondness for sweet scents. She picked up a bag and held it to her nose, inhaling deeply. Lavender, rose petals perhaps, and something more damp, earthy, faintly cloying. It reminded her of walking through the avenues of Greenwich Park and she felt a pang of homesickness.

She nodded at the women, softening. 'I'll take this, please.'

The younger woman nodded, 'A good choice, madam.' She took the bag with hands that looked strong enough to twist the head off a chicken and checked the handwritten label. 'These are for healin', miss. Healin' and protection.'

'Thank you, but I am merely fond of the smell.'

The girl let out an earthy giggle. 'Of course, miss, of course. That'll be two pennies.'

Nancy paid and took the bag, eyeing the trio warily. The woman with the headscarf flashed a swift look at her friends, who nodded. She reached into her pocket, took something out and pressed it into Nancy's hand.

'Take this too. Keep it under your pillow.'

Hesitantly, Nancy put the object, a small muslin parcel, into her bag.

'Thank you.'

Nancy felt compelled to stay. She wanted to know more and the women's eyes seemed to demand something from her, but she could not find words. She made a farewell as polite as she could muster and left the stall. Yet even with her back turned, she felt the stare of three pairs of eyes.

She made her way back to the flower-garlanded stone. There was a tug at her sleeve.

'Ma'am! Ma'am! I got us bannocks!'

Isobel proffered a flat oatcake, marked on one side with a cross. Nancy flipped it over; on the other side was a curious spiked symbol she'd not seen before. There was a hole through the cake. The girl's eyes were wide. 'Bealtain bonnach; that's a Beltane bannock in the old tongue.' She put a finger to her lips.

Nancy returned Isobel's bright grin with a somewhat watery smile. She would not mention her disorientating encounter with the women. They were at a fair and her maid deserved some pleasure on a rare day out of Blackthistle. She linked arms with the girl, and the pair wandered the streets, taking sneaky pinches of warm cake.

The smell of woodsmoke curled its fingers around the town, lingering heavy over the cobbles. The sun sank from the sky, and Nancy pulled her shawl tight around her.

There seemed to be impromptu performances on every street corner; fiddle players and singers, some with remarkable skill. Nancy clapped along, but her thoughts were only of the women. Her fingers closed around the small bag in her pocket.

The clock struck six, and a thrill of excitement seemed to run through the throng. The atmosphere had become purposeful, pointed. As one, the crowd heaved towards the bridge, the insistent sound of drums filling the air, suddenly rhythmic.

Swept up in the crowd, Nancy grabbed Isobel, who looked at her and whispered, 'The bridge, ma'am. We're going to the bridge. It's happening.'

Nancy was confused. The bridge was not a place she wished to be. However, there was no escape from the mass of people in these narrow streets. It was not in her nature to panic, but her conversation with the women in the market had clearly unnerved her, as every sense was now on high alert.

'Fair lady Isabel sits in her bower sewing,
Aye as the gowans grow gay
There she heard an elf-knight blawing his horn.
The first morning in May'

A woman's voice floated high above the crowd, true and strong. It was joined by a deeper baritone from nearby. Then some kind of wheezing reed instrument – bagpipes perhaps.

'He leapt on a horse, and she on another,
And they rode on to the greenwood together.
"Light down, light down, lady Isabel," said he,
"We are come to the place where ye are to die"'

Now the street was alive with melody. It seemed to pour out of every person. The sound grew more intense, louder, more aggressive, as if the walls, the cobbles were shouting;

the echoes sharp and jagged in Nancy's ears. She stood and looked around her in panic, the rhymes circling over and over.

Just as her ears reached the point at which they could take no more, the song stopped.

She kept her gaze firmly ahead as she navigated through the throng. As they reached the bridge, it was packed with bodies, and she had to weave her way through the mob. There was an intense smell of smoke. Jostled and disorientated, she hugged her bag close to her chest, put her head down, and pushed her way through the crush. The crowd pressed closer, chuckling faces distorted next to hers.

She took Isobel's hand and pulled both of them to the edge of the bridge. They gasped in the cool evening air, Isobel's eyes shining. The girl pointed downwards.

'See!'

The huge bonfire was ablaze, spitting sparks into the air, young men dancing through the flames, cheered on by their sweethearts. Couples were kissing, grabbing at each other furiously. A shout went up – 'Sap's risin'' – followed by coarse laughter.

A huge man with a grey pelt hanging down his back took to the stage. His face looked out from under that of a dead wolf. The drums stopped.

'Clann Na Cloiche! Come, Children of the Stone!' he shouted.
'At the turning of the wheel,
As the sun begins to steal,
So she chooses one to take,
Cailleach Bealtane show your face,
To Belenus' fire's warm embrace!
This is to you, oh mists and storms, spare our pastures and our corn,
This to you, oh eagle, spare our lambs and our kids
This is to thee, oh fox and falcon, spare our poultry.'

Five large men, each manhandling a wriggling young boy, burst from the crowd and stood in front of the man. One of the boys had tears running down his face. The man wearing the wolf hide picked up a metal cauldron and shook it. The crowd cheered, then quietened.

Nancy turned to Isobel, her heart racing in panic. The boys seemed terrified, yet no-one was going to their aid. The girl's eyes were round. 'Here come the bannocks. The boy that takes the blackened cake, he'll be the one!' The crowd was now near-silent, all rapt. The boys were pushed forward, towards the man in the wolf hide. He held the cauldron in front of them.

The first boy shoved his hand into the vessel and pulled out a bannock. He looked at it, then held it aloft in relieved triumph. The crowd roared. The boy was released and he danced back into the throng.

'He's safe. He's not the chosen,' Isobel whispered. 'Keep watching, ma'am.' Nancy's gaze returned to the scene. Another boy picked a cake. Again, a roar went up. He too was released.

The third boy was the one who had been crying. Her blood chilled. The boy forced his hand into the pot, and shaking, the boy pulled out his cake.

It was black.

The crowd gasped and then erupted into a roar. The boy's face collapsed in fear.

The drums started again, more insistent, louder than before. All eyes were fixed on the boy and fire. All hands clapping.

The other boys were released, their handlers walking towards the boy holding the blackened cake. Each took an arm and a leg. A wooden bucket was brought forward, and the men took thick ropes and pegs from it and used them to tie the struggling boy down. The crowd laughed.

Isobel took Nancy's arm, her smile broad, her eyes alive. Nancy was in a daze.

The fire seemed to blaze with even more intensity as the man in the wolf pelt stood over the squirming boy. He reached under his cloak and took out a long, heavy sword. He held it above his head, its blade alive with the reflections of orange flames. For a moment he stood there, sword aloft, the crowd holding its breath. Nancy gasped as the sword plunged towards the boy, blood pumping in her ears. However, at the last second, the man twisted the sword sideways, plunging it into the earth a hair's breadth away from the boy's ear.

Nancy shook her head as the boy leapt up and danced into the edges of the fire, darting through the flames, laughing. It became apparent to Nancy that this had been a play-act, although what an actor the boy had been. Her raging heartbeat started to subside, replaced with hot confusion.

Isobel smiled encouragingly. 'It is only a game, ma'am. Now spring really is here, the sacrifice is done.' She bit her lip. 'It happens every year, we got to make sure the sun comes back. She'll fade in time, right enough, and the Call-yack – the old woman of winter – will get her cold bony fingers into the town again. Do you not have anything like it in England?'

'We don't indulge in such nonsense. Come, we must get back to Blackthistle.' The pair trudged back to the house in silence, Isobel wearing a worried expression. Before she pulled the bell cord at the door, Nancy relented and turned to the girl. 'It was a jolly afternoon. I cannot wait to tell Mrs McLoone about the fun we had.'

In return, she received an understanding look. They turned together, smiling conspiratorially as the reliably dour McLoone opened the front door.

★

It wasn't until she was about to get into her bed that Nancy remembered the muslin parcel the woman in the market had slipped into her hand. On the label, a series of pictures depicted the phases of the moon, from crescent to full circle. Nancy wrinkled her nose, wondering why the women had used the symbols of the lunar cycle on a bag of herbs, then loosened the bag's strings. Inside, some leaves. Nancy sniffed them, and immediately recoiled, the stink of rotting, fetid flesh in her nostrils. Goodness knows what they had plucked from the earth, but it smelled as if it had been sitting under a long-dead rat.

She tipped the contents of the bag onto the table. Among the leaves was something else. Gingerly she picked up a knotted, dirty ribbon. Wiping away the filth, she gasped. Yellow and blue stripes. By the stars! It was the ribbon she'd worn on her first morning here, the one those three dark birds had snatched from her hair.

Chapter Eight

A disturbed night. Dreams of fires and swords, of suspicious eyes, choking smoke, and half-human, half-animal figures. A warning, echoing, repeated in a low French accent, rang in Nancy's ears as she stirred: 'Even when you reach your destination, you might need to remain on guard.' It was the most bitter disappointment to wake exhausted and longing for more sleep.

She hauled herself from her bed, catching sight of the contents of the bag left on the table before she had crawled into bed. An acrid scent lingered, a faint reminder of last night's terrors. Dressed, and minded to keep the evidence from Isobel, she swept the now-browning leaves into the bag, along with the hand-drawn label, then used the ribbon – her ribbon! – to tie it shut and put it in her pocket.

Yesterday's sunshine had disappeared, and a May mist hung drizzly and sullen as she took her morning walk, russet dress trailing in the mud, eyes glazed in thought. A familiar path tracked away from the main road and smudged into the hills, and within minutes she was out of the dripping catkins and among the spiky gorse. She pulled her hood tight, but still her face was slippery and hair festooned with pearl-like droplets. Lost in her thoughts about the day before, she let them hang.

As is often the way, the pin-sharp fears of the previous night had been muted by time and sleep. However, the curious bag and its lunar decorations was puzzling.

The women she had met at the market would have known about the phases of the moon, for they were country folk and had eyes in their heads. And yet they were not from these parts, that much was obvious. But the moon was, after all, the lantern that hung above all, and its quartered and halved forms made for a most eye-catching motif.

Similar images were used as shorthand for mystic powers in London. The street astrologers of Seven Dials would hold up signs emblazoned with gold crescents and stars and wheedle empty promises at passers-by: 'Read your fortune, my dear? Find your future in the constellations?' She'd give them a curt shake of the head, and turn away, muttering under her breath, 'I'll put my faith in Copernicus!'

However, as Nancy thought of Caleb and his willingness to bend towards both the scientific and the magical, the faint trace of colour appeared at the memory of her imperious tone at the women's stall. She shook her head. Surely the soft air of Scotland wasn't rusting her cast-iron opinions?

The ribbon was a stranger coincidence. But surely, it was just that: a coincidence. The crows would likely have dropped the trinket, and the women picked it up from the ground; it was particularly pretty. It was probable the trio scavenged for treasures like the mudlarks of Deptford Creek. Yes, the ribbon was a coincidence.

Lifting her skirts, she swung over a rickety stile. Here was her favourite hill, the place on her route that, if she looked back, might ordinarily give her the most spectacular view of the town nestled between the hills. She usually resisted turning around, saving that reward for the summit, but today she stopped halfway to the crest and peered into the rain. Predictably, Inverness was blotted out.

Near the top of the hill sat a large flat rock on which she had made a habit of resting. The stone was darkened and wet, but, nevertheless, she picked a few sodden primroses, then sat, closing her eyes.

Her fingers snaked into her pocket and closed around the bag, marvelling again that the women had chosen to give to her – of all the visitors at the fair – the little parcel that contained her own ribbon! She shook her head at the infinitely huge odds.

There was a crunch on the stony path. A tall figure, its outline blunted by the mist, walked towards her. To her surprise, she recognised Caleb.

Aside from their first meeting, she'd never seen him beyond the confines of the house. His coat was heavy with rain and his gaiters sodden. She ran her hands through her hair which felt suddenly waterlogged, then took out her handkerchief, making a futile attempt to dry her face.

'Miss Lockaby. Nancy.'

This was the first time he'd spoken her first name. He looked amiably surprised to see her. She remembered the copy of Macbeth, bound in red leather.

'Mr— Caleb. I must thank you for your generous present. What brings you here?' she asked.

'The same as you, perhaps. A desire for open space, despite this dreich morning. May I join you?' He indicated the space next to her on the rock.

Away from his books, Caleb seemed easier in his movements, lighter in his speech. Yet this was not a situation with which she was familiar. If she were to be seen even speaking to a man out here, unaccompanied, the scandal would be considerable. Yet the only living being in sight was a morose-looking Highland cow.

'Of course. You are welcome to share my settee, although it is a little hard.'

He laughed and sat beside her. 'I am used to it. This feels perfectly comfortable to me.'

Nancy nodded nervously. 'Usually you can see right across the river.'

He peered out into the grey. 'The Ness. I know. This place is an old favourite of mine, of everyone who has lived at Blackthistle.' For an instant, sadness clouded his face. 'When I was six or seven, I'd come up here and watch the ships blow in and out of port on their white sails. I'd imagine who might be on board and what might lie in their holds. Tobacco. Sugar.' He brightened, and his eyes widened. 'Rum?' He rummaged in his pocket and brought out a small metal flask, from which he swigged. He offered it to Nancy. She accepted it gratefully, taking a large sip.

She passed it back, a glow forming in her stomach. 'I did the same in Greenwich. From the hill in the park next to the house. There were so many boats! Packed together and jostling for space. I'd count them in as they passed up the Thames, try to guess what was on them, give them names and wish them safe travels as they left.' She smiled.

His eyes brightened. 'I still do it now.'

Nancy tried to picture a young Caleb sitting on the rock, smoothing away the creases that worried across his face, softening his widow's peak, replacing those angular lines with round cheeks. It was difficult; he had a face that seemed immovably set.

'Tell me about how Blackthistle used to be,' she said.

Caleb rubbed his foot in the mud. 'When I was young— it— My father, Sir Edward, was a strict man. It was expected that we made little noise, and that I worked hard at my studies. It was a sober place. But up here, in the hills, this is where I came to lose myself in horizons and words. I would read my little copy of *Macbeth* and wander for miles and miles. I found where Duncan made his camp at Forres, the ruins of that old castle at Cawdor. I think I even found the little hill where he met the Thane. Such magic, Nancy. And there I was, in the midst of where it happened.'

Perhaps the coldness of Caleb's father was at the heart of the chill she felt at Blackthistle. Caleb offered her another sip from his flask, and she took it, with a smile, 'I think I understand. Sometimes, when I look through a telescope or lose myself in a chart, I feel as if I'm among the stars. That they are enveloping me.' She gave a small shrug. 'A little fanciful, I know. But your family must have been proud that you went on to such academic heights.'

'Not really. My choice of subject was not what my father imagined would interest his son. "Stories and nonsense!" he called it. I think he had imagined I would find my place in the world of mathematics. Rather like you have, Miss Lockaby. But I left Blackthistle for London, and, despite his disapproval, it felt right. As if I belonged. But eventually, a long time later, I returned.' His voice trailed away, his eyes glassed.

'May I ask you a question, Nancy?' Caleb looked thoughtful.

'Of course.'

'Why did you agree to come to Blackthistle?'

Although Nancy had anticipated this question since her arrival, she was caught a little off-guard. She rubbed a raindrop from the end of her nose, and cleared her throat. 'London was not offering all I needed. My being a woman, at the Observatory…' She looked at Caleb. For a second, she teetered on the brink, then tumbled headfirst into her story. How her love and passion for the stars and figures had been kindled since her early years, the joy of her life with her parents, and her devastation at realising she would never see them again. A life alone at a tender age in London, scrabbling frantically to ensure her life remained comfortable, her staff in employment and a house intact.

She told of the hurt in seeing someone else's name on reams of figures and research – 'In order for it to be read with a serious eye'. The way gentlemen with letters after their names would choose to talk to her male colleagues about new discoveries at academic parties, while conversation with her was limited to compliments on her dress. The humiliation of being ushered into a back room at the Observatory rather than risk the disapproval of the King on his visits.

Caleb exhaled. 'Nancy. I think, in some small way, I understand. My dearest friend in London was William, and he had a twin sister, Cassandra. They had been schooled together, brought up with a tutor and taught as equals. William would marvel at his sister's abilities: how she could add columns upon columns of numbers in the flick of an eye, how she would laugh at his attempts to balance equations. Yet at the age of fourteen, her lessons were halted, while his continued.' He looked distant. 'She married eventually.' His voice trailed off. 'Were there not *expectations* for you too?'

Nancy's cheeks began reddening. It was the unspoken question that had hung heavily over her head in London.

There had, of course, been Charles. She had first spotted Charles Green at one of her father's Royal Society lectures, his eyebrows arching at the sight of the armillary sphere Papa had built for James Stuart. He was nineteen, four years older than her, and his talk of parallaxes and nutations had set her soft, impressionable mind afire. How she had worshipped him.

However, as his visits to the observatory became more frequent, his arch indifference to her puppyish affections became more obvious. Soon he was working alongside her as a junior clerk and statistician so, she assured herself, was bound to fall as hopelessly in love with her as she had with him. These illusions had been shattered, however, the day that he had presented her with a gift, in the form of a little marigold-yellow telescope made from card and vellum.

'Put it to your eye, Nancy, try it!' he had implored her and she had run to the window, heart bursting in her chest. She put the telescope to her eye. It was crude, but she could make out the faces of sailors working on the boats on the river. Delighted, she had turned to Charles, face bright with joy. For the briefest of moments, a trace of shame flickered in his eyes, before a sly smile spread across his face and he turned to his fellow workers, guffawing.

Mystified at the men's laughter, she put a hand to her face and felt something damp. When she ran to the mirror that hung on the wall, she found her eye was ringed with wet, black ink. Ink and grime she could clean, but the shame and rejection were harder to scrub away.

Charles had known of her tender feelings, of that she was now certain, so this public humiliation cut to her core. From now on, it would be only her and the stars. And so she studied, gritted her teeth and went back to work alongside Charles Green and the others who had joined in his laughter, determined to prove herself, even as Charles' star ascended and he was taken on as an assistant to the Astronomer Royal.

Charles was now at the right hand of Captain Cook, as he sailed towards Tahiti on the *Endeavour*. Each triumphal description of the vessel's journey wreathed around her, every gushing description of Charles' well-appointed, hibiscus-scented, tented observatory pulled tightly into her flesh, yet she could not stop reading reports of the journey. If it hadn't been for her bodice and skirts, who knows, it might have been her with Cook on the island.

After Charles' cruel trick, she had pushed any thoughts of marriage to the back of her mind and, a little to her surprise, they had never resurfaced.

To speak out loud of such matters, particularly to a man, might have been considered outrageous in London. However, she was not in London. Still, she spoke carefully. 'There were offers. I misjudged some and sidestepped others. Yet, that choice meant my ambitions were narrowed. You seem to understand my frustrations. I was minded that Scotland might be where I could be free to make sense of this universe that surrounds us. In London, I believe that I was close to uncovering something. I had written a paper…'

Her voice trailed off, and Nancy suddenly realised she was on the verge of exposing the aching wound of rejection that was the result of recalling her treatise on the Fold. Caleb stared at her intently. 'And I—' She stopped, uncertain.

He gave her a thoughtful look. 'To lay your thoughts and theories in writing for others to read is perhaps the most daunting aspect of study, I think. I am still feart each time I send my work to the printers.'

Nancy had spent nights and nights alone, waiting patiently for the stars to wheel again. How she wanted to shout of her discovery to Caleb, to scream it into the sky. Yet without collaborated evidence, perhaps she was as much a charlatan as the astrologers in Seven Dials. 'I am not sure at this moment quite what I have found,' she said eventually.

She looked at his face, wet with rain, eyes wide. Perhaps she was mistaken. Maybe he, of all people, might understand. She thought of the manner in which he had spoken of his friend's sister. 'But I think it is something,' she relented. 'Perhaps to do with,' she paused and swallowed, 'the transit. Something important. Magnificent, certainly.'

'Please, continue,' he said, his expression rapt.

She bit her lip. 'You must understand, this is not easy for me to speak of. I have been ridiculed, my work belittled. You have employed me in good faith.'

'Nancy, if this something is truly magnificent, perhaps I might sponsor a piece of work from you. A paper perhaps? Something to put your name to.'

Her heart thudded. If she were to rework *On an Anomaly*, if Caleb was willing to put his name to it… Now was her chance, perhaps. This is why she had come to Scotland.

'Mr Malles – Caleb – eight years ago, I saw something extraordinary. I know it. I don't expect you to believe me. At the moment I have no more evidence than the truth, and what I alone saw.'

Eyes fixed on hers, he nodded at her to continue.

Something rose in her throat at his words. How long had she wished to be believed, to be taken seriously once again. She felt a sudden blaze of hope. 'I will tell you, if you wish to know.'

She was suddenly aware of how closely she and Mr Malles were sitting. She must present her ideas in a more appropriate setting. Somewhere more *academic*. That they might be taken seriously. Lowering her eyes, she spoke. 'But not here. Not now. Tonight, at study, perhaps?'

Caleb's face registered a flicker of disappointment, but he acquiesced. 'Tonight then.'

Nancy rose. 'Come, let's walk to the top of the hill together. I fear we must return to Blackthistle separately or Mrs McLoone will have conniptions.'

Caleb gave a loud snort. 'I am quite used to McLoone's disapproval, and I suspect Nancy Lockaby cares little what anyone would think.'

The two walked the short distance up the path. Caleb's concern and compassion had seemed genuine, and the way he had spoken so fiercely of his friend's sister, as if he were on the side of all women. And to suggest he could sponsor her paper! It had been a long time, perhaps since the death of James, that she had felt as if she were truly being listened to.

She walked alongside her compelling companion, the mud splashing up her boots and skirts. If anyone was to take her seriously, perhaps that person might be Caleb Malles.

Chapter Nine

The housekeeper's lip had indeed curled as she opened the door to the two bedraggled figures who stepped through it. However, Nancy smiled as she entered her bedroom. Mrs McLoone might be stern, but she'd had the forethought to ensure there was a fire blazing in the grate. Thanks to its glow, her feet were soon warm and hair dry.

Telling Caleb about the Fold would require a strong heart. It had been impossible to keep her frustrations from Cora, so her maid knew the details of her discovery. Yet she had not spoken of it in depth to another soul.

A few sparks sputtered from the fire onto the floor, and she extinguished them with a poker. She picked up the dustpan and brush next to the fire. Beneath it, something gleamed. A ring. Small. Silver. And mounted on it, the most beautiful, six-pointed star, with a ruby at its centre. It looked valuable. She remembered Isobel's strange reaction to the hairbrush. Perhaps this might belong to the same mysterious visitor. Her interest had been piqued, and once piqued, her curiosity did not generally fade away. Ambushing the maid felt cruel, yet her previous reaction had been very confusing. Nancy wrinkled her forehead and put the ring on the dressing table.

Perhaps her flight to Scotland had been in part motivated by cowardice. If she had stayed in London, she would have been expected to anticipate and help document the transit at the Observatory. Here she might continue her studies into the

Fold, to watch for it at the transit without feeling eyes burning into her back. Her mother's scribbles and her calculations and extrapolations suggested clearly that it would appear again during those few hours. She hardly dared hope that on this occasion she might see more, might be able to prove with no doubt the Fold's existence, might perhaps gather enough evidence that she might, with Caleb's help, think about publishing a more definitive paper. But here also, there was no-one to witness any disappointment.

She bit her lip, thinking about tonight. For no matter how open to new theories or encouraging of her studies Caleb might be, she could still not be absolutely sure the promised show would take place. Yet she had made a promise to tell him more, and she always kept a promise.

★

Nancy glanced up nervously as her employer entered the study that evening. She was relieved when he greeted her with a solicitous smile.

'Nancy.'

'Caleb,' she replied lightly, relishing the less formal atmosphere between them.

He put down his books on his desk. 'What you said, this afternoon...'

Nancy looked him in the eye. 'Have no fear. I will tell you.'

A look of relief spread across his face. She took a deep breath and stood, leaning on her desk for support.

'You know already of the transit. But quite apart from the bare mathematics that govern the skies, it's the sight of it, as if Venus has come untethered from its night moorings, determined to plough into the day and across the most powerful symbol of light. That shadow, that dot, moving almost imperceptibly in front of the sun serves as proof we are on the correct path, our calculations aren't some abstract concept, that they have meaning. And it reveals the majesty, the logic of the universe.' She smiled, reddening a little. 'Of course, some would say that's a rather egocentric view; it's only from the Earth-bound viewer's perspective that anything spectacular has taken place.'

'Your humility is admirable.' Caleb was listening intently. 'And you paint quite the picture. We ought to watch the next one together. Will we see it here?'

She swallowed, but spoke as lightly as she could, 'Yes, we should, I hope, if it's not cloudy, but the sun will set before the transit is complete. It's rather frustrating, and why Captain Cook and his crew have made their long journey across the Atlantic. They will see the whole thing from start to finish, and paradise is rarely clouded.'

'But there was something else, wasn't there? You told me that you saw something else that night.'

She took a deep breath. 'I did. It was extraordinary. A whirl, a movement, a phenomenon – a shift of the skies undocumented anywhere. Unlike anything I've seen, before or since. The stars moving, spinning.' She spun her finger in the air. 'Like water swirling down a hole, a vortex. But instead of water, hundreds of pinpricks of light. And at its centre, something bright spilling through.'

'From behind it?'

'Yes, I think so.' Of course she could remember what she had seen all those years ago with pin-point accuracy, She had turned over the visions in her mind a thousand, two thousand times. 'A brightness, pushing, pulling perhaps at a rift. And then, rays, beams spilling out. From start to finish it lasted for thirty-seven minutes,' she added with a self-deprecating roll of her eyes. She was always the accurate timekeeper.

She took a deep breath, 'I think – no, I am almost sure – that I have discovered something, something *new* in the skies. I've seen it only once, but I am convinced that it will appear again. If my calculations are correct, a month hence, at the time of the transit, on the third day of June. I wrote a paper.'

Caleb's eyes were fixed on her, and he spoke carefully, 'Would you let me read your treatise perhaps? Would I understand even half of it?'

Nancy shook her head slowly, her thoughts still bruised. 'Perhaps. I'm not sure. Nothing, as I have been reminded again and again, has yet been proved.' She sighed.

'I believe that you saw something.' He looked her in the eye. 'Since your arrival at Blackthistle, you've shown diligence, integrity and, in my humble opinion, extraordinary academic ability. I can see no reason for you to lie about this, of that I'm sure. If you claim to have seen such a spectacle, then of course I believe you.'

The relief that surged through Nancy almost unbalanced her. To hear someone – even if that someone was a scholar of words rather than mathematics or natural philosophy – give credence to her theories was a thrilling moment.

'Thank you, Caleb. I appreciate your words of encouragement. I've told very few people what I saw that night.' Caleb smiled broadly, his eyes shining. Nancy tilted back her head and narrowed her eyes, 'Tell me, do you think my research into the Fold – as I have termed it – might be in some way useful to you?'

He cracked his knuckles. 'I don't think so. But perhaps we will learn something to each of our advantage as we come to discuss this more.' He pulled out a copy of Horrocks' *Venus in Sole Visa*. 'Now, I must learn more of what will happen in June.'

★

In contrast to Caleb's leaps and bounds, Isobel's education in mathematics was not progressing particularly swiftly. That evening, Nancy tried again to teach her the basics.

Isobel sighed. 'You are so patient, ma'am. I can scarcely believe that you, with your fine mind, would spend time on someone like me.'

Nancy smiled. 'Seeing you advance, however slowly, is a joy. And, I find, that through teaching, I learn something more of myself. As a girl, I wanted to know everything of the stars. I haven't really changed. I'm still learning.'

'Are you?' said the girl. 'Really? I thought you were teaching Mr Malles.'

'I suppose we are both still learning. The cosmos still holds so many secrets.' Her eyes drifted to the ring she had placed on the dressing table. She swallowed, 'Look what I found.'

'Ah me! It's the ring! The one Mrs Malles loved so much.' Isobel gasped before she could finish her sentence and covered her mouth with her hand.

'*Mrs* Malles? What do you mean?' Nancy turned and faced the maid, who looked terrified.

'She… she… I can't say. The staff turned the house upside-down looking for this. I remember my mammy—'

'Calm yourself. Breathe deeply, child. Now, tell me, of whom do you speak?' Nancy's words were as soothing as she could make them. 'Isobel, you may speak freely. I shall not mention this to Mr Malles or Mrs McLoone. You have my word.'

Isobel gulped. 'She was here before – Mr Malles's wife. She lost her ruby star ring. My mam had to work late lookin' for it.'

'Mr Malles had a wife?'

That neither Caleb nor Mrs McLoone had mentioned her was strange, but it was stranger still that any evidence of her existence in the house had been removed. There should surely have been clothes, a piano or needlework? It seemed as if the woman had left no echo at Blackthistle, and that any trace of her had been scrubbed from its walls. She thought of the blank spaces, where paintings had once hung. This, perhaps, was why she had felt so disconcerted by the atmosphere of the house. Here was the missing actor. The ghost at the feast had a name. But not yet a face.

She faced Isobel with an intent look, 'Tell me more, child.'

The maid looked as if she were about to cry, but Nancy endeavoured to give her some encouragement. 'I will not breathe a word to anyone.'

'It was easier before. Mr Malles is so kind, although you might not always see it, ma'am. He and Mrs Malles. My mam told me that they were so happy together when they first arrived at Blackthistle.'

She looked at Nancy, her eyes wide, 'I weren't born then, but ma told me about them coming up the drive, past our little house. They were blithe, in love. They'd dance in the hallway every night, she said, just the two of them. Whirling and twirling and reeling together.'

'Doesn't that sound wonderful, Isobel?'

'It must have been, ma'am. Ma said that for that first Hogmanay they were here, you could hardly see the walls for the ivy and the holly they'd made the help bring in and put up. And then the wassailers came round. She said Sir Edward would ha' got the staff to chase them away with sticks, but Mr Malles asked them all in and they sang until the hallway rang and rang with a wappin' din, and they all jigged.'

Nancy tried to imagine the bare, silent rooms of Blackthistle echoing with laughter. She turned to Isobel. 'It's hard to imagine. It seems so quiet here now. Such a big place to live in alone.'

Isobel lay down the blackboard on the bed. 'Yes, ma'am,' she said, impassively, 'The house changed very much after Mrs Malles went away.' She stopped.

'What do you mean, *went away*?' Nancy asked, confused. 'Where did she go?'

Isobel had gone pale. She muttered, 'I cannae tell you more. I've said enough already, like a fool. I was so young, I dinnae ken what happened. I am so sorry, ma'am. I have your hearth to clean.'

She took the brush from beside the fireplace and started to brush the ashes into a little pan, her eyes fixed on her work.

Nancy stared at her back, confused.

Chapter Ten

It had been five days since she had told Caleb about the Fold, and there was a new focus to his work. His eyes gleamed brightly, the skin below them bruised with tiredness.

He would change the subject of their lessons to ask questions about what she had seen. 'Tell me. For how long did the stars circle?' Her answers had started to become non-committal, her replies a little obscured, and she would attempt to steer him back to the task in hand.

Caleb's state was not unfamiliar to Nancy. She had lost untold weeks, months, to the madness that took hold when consumed by a new discovery. She had barely eaten anything more than platters of hardening bread and meat in the weeks following the first transit. But Caleb seemed to be brewing a mania. His enthusiasm for her discovery was, in some ways, most flattering, yet she felt loath to fuel it more, and although she could barely admit it, she was protective of the Fold.

For the first time since she had made the journey to Scotland, Nancy found herself questioning whether taking the position at Blackthistle had been the correct choice. She missed Cora, she missed the huge quadrant at the Observatory made by her father, she even missed the stale blast of old beer that wafted from the Plume of Feathers tavern. Perhaps leaving her comfortable life, predictable as the Earth's orbit, and plunging into the unknown had been wrongheaded. Yet the thought of returning to Greenwich, spooked by the first hint of someone showing a sincere interest in her research, was unthinkable. It would be impossible to step back into the Observatory, head down. The humiliation. She must remain here until at least after the transit was over.

It was not just Caleb's intensity that disconcerted her. The ribbon from the market snaked and flittered through her dreams as if it had a life, a will of its own, beckoning and leading her round misty corners and blurred passages towards the women who had given it to her. She could not forget them.

The bag around which it was knotted lay on the small table next to her bed each night and in her pocket every day. Somewhat bizarrely, its rancid, herbal scent had started to settle her nerves, and she had got into the habit of taking it out of her pocket and sniffing it when she felt a fret come upon her.

A week after the fair, rather than taking their habitual afternoon country walk, Nancy steered Isobel left at the end of the drive, into Inverness. After all, she told her companion, she needed to ask Mr McBride if he had taken delivery of the newest edition of *The Mercury*, as it was surely time for another update from HMS *Endeavour*. She found her breath quickening, her hand gripping the little bag that she had tucked into her dress.

The trees, so stark in winter, were now weighted with thick, heavy blossom. In Greenwich, she had taken joy in the pink clouds of flowers with their promises of picnics and parasols, but here, today, they felt almost vulgar, their scent overly sweet. The pair crossed the bridge into town.

The stores hadn't received *The Mercury*, so they strolled a little. Here was the market square that had been so busy last week, now with just a few wizened apples rolling in its gutters. She glanced up and down the street, and fancied she heard the distant echo of the high-pitched whine that had heralded their previous arrival humming in her ears.

A quick movement in the corner of the square caught her eye. Something lurked in the shadows of the arch in which the women's stall had stood. She peered into the gloom, then gasped. Two eyes gleamed in the shadows. Out shuffled the oldest woman, leaning heavily on her staff.

Nancy started, then glanced around. Isobel was standing back ten paces, her eyes round with fear.

The woman spoke in a brittle voice. 'Here you are at last, child.'

Taken unawares, Nancy could barely form words. 'What do you mean, here I am?'

'We've been expecting you. There is something we must speak to you about.' The old woman whispered, 'At our home. We are waiting.'

She came closer. Nancy could hear her lungs whistling like wind through a loose casement.

'Why? Where do you live?'

The woman put her finger to Nancy's lips. It felt twig-dry. Horrified, Nancy pushed it away.

'You will find us. You know how.'

The woman turned and scuttled off down a little alley that snaked from the square. Nancy followed, yet when she reached the column that stood at the corner of the tiny road, could not see the crone.

She turned back to Isobel, her heart pounding, half in fear, half in excitement. Now she could admit to herself she had come here hoping that she might see the women again. She attempted to hide her hands, which were shaking in anticipation.

The girl shook her head, her eyes in shadow. She spoke quietly: 'Those women... they're not ones to be messed with, ma'am.'

'What do you mean, Isobel?' Nancy asked. 'They simply hoped to speak to me. Now, where should I find their house?' She spoke as brightly as she could.

Isobel snorted and muttered something under her breath, prompting a stern look from her mistress, 'I will not stand for rudeness, Isobel.'

'I don't know where they live.'

The girl was patently lying, but Nancy could see the fear in her eyes and didn't push further.

'Very well. I will find someone who does.'

'I wouldn't go near 'em, ma'am.'

'Why is that, girl? What have they done to you?'

Isobel rubbed her head, her brow furrowed,

'Everyone knows to stay away from that place. You might buy herb pockets from 'em at market, or get 'em to charm your wart, but go to their house alone?' She shivered, dramatically. 'You know what they say, ma'am?'

Nancy had her suspicions. 'Tell me.'

The girl eyed her seriously. 'They say they have special powers. Magic.'

In London, flushed with the unshakeable confidence bestowed by youth and wealth, Nancy had treated the opinions of those who blurred the lines between hocus-pocus and science with disdain. Yet perhaps a lifetime spent coddled in observatories had insulated her from the beliefs of many of those who lived further than a day's ride from the Thames. Perhaps this supernatural dogma existed to give reassurance and hope to those who might need it most.

'Ma'am. You ken the wasting disease? You get the withering, they'll cut off your nails and bury 'em and the ague will disappear.' Nancy raised an eyebrow at this, but Isobel was undeterred.

Her fingers splayed. 'A few of the townsfolk go to 'em and spend a few pennies on mushrooms. make 'em into a tea and see visions! Peep the future! Some of the boys'll do it for sport, before the May or the October fires,' Isobel said.

Nancy tutted. 'They are clearly accomplished cunning folk, and I don't doubt their simple remedies work wonders for those good people of Inverness unable to afford or access a physician. But a rounded knowledge of herbs and roots and a silvered tongue is hardly magic, is it?'

Isobel whispered sulkily, 'They say they make love to the devil.'

Nancy flinched. 'You would do well to hold your counsel, girl, as such whispers have sent many to their deaths.'

The girl shifted from foot to foot. 'As you will, ma'am.'

The girl's dislike of the women and her wild allegations unnerved Nancy, and set her off kilter. She tutted again loudly, as if the tsk-tsk would restore her usual logical balance. It almost did.

A lad ran across the square, barefoot and grinning. She called to him.

'Aye, ma'am.' He looked at her with a curious expression.

'Tell me, young man, do you know of the three women who have a stall in the market? Right here?' She indicated the spot with a jabbing finger.

The boy looked warily at her. 'Aye, I do.'

'Do you know where they stay?'

The boy looked even more suspicious.

'Mebbe.'

'Oh come, boy. Answer me straight. Do you know where I might find the three women who have a stall here?' She held out a penny.

The boy's eyes lit up.

'Aye, I ken. I'll take you near. But I'll not go close.'

'As you will. Just accompany us as far as you can.'

Isobel shook her head. 'I'll no' go, ma'am. Please.'

Nancy looked at the girl's face, eyes widened in fear. 'I understand, Isobel. You go home to Blackthistle. I will return home alone.'

Isobel's mouth dropped open. 'Ma'am!'

'Really, Isobel. I will be fine.'

The boy led her down a street that led away from the square and away from the centre of town. Here the houses were squatter, unpainted, with tattered curtains across doors, dogs sniffing at corners. Nancy gripped her purse a little more tightly. Indicating a dirt road leading out of town with his thumb, and clearly unwilling to go any further, the boy grunted.

'Last cottage down this wynd, ma'am.' He held out his hand. 'The one beyond all the others.' Nancy handed him a coin and he ran swiftly back up the track.

Although dark, the lane was otherwise unremarkable, but her heart was fluttering in her chest like a trapped sparrow. A prickle of nervousness ran down her spine, and her fingers tightened around the bag. She brought it to her nose and sniffed it.

She steeled herself, then walked past three or four grubby shacks in the direction the boy had indicated.

The house, if you could dignify this hut with such a name, was almost hidden behind a tangle of thorns that acted as a spiky barricade. A yew tree, leaves spread like fingers, stood in the corner of the front garden. Someone came down the path and out of the gate: a roughly dressed man, eyes shining, stuffing something brown and dried into his bag. He rolled his eyes at her. ''Tis more pennies than ever, ma'am. Worth it though.' She wrinkled her forehead and let him pass.

She entered the gate, the brambles folding behind her. The roof was turfed and hooded a small door, and the windows were open, glassless, hung with thick, brown sailcloth. Nancy realised guiltily that she had never before entered a house that didn't have glass windows. She stepped over a skinny striped cat stretching in the late-morning light, and knocked gingerly at the door.

A rustle came from inside the house, but nothing more. She knocked harder. Muffled laughter drifted through the window, followed by a hushing. The cat turned its head towards her.

And then the door creaked open. In the darkness she could make out a face. The oldest of the women. 'You're here then.' She beckoned. 'In you come.'

Chapter Eleven

Blinded by the room's darkness, the thick smell was the first thing Nancy noticed; grassy and soporifically sweet.

The only light was cast from the glowing hearth, bathing the three women who stood beside it in claret-red. They stared at her for a good half-minute. She felt as if she were hanged from a tree, twisting in the wind in front of them.

'She was right then – you have come,' said the gap-toothed young woman, but she was quickly hushed with a hiss from the oldest. The younger woman's hands were slick with blood. Nancy swallowed and shot an anxious glance at the front door, which the old woman had shut behind her.

Her eyes darted around the room. A small skillet of pottage bubbled on the fire. Above the mantel and from every beam of the roof hung bunches of dried plants the size of small bushes. Lavender, hops, spiked and downy thistle, white sticks bristling with tiny, desiccated black berries, and many more that Nancy couldn't name. A huge warty toad sat impassively in a wide-mouthed jar.

The room was dominated by a rough, heavy table. On it were a brace of rabbits, skin half-pulled loose, heads lolling, eyes misted. Evidently, she had interrupted the preparation of a meal. She summoned up her flintiest voice. 'My name is Nancy Lockaby.'

The young woman used a rancid brown cloth to wipe her bloody hands and pointed at herself, saying, 'We are Daughter,' then at the woman with the dark skin and silvering hair, 'We are Mother', and finally indicated the oldest of the three,

'We are Granny.' Nancy nodded quickly. The names were universal, yet each clung to the women like ivy.

'I need to ask you about something,' Nancy began, fumbling a little, taking the bag from her pocket. She took off the ribbon and dangled it in front of them.

The young woman giggled. 'Tis pretty.'

Nancy's voice rose. 'I know it's pretty. I picked it out for myself at Greenwich Market. This was in the parcel you gave me at the fair. How did you come to have this? How did you know it was mine?'

Mother took the scrap of material and rubbed it between her fingers. '*Oui.* It was needed for that bag.' She chose her words carefully, and her companions eyed her warily, as if worried she might betray some secret.

'Needed for what? Where did you find it? This is mine.' Nancy had not been mollified.

The woman put her finger to her lips. 'Hush now. Have you been keeping the bag under your pillow?'

Nancy nodded.

'As you should.' Mother sighed.

Although the women were more talkative than at their first meeting, this was less than straightforward, and nothing infuriated Nancy more than obfuscation. She hoped that the woman might soon start to make sense.

Mother continued. 'You should hearken to us, girl. It will help us all if you listen. Not all truths are written by men's hands. Many come from women's hearts.' Mother spoke in her sing-song accent. 'But you know that already, child. The time will come soon when you understand everything. Not yet perhaps, but soon it will come.'

The younger woman nodded. 'Listen well.'

If anything, the conversation was only becoming more confusing. Nancy wondered if it would help if she were more direct.

'Tell me where you found the ribbon.'

Granny nodded approvingly and beckoned to her. 'Come with me.' She walked to the back of the room and pushed open a rough wooden door, letting the bright, late-afternoon light pour in. The older woman shuffled out of the opening, leaning heavily on her stick.

Nancy shaded her eyes. There was a large garden at the back of the cottage, lined with neat rows of plants: herbs, berries, some purplish-white flowers. Trees hugged the edges of the plot protectively. It was surprisingly ordered and well-kept. A great deal of care had evidently been spent on the plot. The woman tugged at her sleeve. 'Come!' She dragged her to the end of the garden, towards a tall table. Her hand scuttled across its rough top, and she held up a piece of blue sea glass with a gleeful expression.

'They've been,' she said. She reached into her pocket, pulled out a handful of dried worms and scattered them on the table.

'Thank you, old friends!' She made a little bow.

There was a harsh caw. Outlined in the budding branches of a nearby tree were three dark silhouettes, sitting like judges in black caps. Nancy shuddered at the memory of flapping wings beating about her head.

The old woman eyed her. 'The cleverest and most generous of birds.'

Nancy's lip curled. 'I've met them before. They attacked me. They tore that ribbon from my head.'

'That was not these birds.' The woman smiled. 'And no crow would hurt you. Not you.' She handed over the sliver of sea glass.

The crone was already creaking up the path, back towards the cottage. Not wishing to be alone with the crows, Nancy tucked the blue glass into her pocket and followed.

Granny's words floated over her shoulder. 'It was time you came, child. We've been waiting for you for many moons.'

She tapped her stick on the rough mortar wall of the cottage, then hobbled through the door. Nancy stopped in her tracks. There, painted crudely, were the crescents and half-circles that represented the phases of the moon, rather like those on the label of the bag the women had given her.

Next to the symbols was a portrait. It depicted a woman with green eyes and a cloud of bright-red hair. Around her head traced the orbits of five planets, the solar system; all precisely rendered. The peeling paint and faded colour indicated that it had been there for many years, decades, centuries even. Her legs buckled. It was… *her.*

She stared at the likeness, tracing the outline with her fingers. The ancient paint flaked away a little. It felt as if she were teetering on the edge of a gaping abyss, looking into the clouds and considering whether to step out and over. She might leave now, Nancy thought, without comment, and never speak to the women again. But there was not a chance she would walk away.

She tore herself from the painting and ducked under the lintel back into the cottage.

Blood rushed in her ears, and her voice shook. 'That picture. It's— Is it me? Who painted it? When?'

Her voice trailed off. Granny was in a chair by the fire. Daughter was at the table, her hands bloody once more, pulling tiny bones from the rabbit flesh.

She looked up. 'I did. A long time ago.' She dipped her hands in a bucket of water on the table, then wiped them on her skirts. 'Let us tell you some more about ourselves. Make sense o' things.'

Chapter Twelve

Daughter picked a shiny copper bowl from the shelf, then pulled back the rough brown curtain. She held the dish in the sunbeams and spun it about, sending rose-gold glints whirling around the room.

'Here we are. Come, Mother! Come, Granny! 'Tis time to tell her some more.' She opened the back door and ducked into the garden, not a glance behind. Nancy and the two other women followed. The girl walked down the long path to the end of the neatly planted herb patch, then bent her legs. She was kneeling in a stony stream, clear as the lenses crafted by Nancy's father, filling the vessel. A few drops of water spilled over the side. 'Damn,' the girl muttered as they sparkled in the sun, then beamed, broadly.

She held out the bowl to Nancy, then sat down awkwardly, spreading her skirts. The girl leaned towards Nancy. Her breath was ripe. 'I use my bowl to help me peep. Sometimes I peeps backwards, sometimes forwards. Let's go back. Way, way back. Many years.' She let the water settle until it was like glass, then her top teeth bit on her lower lip and she closed her eyes for a few seconds. Then they flashed open, wide, and she bent over the bowl, muttering. Nancy leaned in, fascinated.

Later she would tell herself that the shadows beckoning her were broken reflections of Daughter's face, but at that moment the tangle of eyes and beckoning hands seemed solidly real.

Suddenly Nancy could see a cart, lurching along a boggy track through a series of brown, flat, furrowed fields. In the vehicle rode a child whose wide face and gapped teeth matched Daughter's, but whose blue eyes looked beyond and through her.

The Daughter peering into the pot whispered, 'Here I was with my dear ma.' Nancy saw a woman, broad as a carthorse, sitting beside her daughter, a baby in her arms. All wore dark-blue tunics in the same style as the girl's, and simple leather boots.

The cart drew up at a little grey-thatched timber hut. Around it scratched a few chickens, and as they climbed down from their cart, Nancy blinked.

They were inside the hut. The other Daughter ran to an old woman on a truckle bed, shivering under a blanket the colour of slush. Her eyes were clouded and pearl-like. The old woman groaned. 'I've not got long now.'

Nancy watched as the girl knelt beside the old lady. She ran her smooth, chubby hand over the old woman's brow. 'Hush, Granny, go quietly now, into the dark.' A smile spread across the ancient woman's sun-cracked face. 'Winter time is nearly done, the final frost is coming. Take my hand. I'll lead you.'

The old woman's head fell back, her chest rattled, then nothing. The girl looked up and smiled. 'She is beyond the winter now, in the dark,' she chirped.

'That was the first time it happened,' said Daughter dreamily. 'I can still remember the smell of my Granma's spirit, like bitter hops. She was my first. I helped her pass through. She wintered. Others weren't so lucky. They got to autumn, summer... spring if they were awful unlucky.'

More visions flashed on the water. Death upon death. 'I saw 'em all through,' said Daughter, 'and welcomed the new too.' In the water, Nancy saw Other Daughter, older now, bent over a bed, helping a woman ease her baby into the world, raw and bloodied.

'There at the dawn, there at the dusk,' said Daughter. 'It felt a rare gift. I knew I had to hold it careful in my hands like a winter-lost bird. And, of course, I got pennies for my work. And I could peer into the past, into the future. People liked that.'

Another starker image, Other Daughter dwarfed by three stern men, cloaked in black with tall hats. Nancy watched in horror as they bundled her away, then plunged her head into a barrel of water, into the deep, dark wet. Her body squirmed as the men held her tightly until she went limp.

Then a bright, searing flash. They watched as Other Daughter's head jerked up, bedraggled, confused. Then she threw her head back and cackled. From the dark came a shadowy figure in black robes, a flaming torch in each hand, standing behind the sitting girl, blowing gently on the top of her head. Daughter looked up from peering into the pot. 'The end of my mortal years. Heggity came. She pulled me back to this world and popped me back in my house. I became forever a witch.' Daughter's eyes grew wide. 'Immortal, thanks to her.' They looked back into the water. Nancy saw Other Daughter, back in her hut with her family.

She sighed. 'I had to watch my family grow old and leave me one by one, while I stayed the same.

'I found my place. I was the one people came to, the one who birthed, the one who closed the eyes of the dying, then cleared up the blood, the piss, the shit. I'd peep what was coming, what had gone for 'em.'

Nancy watched, the scenes flicking through the years faster and faster. Winters frosting and suns rising again and again. Centuries. Tens of centuries perhaps. Gradually the clothes changed, tunics exchanged for dresses and breeches, but Other Daughter's face remained the same.

'It weren't all easy. Far from it. I watched as the churches were built, stone by stone, village by village, and one by one the old lords fell in with them. Hundreds of years later came the bishops and priests, whispering of girls and women who were baby murdering and dancing with the Devil, bringing the hail and makin' the crops fail, stirring up the flames.

'Where there was one witch, there were dozens,' Daughter said. 'The fires. The stakes. That smell of hair in flames and blistered flesh like a slaughtered pig on the spit. All of it with me every day.'

She rubbed her bare feet in the soil of the garden.

'I could protect myself. I had charms, spells, this an' that. I had powers. I was real. Those poor other girls din't.'

'That's how it is for us. All three of us. Here forever. We come together when Heggity calls. And when we're done, we go back to our people, until we're needed again.' Nancy thought of that shadowy, torch-bearing figure she'd seen. Heggity. Hecate. Could she mean Hecate? Nancy knew of the witch-goddess through Caleb's readings of *Macbeth*. The one who brought the three crones together, led them, commanded them.

She shook her head slowly. 'You spin the most wonderful fantasies, Daughter. Truly, I was absorbed.' Yet still the visions refused to fade from her mind.

The girl glowered at her. 'This is no fireside tale. This is my life, has *been* my life, *will be* my life. But mine are not the only words you need to hear. I am but one. There are two more lives, two more stories.'

★

'Quite the tale, *non?*' said Mother. 'Now I too have something to show you.' Her fingers ferreted around in one of her bags. Quick as a hare, her hand flashed towards Nancy, and she blew a pinch of powder hard into Nancy's face. Her eyes red-hot in agony, Nancy cried out and her hands flew to her face, then just as quickly, the pain subsided. She opened her eyes and tilted her head back and looked into the sun. Its beams flared rainbow colours that swirled and throbbed. Nancy looked back down. She was no longer in the garden, but somewhere else entirely.

It took a while for the glare to subside. A sun more scorching and intense than she had ever experienced shone bright over a village formed from round, thatched huts.

Mother took her hand and spoke quietly. 'Come. See where I was born.'

Nancy saw a group of women, singing and talking as they pounded grains into flour. Their skin shone like obsidian, their limbs lithe and strong.

A skinny-legged girl shook her head, singing along with the older women. Then she jumped up and ran outside, into a little garden, took a jug of water and splashed it on the green herbs sprouting in the ground.

Mother hummed approvingly. 'I always could make anything grow,' she whispered.

A flash. Drums started to throb through the night.

'We did this for the water goddess,' Mother whispered. 'Mami Wata.' She pointed to a wooden shrine – a series of rough boxes piled high with shiny fruit, jewellery. At the top was a mermaid-like figure carved in wood and painted jay-bright.

People gathered in a circle and started to shuffle faster. Heads were thrown back, eyes open and staring as if lost in a trance. Their feet moved together, the ground resonating with each massed step.

The hubbub faded away into an inky night, lit only by the moon and a blanket of stars. A figure crept slowly out of the hut, dressed in white. Other Mother! Two men emerged from the dark. She watched in horror as one of the men grabbed Other Mother, holding her arms behind her back. There was a glint of moonlight on a huge knife. Nancy cried out, but it was too late. The man with the knife drew it across her neck. Blood bubbled from Other Mother's throat. The light in her eyes started to fade.

Two glowing lights in the dark moved swiftly, silently, quicker than a human might run. A figure in a black robe. Hecate! Gently, she stroked Other Mother's neck and the wound healed. The shine came back into Other Mother's eyes and she jolted into consciousness. She started laughing, rubbing her neck in astonishment, then turned and embraced Hecate, half-laughing, half-crying.

Nancy turned to Mother, who was watching the scene, tears streaming down her face, her arms reaching out towards the mirage, which was slowly fading away.

'Hecate gave me fifty years, fifty more years with my children before they left me. I saw 'em grow, have children of their own, and took care of those children, and their children's children,' she sighed. 'When they had gone, when I had forgotten which children's children were my children's children, I was still there. I was called, of course. We three came together each time Hecate called, but we always went back, always looked after our people.'

Her face clouded. 'Even when the real darkness came. The darkness even I couldn't hold back.' The scene blurred. Nancy heard terrified screams, saw the flash of blades, made out bound legs and children wriggling in sacks. Even as the scene faded entirely, the cries of torment still rang in her ears.

A lurch in the darkness. The sounds of creaking timbers. A low murmur. The rank smell of sweat and rot. Mother shook her head. 'We got taken on ships, taken over the sea. Taken a long way. Many of us didn't make it.'

The view shimmered and changed. They were no longer at sea but among fields of violet flowers undulating in rows as far as Nancy could see. Women and children bent over, picking the blooms, silently, swiftly, precisely, their hands stained a sore, sticky blue. Behind the workers, ruddy white men stood laughing and smoking cigars, dark-wood guns held beneath their arms. One of them swaggered over to the line of women and tapped a picker on her shoulder, taking his cigar from his lips and shouting a torrent of curses at her. Nancy watched, horrified, as he lifted his gun and swung it into the woman's face. She fell, bleeding, eyes closed.

A line of women trudged to a field filled with huts in harsh lines, each with a sad little veranda. The injured woman sat on a chair, head tipped back, and Mother used a glass dropper to drip something into her eyes, smoothing her hair while whispering in her ear. Mother smiled. 'I do my best for them. I conjure. I give them salve for their sore hands, herbs to help them try to survive the cruelty. I tucked seeds in my pockets when we were taken, look.' She pointed at a row of pots on the sill, bristling with angular, spiky plants. 'We got the old country inside us. We took the earth in our shoes. The magic is still hidden in our bellies. We might call it root-work now, but it's still magic. Our goddesses still look over us. They might wear the masks of saints, and we may mouth the names the Christians want to hear, but beneath, they're our goddesses. We know their true names.'

It felt as if Nancy was surfacing through dark water, towards the light, faster and faster. A shake, and she was back sitting on the bench in the garden, Mother stroking her hand. The sun was dipping behind the trees.

Nancy had thought she was fully aware of the horrors of the slave trade. She had heard enough chatter through the drawing room doors of Greenwich to know that the practice formed part of that opaque world of 'merchantry', but never had she imagined that those bland terms sealed and glossed such raw horror.

'I had no idea,' Nancy sputtered. 'That pain, that cruelty.' She thought of her night-coloured cloak, dotted with stars. 'For blue clothes?'

'*Oui, ma chérie.* Indigo for your beautiful starry cloak, tobacco for your pipe, sugar cane for your tea. Picked by hands that bleed, by captives torn from their country. All that industry built on the slashed backs of my people, my descendants. Nancy looked down at her feet, guilty at her complacency.

The setting sun cast deep shadows on the women's three faces, painting them orange-pink. They sat like magistrates, watching her impassively. Nancy regarded the women with wary eyes. The day had left her senses bruised, the neat filing system of her brain in disarray.

A tiny spider was descending from the branches above on the thinnest thread of silk, spinning in the evening sun and Nancy watched it as it descended onto Mother's waiting hand. Gently, Mother lowered it in front of the toad on her lap. 'For you, Paddock,' she whispered. The toad's tongue flicked out and took the creature.

*

'One more story,' rasped Granny. 'I've been on Earth longer than all you put together and more.' The sun had sunk below the horizon and the first stars were blinking into the greenish glow of the sky.

A hum, mournful and rich came from between her closed lips, one note unchanging. Then her lips opened, but still, the noise was wordless, linear. Nancy swore she could see the tone writhing and arching across the lawn, twining around the tree trunks then spiralling high into the sky. She followed its smoky trace into the stars, heard its crystalline echo fade. And when she looked down, it was night. A few feet away stood a little red hut with glowing windows. They were among fog-wreathed mountains that plunged steeply into mirrored waters.

Instinctively, Nancy tilted her head towards the skies and gasped. They were the darkest, most star-hung she'd ever seen. Hearteningly, she spotted Cancer, Hydra, Hercules, the Seven Sisters. She crinkled up her eyes. Granny saw her confusion. 'Back when the six sister stars were seven,' she chuckled.

They walked over to the window of the hut and peered in. Inside dozens of tallow candles lit simple wooden furniture softened with thick, silvery furs. At the far end, on a little platform, was a wooden seat, spindly legged and tall as a person. On the wall hung a large drum, decorated with feathers, and near it leaned a thick stick topped with a silver crescent. Granny's staff. In front of the fire was a large square loom, and working that loom was a woman, fair-haired and furrow-browed, singing a wordless song to a little girl sat beside her on a stool.

'That's me. My mother taught me it all,' murmured Granny. 'The warp and the weft. The wax and wane of the moon. We'd pick juniper when it was full, plant dill when it faded. We found mushrooms that glowed like tiny lanterns and willow bark that took away the pain. Look.' She pointed at a black book on the table. 'It's all in there.'

Granny took the book from the table and flicked through it. Sketches of plants, and what looked like stanzas of poems. Granny paused at a page and opened the book on the table. 'You'll like this!' Nancy moved next to her. Unmistakably, there were astronomical diagrams. The moon's phases, mapped, eclipses, constellations. Nancy turned the page. A diagram of the solar system? How? Surely wherever they were was a time before Copernicus had even been born. Granny put her hand on Nancy's. 'Enough now. Think later. Watch. Forward a few years.'

The candles flickered, the hut shimmered for a few silvery seconds, and the air was now alive with the sound of chatter and laughter. A young woman with plaits in her hair stood at the fire, stirring a seething pot which filled the cottage with muggy, mossy sweetness. The loom had been pushed to the wall, a tapestry half-completed. Another girl stuffed a cushion with feathers, and a smiling woman shook out a heavy cloak embroidered in blue and gold. The chair was missing, but the drum was on the table, being polished by another woman with thistledown hair and high cheekbones. Granny grinned, 'Oh, look at me. At us. The joy we found in the preparation.'

Other Granny picked up a bottle of herbal liquid and poured it into four wooden cups, giving one to each of the other girls and keeping one for herself. They stood in a circle, held their drinks high and brought them together, then knocked them back in one draught. Other Granny wiped her lips, picked up her staff and nodded. One of the girls picked up the drum, slung it round her neck, then started to beat it with her hand, steadily, slowly. All humming, they left the hut.

The night air was fresh and cloud-free, with a splinter of new moon. A fire sent sparks into the cold air, a group of men silhouetted against the flames, heavy in furs. The drumming became more urgent, the singing louder. The girls' eyes shone like wet pebbles, broad smiles on their faces. Other Granny tilted her head back, ecstatic, screaming, wailing, the words whipping away on the wind. Louder, and louder, like a hurricane from her belly. It was as if the scream was outlined, eddying, swirling, growing, its tail snaking from deep inside Granny, leaving her lips like a serpent and whipping round and round until it became part of the air and the sky and the stars. One final scream and then Granny shouted once in triumph. The drums and singing stopped. Nancy felt her eyelids drooping.

When her eyes opened again, she saw a narrow lake, mountains plunging each side, the sun disappearing between them, sending a shimmering, orange path across the water. At the edge of the lake were hundreds of people carrying torches, pushing something – a long, thin wooden boat. On the boat was the body of a frail old woman. Other Granny. On top of her lay her staff.

Nancy bit her thumb and turned to her companion, who took her hand. 'Don't be afraid, Child of the Moon. I was so old. It was my time.'

They watched as the boat was set alight, then pushed into the water. It glided through the still surface, smoke spiralling into the liquid sunset, the only sound the crackle of flames.

From out of the melting sun came a figure, silhouetted, gliding steadily towards the boat, getting bigger as it approached. Its hands were outstretched, a torch in each. She felt Granny squeeze her hand harder and sigh. 'Heggity. Oh, Heggity'. The scene crackled and crumpled, burning away.

'Hecate saved me, brought me back to life. I took myself from village to village, seeing, healing, working charms,' said Granny. 'Walked until my feet hardened and my eyes disappeared. It was a hard life, a long life, that is true! The years! The thousands and thousands of years. But, oh, the sweet rewards.' Nancy watched the figure shuffle into the distance, alone, until she was swallowed up in white dazzle.

'I think I was lucky. Mother and Daughter… their lives were tough. Hounded, tortured, blamed for the sins of the world. Ripped from their time before they were meant to go. But I was always adored. People would come to me, they heeded my words, gave value to my work.' She sighed.

★

They were in the garden once more. It was almost dark. The windows of the cottage glowed, smoke poured from its chimney. The women got to their feet, and walked up the path to its low door. Nancy followed them into the cottage.

She felt chastened, remembering uncomfortably how she had stood on this spot several hours earlier, airily dismissing these women as frauds. How she had been unwaveringly secure in the knowledge that science was the bedrock of everything, buoyed by prim facts and smug reason. Now she barely knew what to think. To all appearances she was the same person who had walked through the front door of the cottage that afternoon, but it felt as if her thoughts were shifting in the most fundamental fashion, her certainty was starting to crack. She could scarcely bring herself to admit it – these women were telling her, proving to her, that they were witches. Witches. She could barely let herself form the word in her head, let alone say it aloud. She shook her head and closed her eyes.

Mother looked up as if scrying her thoughts. 'It can be hard, can it not? Letting yourself believe the new. Havin' your head tipped upside-down. You've heard our stories. Thank you, child, for listening. You needed to hear.'

Her arm fell around Nancy's shaking shoulders. She smelled of orange blossom and woodsmoke.

Nancy shook off Mother's arm and turned to her. 'What's happening? Tell me about that painting. How long has it been there? Who are you really?'

Mother reached out and tucked a strand of Nancy's hair behind her ear. Nancy did not move or complain, loath to break the silence. Mother exhaled. 'Very well. We will tell you.'

Chapter Thirteen

Mother patted a stool next to her, an earring glinting in the light of the fire. Nancy noticed strange markings up her arms, a little like the tattoos she'd seen peeping from beneath sailors' shirts around Greenwich.

'Sit down. Have some tea. You'll likely be here longer than you think,' Mother said.

It was getting late, but she would tarry and speak to them. She was still dazed by the stories they'd shown her, the painting on the back of the house. How did a woman who had never stepped over the threshold of a schoolroom know the order of the solar system?

The stool was hard, but Nancy perched on its edge, back rod-straight, and took a mug of something steaming. It smelled like buttered toast. A cup of tea was always welcome, particularly when one was at ones and twos. 'Very well,' she said.

Hot and strong, the drink sharpened her blunted senses a little. These women were just that – women. Women that she might spy gossiping around a water pump or bustling through town. Nancy lowered her voice. 'You may be shrewd. You may be able to grow herbs to give relief for the ague, and have learned the phases of the moon, or how to glean from a man's shoes what his future is likely to bring. You might forage in hedgerows for weeds to sell at the market, but you are not witches! You have no magical powers.'

The women laughed.

Mother spread her arms wide. 'Of course we have powers, child! What would we be without our powers?'

Nancy stuttered. 'I know you possess knowledge. Your remedies have quite a reputation.' She paused, thinking of Isobel. 'But, please, afford me some respect and be truthful. Out of sisterliness, if nothing else.'

Mother made a tutting sound, '*Bébé*, we tell only the truth.'

The room held its breath. Three pairs of eyes met Nancy's gaze. Daughter's wide and watery blue, Mother's green, flecked with gold, Granny's so hooded and creased her black irises struggled to peep through.

Mother tilted her head. 'This might seem curious. We understand your fear. Your mind shines as brightly as those stars you stare at every night.' She scratched symbols – a cross in a circle, some arrows – in the ash near the grate with her foot, then looked up again.

'How do you know what I study?' Nancy asked sharply.

Mother ignored her and continued. 'We understand what it is to carry that learnin', to be blessed with that power to understand. Sometimes women have to tuck that power away, to shade the white light of our precious gift in order to stay at peace, free from men's ridicule. But we don't have to hide in the shadows. Here your light can shine. We are sisters. We are three. Together we are one.' *Men's ridicule.* Nancy shot her a sharp look.

The old woman, Granny, smiled. 'The moon leaves its trace on you.' She reached out a bony hand and stroked Nancy's hair.

Daughter leaned forward. 'We knew you'd come, Child of the Moon, Daughter of the Stars. I made your likeness.' The portrait on the back of the cottage lay but six feet away. 'I saw it in the bones. I scried it in the entrails. And Granny glimpsed it in the skies long ago.'

'Long ago,' wheezed Granny. 'Back when I had a real name.'

The skin on the woman's face drew back tightly around her temples. 'And now, now you are here.' She grasped Nancy's cheek between her finger and thumb, and turned to the others. 'Now she is here.'

Nancy pulled away and rubbed her face. Their stories were absurd and she was tempted to leave, but walking away now felt as if she had failed somehow to prove a hypothesis, and – she hated to admit it – there was an unsettling whiff of conviction about their words. And the dusty, cracked painting on the back of the cottage was unmistakeably her.

She threw a hand in the air. 'This makes little sense, but please, go on.'

Daughter nodded. 'We are three, three into one. We are the weaver, the Earth-tiller, the moon-watcher.' She jabbed a thumb at her chest, then pointed at Mother and Granny in turn. 'Many stars died before we found each other. Our mothers and our daughters and our daughters' daughters bones in ashes. It took all of time and a few years more. We were humans like you. Then we came alive once more. You saw. Hundreds, mebbe thousands of years ago we died, yet we continued to live.' She squeezed Granny's hand, 'But together we is one.'

Mother placed her hand on Daughter's. 'Together we are one. Each of us so different. Each of us needed. My hands turn dust into soil, coax seedlings from cracks. I can grow herbs that can protect you from the sharpest blade, or that will seduce the stoniest heart. She,' her finger jabbed in the direction of Daughter, 'can scry the future. In bones, in chitlins, or from the shine on a bowl of still, cool water. And more. She'll see your child born, help you deliver, help you pass on beyond too. This one,' her voice lowered to a sonorous whisper and she jerked her head at Granny, 'flies among the stars. When she passes by, the moon bows and whispers his secrets. She bears witness to all. We started our journeys so far apart, but we was needed. Called upon. By her.'

Nancy shook her head. Who did these women believe had called them?

Mother continued. 'We come together every few hundred years, back here near the roof of the world. Help save folk.' She shrugged. 'Over and over. Fought battles, held off evil, and brought that prophecy to the Thane.'

Nancy's ears pricked up at the word. The Thane. Macbeth?

'What do you mean *the Thane*?' she asked. Indulgence would be her weapon. 'You believe that you are somehow related to the witches in Shakespeare's play?'

Daughter smiled. 'We is them. We was. We always will be.' She started to intone flatly,

    'The Weird Sisters, hand in hand,
    Posters of the sea and land,
    Thus do go about, about;'

The three women's voices keened together, thin as scutch grass,

    'Thrice to thine and thrice to mine,
    And thrice again, to make up nine.
    Peace! The charm's wound up.'

The rhyme snaked around the cottage, wrapped around Nancy. She swallowed, recognising the lines from *Macbeth*.

'This is poppycock. *Macbeth* is a play, a diversion that sprang from the mind of one man! And besides, we all know that the events Shakespeare described took place hundreds of years ago.' The women nodded. 'And yet you are here, still walking this Earth.'

Daughter bent over the sputtering fire, took a poker, then jabbed at the white-ashed logs.

She stood, turned to Nancy, and smiled.

'We are as different as the morning sun, the afternoon star, the midnight moon, but we're sprung from the same field. Heggity saved us, didn't she? Each of us. She called, as she always does. We heard her. We came here, and found the Thane just a few miles over, on the moor. We was to bring him a proffercy, y'see?'

Hecate! Macbeth! The play felt inescapable, as if its lines twined around her, snaked around this place. Hecate's blistering speech, scolding her three weird charges for meeting the Thane without her blessing. Caleb had taken down a book and showed her a picture of this ancient deity, who dressed in flowing black robes, and roamed moonlit graveyards with her she-dog and polecat. He told her she was the spirit who unlocked doors between this world and the next.

Nancy pinched the top of her nose. This miasma of fantasies was drawing her in. Yet she felt compelled to remain here, untangling these women's riddles.

She spoke slowly, humouring the girl. 'How often do you see this Hecate, Daughter?'

The girl scowled. 'As often as we need and no more. She was the one who told us that we must come together, that we must become one. Three into one. Stronger, y'see. She told us to be up here, in this wet tip of the world, to give him his prophecies. That we had to be in this place for a little while to stop the worst happening. He must be King, if only for a whisper. We had to be sure it all played out.' She spat on the ground. 'But she got the gripe with us, didn't she? Got the gripe cos we didn't tell her we was going to meet him on that moor.'

Nancy looked at the grub speaking to her, her dirty toenails, her reddened hands, her grubby apron. How could this farmwife know of *Macbeth*? Of Shakespeare and Hecate?

The girl was a convincing liar, that was for certain. Perhaps she was deluded. Nancy looked to the other women. Who then, was at the heart of this deception?

She remembered the intensity on Caleb's face as he read the scene where Macbeth first met the witches. How the first witch had told of her vendetta against a sailor, and that she would, 'drain him dry as hay'. She recalled the hag's threats:

> 'Sleep shall neither night nor day,
> Hang upon his pent-house lid.
> He shall live a man forbid;
> Weary sev'nights, nine times nine,
> Shall he dwindle, peak, and pine.'

Bloody, vengeful, terrifying. For all their oddness and lies, she couldn't imagine these words coming from the mouths of any of the women drinking tea with her in this kitchen.

Yet there was something compelling about their spiel. She held the tin cup more tightly and turned to the oldest woman. 'Very well, let us play this charade for a few minutes. Macbeth has now been dead for over seven centuries. Why did you stay in Scotland?'

Granny tilted back her head and looked from under her hooded eyelids. 'We didn't stay. We left, back to our people, as we always do, then returned. Heggity, my child, brought us back here again. As she likes to.'

Nancy wrinkled her nose. 'Why? What is there for you here now? Macbeth is long gone.'

'She brings us back when we're needed,' said Daughter, keeping her gaze carefully on Nancy. 'And so we return, every few hundred years. Come together. Because three of us is strong. But this time, she told us four of us is needed. There is something bigger to come.'

Granny nodded. 'We are but strands of rope. Each of us is steady, but braid three of us together, and we have enough strength to hold fast planets. Daughter, Mother, Granny. Planting time, harvest, barren winter.' She pointed at each in turn with her stick. 'We returned to wait again patiently, to do Heggity's bidding. If we have nothing else, we have time. We left our people once more, and came back here, to this cold, damp town, and have been waiting here again ten years – ten times around the sun.'

Nancy closed her eyes. Her face burned hot in the glow of the fire and she felt dizzy. These women were so practised in their wheedling lies, their stories as neatly aligned as a total eclipse. Yet the words 'Child of the Moon' rang in her ears. The name given to her by the women. Their tales. And the crows. The silhouettes of those vast, flapping birds from that snowy day seemed to flicker up the sides of the room. She glanced towards the back of the cottage, where she knew outside lay the painting of the red-headed woman and the planets.

Mother laughed, hard and loudly. 'Oh child, we know you've peeped that picture, the one that Daughter painted last time we were here – sometime last century, when Hecate told us when she needed us next. That hair! Those eyes. So the day we first spied you, we knew you in the shake of a rabbit's tail!'

The woman touched her gently on the arm. 'You are right, child. We came back for you. *You* are why we are here.'

Chapter Fourteen

The skies were clouded and dark on the walk back to Black-thistle. The women had vouchsafed little more, although, as she had been led to the doorway in a surprisingly strong grip, Mother had whispered that all would become clear soon. Nancy trudged slowly. Maybe the women had painted the image after their first meeting at the market and applied something – dust perhaps – to make it appear more ancient. Or perhaps it was merely coincidence that the painting so resembled her, and that the likeness had prompted the women's initial interest in her. But then, there was the ribbon. And Hecate. She exhaled, loudly. No, they were ought but charlatans. Cheap tricksters. Perhaps they had slipped something into her tea. Ergot, or those mushrooms the people of Inverness seemed so keen to pay good pennies for. Her head started to ache.

She must make no mention of her visit to the cottage to Caleb. She winced at the thought of how he might react, picturing his incredulity that a woman he'd employed, pre-cisely because her work was rooted in reason and life in logic, would give any consideration to a trio of herb-pedlars and tricksters, a silly ribbon, some well-spun words and a rough-hewn sketch. And that the women claimed to be those in the play with which he was so obsessed? She had seen how his eyes had gleamed at her revelations about the Fold. Now the swirls of Shakespeare's tale were rising around the town, into Blackthistle, like an infection. The nature of these women's claims surely might lead him to the madhouse. No, he must not know that she had ever visited that run-down cottage.

It was now late. She had stayed out a lot longer than expected. As an astronomer, she knew precisely when darkness would fall, yet something had compelled her to linger in the cottage past the end of the day. Inverness was much darker than London, with its columns of oil lamps. Here, only the odd corner was lit, although there was some illumination from open casements and candles in windows. She picked up her pace and tried not to think of drone-like chanting, flaming boats being pushed into ice lakes and shadowy, lantern-bearing figures. Even though she spent more time in the dark than most, the thought of crossing the bridge across the river and navigating to Blackthistle with only moonlight to light her way, and on her own, filled her with trepidation. She cursed herself for not bringing her lantern. She cast an anxious glance down a narrow path between houses, heard a rustling in the shadows. She shivered, despite the warm night, and gripped the little bag in her pocket tightly. Darkness had never held any fear for her, but tonight it loomed rather than embraced.

For a moment she wondered about turning into the brightly lit tavern on the corner and asking one of the men to accompany her home. Yet that might be inviting more trouble. No. She was well used to the gloom and she would walk home. This was a route she had followed many times, after all. However, as she approached the bridge, she felt a tightening in her chest. The moon gleamed on the flagstones, but beyond, the trees enveloped the path in blackness.

At the bridge she stopped for a moment, breathing heavily. Every part of her was alert. She looked upwards, finding the North Star. Whenever her world threatened to teeter out of control, she took comfort in the reassuring permanence of dear Polaris. Blood thumped in her ears as she started to walk across the bridge.

'Halloo!'

A shout. Across the bridge, a shadowy, skinny figure, lamp in hand.

'Nancy!'

It was Caleb. A wave of relief swept over her. She picked up her skirts and walked as swiftly as she could towards him. He smiled as she drew closer.

'How did you know?'

He shook his head. 'I expected you at study, but there was no sign, so I asked Isobel where you might be. She told me she'd left you in Inverness this afternoon. So I thought I'd come out to find you. It's a bonny night, make no mistake, but walking alone after dark is never a good idea.'

Evidently, Isobel had not mentioned the women to Caleb, for which she was grateful. She nodded and spoke as evenly as she could. 'I know. I stayed out far later than I expected. I feel so foolish.'

He pushed back his black curls. 'Easily done when you get caught upon something.' It appeared he knew nothing of why she was so late in town.

The intensity that had lit his eyes last time they had met had subsided, and this calmer Caleb was far more agreeable. He indicated his arm, and Nancy took it. It was dark, and there was thankfully no-one abroad.

'Thank you.'

'My pleasure. This must be quite a novelty. I can't imagine you need rescuing very often.'

Caleb was right. For more than ten years she had faced life alone, consumed with looking after Crooms and pursuing her research.

'It's rare. But when it's needed, very welcome.'

They were across the bridge. Now Caleb's lantern cast shadows into the trees, which stretched backwards into gloom and pitch. She jumped at a crackle, but the creeping fear that had consumed her but five minutes previously had left her. She shook her head at how rattled she had been.

'I'm sorry, Nancy, if my questions about your research have caused any... *awkwardness* for you. I know I can be demanding.' Caleb coughed. 'You have made yourself invaluable, to me, in many ways. I needed someone who had studied astronomy to show me the intricacies, the machinations of the universe, and you know, you can tell me that. Yet I hoped I might find someone who was open to something further than merely received knowledge. And I believe that I found them.'

Nancy was glad that it was too dark for Caleb to see the colour rising in her cheeks.

'Thank you. I truly appreciate the opportunity you have given me.' With a jolt, she realised that she spoke the truth. When he was in this mood, there was something in Caleb's manner that reminded her of Uncle James. A straightforward openness and questions that showed a willingness to collaborate as equals. All that Nancy had longed for. Perhaps he was right. Imagine what they might discover together. He might even be the perfect study partner to help her discover more about the Fold.

Blackthistle's silhouette now seemed sharp and oppressive. Perhaps it was the house itself that tormented Caleb: its winding, cold corridors, the walls that echoed with the whispers of those long-vanished. For a moment, Nancy considered asking Caleb about his wife. Yet his steps seemed lighter tonight, and she knew that to seek answers now would risk the collapse of this carefully rebuilt friendship.

Caleb rang at the heavy bell-pull and turned to Nancy. 'I know your head must be aswirl. Blackthistle is an uncommon place, and it has its,' he paused briefly, 'ghosts. Yet I believe our studies will bring the life back within its walls. Please, trust me.'

Nancy exhaled. 'I think I do.' And she did.

It had been a long, confusing day. She was still unsettled by the stories the women had shown her, but Caleb's kind words meant her nerves jangled a little less harshly. Nevertheless, she left her candle lit that night.

Chapter Fifteen

Once more, the night's dreams had been phantasmagoric; she'd woken, arms pinned to her side, unable to move or to form a scream as the faces of the women loomed above her like succubae, arms branch-like and outstretched. There were glimpses of masters beating the sweating workers in the indigo fields, the shimmering glamour of the northern lights, a girl, head held underwater, a small boy, a woman with black, shining eyes. Night terrors, sure, but the illusion was disconcertingly persuasive, the ghosts lingering around every corner, their fingers creeping around doors.

However, the chance of Caleb finding out about her encounter with the crones worried her almost more than the women themselves. She felt strongly, more strongly than anything, that she must keep him from that cottage, that he must not find out about the three, and who they claimed to be. So, when she was with Caleb, she attempted to banish all thoughts of those strange few hours, tamping down the unease that had started to foment inside her since her visit to that shack on the outskirts of the town.

Yet if anything, the next few days' studies passed a little more easily. Her student's eyes had lost the trace of desperation they had held, and he even, on occasion, cracked a wry smile. He was, however, still engrossed in his studies, and worked with a crisp vigour. His appearance on the bridge had been a godsend, his kind words had warmed her heart, and, yes, the strange light in his eyes when she had mentioned the Fold might well have been just excitement and encouragement. For did she, of all people, not know the potent thrill of uncovering something new? Something previously undiscovered? She felt as if she had not extended the same kindnesses to Caleb as he had to her, and resolved to be a little less guarded with her pupil.

The last two days had been spent studying celestial coordinates – those numbers that placed stars, pinned them down like butterflies in a case. Caleb was a swift learner and seemed determined to master the theory, but even he found grasping the system of charting, using right ascension, declination, hours and degrees challenging. It was grinding study, yet they savoured their slower progress, heads bent together, tutting together at Caleb's mistakes. After four days of hard toil he had mastered the method, so Nancy resolved to make their next session a little more agreeable.

She had been remiss in not yet taking him outside to stargaze. Field study was, she considered, the most rewarding aspect of her work. Spending time directly under the heavens felt elemental, as if she were just an arm's reach away from creation. Caleb had shown her the wonders of verse, and tonight, she determined, she would open his soul to the sight of stars. At the very least, she reasoned, he would be company on a dark night in a damp field.

Tonight, she heard the clock in the hall chime nine just before Caleb entered the room. Nancy indicated the greenish-blue skies through the window.

'Good evening, Caleb. I thought tonight we might take my telescope into the fields. We have, after all, studied the theory in depth, but never ventured beyond these windows. I would like to show you the heavens, for you to drink them in as I do.'

He smiled eagerly. 'I would be honoured. As you well know, I am always eager to learn more.'

At the last transit, she had relied, to her regret, on a small telescope, which, she had concluded, had not helped her cause when it came to gathering hard evidence. At the second transit, she could take no chances. So, as her dear father was no longer alive to build another for her, she had commissioned his fiercest competitor, John Dollond, to make a fine Gregorian reflector, which he had described to her as, 'His crowning achievement'. As requested, Cora had sent the telescope up by boat and Nancy looked through it before retiring to bed every night. The last image she saw before falling asleep was its silhouette against the stars.

Nancy entrusted Caleb with the telescope, and took down her little lantern and tinderbox. They walked side by side across the damp, slippery grasses, the light of the house fading into the night.

Caleb hummed a half-familiar song.

'There was three men come out o' the west their fortunes
for to try,
And these three men made a solemn vow, John Barley-
corn must die.'

Nancy shivered, although the night was warm. A still-plumpish moon hung above them, its honeyed beams spilling into the sky, flattening the weakest stars, but still she knew there would be thousands of pin points of light to be seen. Many of her colleagues wouldn't countenance charting when the moon was this bright, but Nancy liked being outside and seeing her night shadow. It reminded her of the elemental nature of the Earth's satellite. They passed through the little gate that led from Blackthistle's formal gardens into the wilder fields beyond. She slipped red glass into the windows of her specially adapted lantern.

'We must wait until our eyes get their night sight. Be patient, and you will be rewarded.'

They stood, silent, heads tilted back. A screech close-by broke the stillness. Nancy squealed.

'Just an owl, Nancy.'

Both laughed at her shock. 'I'm not usually so easily frit,' Nancy mumbled.

'It's a dark night,' offered Caleb gallantly.

This wild, cold trawl of the skies felt a million miles from those insulated, stuffy nights at the Observatory, the smell of whisky and machine grease in her nostrils and the harrumphing of Dr Maskliss in her ears.

She smiled in the dark. 'I wonder if this might be the most perfect place to stargaze?'

'It's a lovely dark spot,' said Caleb, 'I can think of few better.'

Nancy bit her lip. 'There's a place in London – perhaps the best place in the world from which to watch the heavens. On top of the Observatory, the roof of the Octagon Room. So secret that even the astronomers beneath your feet have no idea you're above. I used to spend night upon night there when I was a child, slipping through the green-painted door behind the rose hedge in the outside wall that was never locked, tiptoeing up the back staircase. Oh.'

It was time. Twenty minutes had passed and their eyes had softened, become receptive to every nuance and billow of sky. A thick blanket of stars revealed itself. Countless pinpricks, like sparkling dust on velvet. Scotland's skies were infinitely richer, more generous than those of the south. Despite having spent a life with her eyes cast heavenwards, tonight, the sky was newly mesmeric.

'What a sight,' she breathed. 'Truly, the skies here are magnificent.'

'I know,' said Caleb. His voice sounded a little choked.

Nancy could see his outline. He was pinching his nose. 'It can be overwhelming, I know,' she said. 'Let's try to make some sense of what we can see. Here.'

His height meant that he was required to stoop further than she in order to put his eye to the glass. She put her fingers on the back of his head. He started at her touch, but she kept them in place. Her other hand closed over his on the telescope, gently guiding a sweep of the darkest areas of the northern horizon, pausing to point out some familiar friends. 'Ursa Minor, Draco. There's Ursa Major.' She took away her hand and pointed at the constellations. 'Orion. See the stars that make up his belt? There's his dagger, his tunic...'

'I see them,' he whispered. 'It's easy to forget how simple and beautiful they are.'

Something in his voice made Nancy look up again at the outlines in the sky. Caleb was right. She had seen these stars, these configurations, countless times, yet tonight it felt as if she was coming to them afresh, that it was the first time she'd seen them properly. Now they seemed to sing from the sky, to nod and bow to them both, moving like a bear, a hunter.

Caleb turned his head from the telescope. 'I feel that we could gaze at these stars every night and still see something new each time.'

'I feel the same,' Nancy murmured.

There was a flash, a bright light arcing in the direction of Inverness. So bright, it left a greenish trace in her vision.

'A meteor,' she said, pointing.

'I saw.' Caleb gasped. 'Shakespeare writes that they are "exhaled from the sun".'

Nancy smiled. 'A graceful description.'

'Were you aware that his wife was a stargazer? I once visited her grave. Her epitaph translated reads:

"Come quickly, Christ,
That my mother, though shut in the tomb, may rise
again and seek
the stars."

Women and stars, Nancy. It's a formidable union.'

She nodded to herself. 'I shall be forever grateful for this opportunity. Truly.'

Caleb exhaled. 'Thank you for showing me the skies, Nancy. Tonight it felt as if we danced among the galaxies.'

She heard his boots squeaking in the grass as he stood back from the instrument, 'This telescope feels powerful, Nancy. I presume your father made it?'

A surge of sadness coursed through her. 'Sadly not. Yet had he been alive when I needed it, he might have made one even more magnificent.'

Benjamin Lockaby's family was unimaginably wealthy, but unlike many blessed with similar fortune, her father had had a strong sense of purpose. While his brother steered the family business, sending ships around the world, Benjamin's Grand Tour had taken him across Europe and through the Ottoman Empire to Persia, where he became enamoured with astronomy, and in particular, its instruments. Few knew how many hours, months, he had spent learning to patiently grind the speculum metal in order to make unflawed mirrors for huge reflecting telescopes, most were unaware of the years he had taken to experiment with brass, until he was capable of crafting precise sextants, engraved with whorls and waves and tiny moons to help sailors find their way home, and exquisite miniature gold astrolabes that ticked and whirred and distilled the secrets of the universe into something you could hold in the palm of your hand. Those instruments found their way into the grandest of houses, even to the palace and the care of the King.

'Mr Dollond made this for me. I needed the most powerful instrument possible, you see? To see the Fold.' Her voice quivered a little. Since the night she had described her discovery to Caleb, they had not discussed the topic.

She heard him take a sharp intake of breath, yet his reply was even. 'Time is passing fast, isn't it, Nancy?'

She nodded in the dark. 'The transit is only weeks away.'

He continued quietly. 'Can you tell me more about the transits? Am I right in thinking that there are pairs of transits, but hundreds of years apart? I'm not sure I fully understood when you last told me.'

Nancy quickly led him through the strange sequence the transits sketched. 'So, a transit took place, of course, eight years ago. Before that in 1639, when it was first predicted by Kepler and Horrocks. But before that too. Way back in time. Let me see... in 1518 and 1526. 1275 and 1283, 1032 and 1040.'

There was a silence. Then Caleb muttered darkly. '1040.' He stood back from the telescope. 'The year that Macbeth – the *real* Macbeth – slew Duncan and became King.'

Macbeth! She thought of Daughter, and what she had said, 'We had to be in this place for a little while to stop the worst happening... He must be King, if only for a whisper.' The women had claimed to have been here to meet Macbeth. And in that year, all those centuries ago, the real Macbeth had became King. Somehow she managed to control the gasp that rose in her throat, for she knew more than anything else she must not reveal the existence of that strange trio to Caleb.

He was silent, seeming lost in thought. Tonight she had almost found him, he had come so close to revealing something of himself, only to turn his head at the last minute.

'I should get back to the house,' he said abruptly.

His reaction had unnerved her further, yet she knew she must remain calm.

'Very well. I will stay here for a while. I have stars to chart.'

His hands shook as he used his little tinderbox to light his lantern, then he turned and stumbled back through the fields towards Blackthistle.

Quietly she called after him, 'Good night, Caleb.' But there was no reply.

Chapter Sixteen

The sky was now full of clouds, silvery at the edges, scudding across the moon. Each sweep of the horizon felt half-hearted, every attempt to chart feeble, her thoughts entirely of those women and their claims. Caleb had once told her that Shakespeare's version of events differed from those in the history books. 1040! 1040! The date seemed to ring into the heavens, taunting her. Connections were being forged, evidence stacking, leaf on leaf. There appeared to be some connection between the transits and the years that the women had claimed to have been called back by Hecate. She shook her head in disbelief. What was she becoming?

Something gleamed in the dark. She glanced up at the turret. There. There again was that light. It shone that bloodless, queer white, with none of the flicker or yellow of tallow or wax, and unlike any glow she'd seen before. It was enough to send anyone half-mad with fright. It could only have been lit by Caleb. She stared at it intently for a few minutes, yet could make very little out, bar a few flickering shadows, then the light went out, leaving the turret in darkness.

Nancy shivered. She was tiring. Time to pack up her instruments and light her lantern. As she made her way back across the slippery, damp fields she heard the thud of the front door. Peering into the dark grounds of the house, she saw someone stride away, his boots soft on the drive, a lantern in his hand lighting the thick night. His coat collar was turned up, a hat pulled down, but that hunched gait was familiar. Caleb.

His corvid figure smudged into the darkness. She must know what he was doing.

She hid her box of instruments and notes behind a tree and flipped the hood of her indigo cloak over her hair. Caleb disappeared around the corner and she followed him into the brackish night.

Her footsteps made only the barest of crackles as she hurried behind him. His wheat-slender figure dipped in and out of the moonlight, over the bridge and into the shadowy streets of Inverness. The town. For a moment, Nancy wondered if he might be headed to a late-night alehouse, but it was one o' clock and far too late for any tavern doors to still be open.

Every so often, Caleb turned and glanced backwards. At each pause, Nancy pressed herself into the shadows, against houses and walls, holding as still as she could, willing her breath silent then tailing him once more. By the church, he stopped and leaned against the wall, as if to cool his head on the grey stone.

After what seemed like an eternity he raised his head, inhaled, and started walking again, slowly at first, then with more purpose. His hobnails clinked across the gleaming cobbles of the market square, the sail-like tails of his long coat billowing behind.

Nancy followed as quietly as she could, into the darkness of a small street that led from the square. These were the roads she had scurried down only a few short days ago, now lined with shuttered, sleeping houses. They reached the top of the street down which the boy had been too scared to walk. There could be no mistake: he was visiting the women. Her mouth prickled dry.

Something seemed to focus – a clearer image appeared where before there was a blur. Caleb, the women, and her, bound together. Not by fate, Nancy reasoned with herself, but by an alignment like that she might find in the skies. Planets moving into formation.

She slipped into a dark alcove, watching as Caleb paused outside the thorn-wreathed cottage, eyes scanning the street. Head down, he gripped the gate with both hands, shoulders rising and falling a little. The moon silvered him like a marble statue. With a determined shake, he opened the gate into the prickled embrace of the brambles.

She crept down the street towards the cottage, slipping along the alley alongside the front garden, feet feeling their way as she peeped over the top of the wall. Caleb was standing on the step of the cottage, eyes shut, head thrown back. She was close enough to see a pearl of sweat trickling down his throat towards that silver locket. She slowed her breath to almost nothing. What hold might these women have over him, that he looked so afflicted?

The bang of Caleb's fist on the door was loud enough to raise the dead. Nancy feared he would wake the entire street. The thuds echoed away into the night air, followed by silence.

Stark black and white in the light of the moon, Caleb leaned against the door, his face pressed against the rough wood. His eyes cast towards Nancy, and she shrank back, but it was apparent that his focus was somewhere far beyond the wall. The street was silent. Perhaps the neighbours were waiting behind their shutters, accustomed to such disturbances.

Much as she wanted to run, she was unable to tear her eyes from Caleb, let alone move her feet. His lips were moving, intense whispers she could barely hear. The night was still, but it was as if the words were being blown into the night. She strained to hear more clearly but any meaning danced just out of reach.

The door opened a crack, a sliver of flickering yellow light. Caleb's face was pressed close to the narrow opening, his muttering now directed towards whoever had opened the door. Nancy made out a dim murmur in reply.

Caleb was now scrabbling at the door, forcing his fingers into the gap, and attempting to push it open. His whispers became angrier: 'Hail one! Hail two! Hail three!'

There was a deep chuckle from within the house, and Caleb's voice rose.

'Tell me what you gave her. Tell me what she used. Tell me what I need! I know who you really are, filthy hags! You were here for the Thane, back all those years ago! Now I know that beyond all doubt. I have proof. Verifiable, scientific proof. Numbers! I know the dates of the transits and I know you were there! And now you are back again and have taken all that I loved!'

From the house swelled a fierce cry, as if all the anger in the world had been distilled down into one, vengeful, half-animal sound. Caleb dropped to his knees, fingers over his ears, but Nancy remained standing, frozen by the blast of noise.

The door slammed shut. The unearthly noise abruptly stopped, and it seemed the world stilled and held its breath. Caleb remained as if in prayer, head down. Overhead, the moon watched impassively.

From behind the house, the striped cat appeared, and sauntered towards the kneeling figure, mewing. Caleb's head jerked up as if woken from a trance, and he rose to his feet then stumbled backwards from the garden. Steps echoed down the street.

Let him run. Nancy leaned against the wall behind her, eyes fixed on the silent cottage. There was no sign of life, nothing that indicated the source of that unearthly noise. That sound and fury. The clack-clack-clack of Caleb's boots faded into the distance.

She pulled her cloak tight and hurried up the road, her hands damp from fear. His torment had been obvious, as if his soul was being twisted by some unseen hand. He'd spoken of some object they had given someone, and screamed. 'I know who you really are. Filthy hags.' *Filthy hags*. She had heard those words from Caleb's mouth before. It was a speech from *Macbeth*, from early in Shakespeare's play.

She stopped dead in the street.

The words were from the scene in which he first met the witches.

Chapter Seventeen

Blackthistle House,
Inverness,
Scotland
May 16th

My dearest Cora,
I write from my bed. I cannot sleep. If I do close my eyes,
they are imprinted with images most dreadful. If I lay my
head on the pillow, a noise so hellish jangles in my ears.
Cora, I wish I might tell you more, but you would think
me to have quite lost my mind.
Do not fear. My fingers retain their grip on rationality in
the face of a storm of superstition. However, it seems as
though those around me are struggling to stay on course.
Please, not a word to a soul, but I fear for Mr Malles's
health. His behaviour is disturbing beyond belief.
Although I want nothing more than to jump into a
stagecoach and ride back to Greenwich, away from this
superstitious town, I must, of course, stay. I feel that he
is a good man, Cora. A good man who I am determined
to help. I need to attempt to wrest Mr Malles from the
delusions under which he labours.
Also, I have given my word, and you know I always
keep my word.
I do, however, dearly wish you were by my side.
Give my regards to Greenwich, and please, send me
strength!
Nancy

★

It was no use. Nancy could not rest. The plaintive bleats of sheep in the fields beyond rang in Nancy's ears like cackles. She rubbed her eyes. She would rise early. A walk might clear her head. Perhaps Isobel might be persuaded.

A wide-eyed Isobel could indeed be persuaded and was eager to get out of the house. 'It feels queer in here today, ma'am,' she whispered. 'Heavy. Like a pot on the fire that's about to boil over.'

Outside, it was already uncomfortably hot, the sun casting a harsh shadow. The only sound came from the rookery at the end of the drive. The birds cawed even more loudly as the pair came out of the gates and turned towards the open country.

'I'm glad we decided to take a walk, Isobel. You are right, the house feels more steeped in melancholia than ever. I hope this sun might chase that gloom away.'

'Yes, ma'am.'

Nancy turned to the girl. 'I feel more than a little countable for that suffocating atmosphere. There is something about Blackthistle that disturbs me.'

The girl looked nervous.

They walked along a path between two fields. The unseasonable heat had already leached the colour from the grass. 'I have an inquisitive nature, Isobel. The thinnest thread of something that interests me will mock me until I pull at it.'

She put out her hand, and the girl smiled nervously and then helped her over a stile. They were in a meadow edged with thorn bushes. The two walked on, Isobel leading the way, Nancy bustling behind her, sweat beading on her brow. They made it up to the flat rock, that rock on which she had sat with Caleb in the driving rain. The girl waited patiently until Nancy had regained a little composure, then they stood together, in companionable silence, looking across the shimmering valley to where the Ness glittered in the sun.

'Isobel, tell me. What more do you know of those women in town?'

The girl looked at her with fear in her eyes.

'I told you. They're not to be trusted.' She glanced around nervously and lowered her voice. 'They'll empty your belly of a baby if you ask. They will. Mhairi Mackintosh told me they gave her tea and she went flat the next morning. They did that. And I heard they get buck naked in the moonlight!' She splayed her fingers and spoke so quietly Nancy strained to hear her. 'Some say they have a taste for the blood of bairns.'

Nancy shook her head. 'And has anyone seen them drinking this blood? Or witnessed them making magic?'

The girl's eyes were saucer-wide with fear. 'I ain't. But others have.' She looked around again and whispered, 'I can speak no more of them. Mr Malles—'

'Mr Malles?' Nancy tilted her head and looked at the girl.

'He says that we are not to speak of them in the house.' She was trembling.

'Do not worry. I will not breathe a word to him or Mrs McLoone. Why will he not tolerate talk of the women?'

A look of relief, yet the girl still kept her voice low. 'It's Mrs Malles, ma'am. He is sure that they had their fingers in her goin'. But I was still a wean when she went. I can hardly remember anything.'

Mrs Malles. Dread crept up her back and her voice lowered. 'He thinks they had something to do with her disappearance?'

'That he does. I remember that she got awful skinny, that she would pace up and down, up and down. At night, she'd walk the corridors. Mr Malles was out there too, fair spare with worry, poor man. Ma said they put a hex on her.'

The girl gulped. 'I'm so sorry, ma'am. I should have said something about them women and Mrs Malles before. I just... I was told when I came up to work at the house never to mention them. Mr Malles was—'

'There's no need to apologise, Isobel. You are a loyal girl.' She stared into the yellowy haze where the sea met the sky. Here, perhaps, was the mystery, the cloud that hung above Blackthistle. Caleb blamed the women for whatever had happened to his wife. That last night he had been seeking answers. Apologies. Revenge even. Goodness only knows what he imagined the three had to do with her vanishing. She felt, however, somehow obliged to tug at that loose thread, to find the reasons behind Caleb's wild accusations.

The pair walked back through the fields, sun-hardened after their winter bogginess. Isobel walked a little more straight-backed than was her habit. She was now almost as tall as her mistress.

Nancy was silent. As they passed the little hillock, now greened by the spring, she thought of the crows, attacking and pulling at her, then remembered the chill she had felt on seeing the portrait on the back of the cottage and her rising unease at the witches' wild claims to powers beyond this realm. She glanced at Isobel. The girl seemed determined in her fearfulness of the women. Only days before she had shaken her head at the girl's skittish ways, yet now... She sighed. Now she was not sure what she believed. Her philosophy itself was being tested. Her faith in science, in numbers, was in the dock. And that uncertainty, more than the women's stories, more than Caleb's desperation, more than the mysteries that tangled around Blackthistle, terrified her.

If she were to retain her sanity and her sense of righteousness, while, perhaps, extending a helping hand to that poor, troubled man who so believed in her, she must make sense of everything. It was becoming obvious. She must go back that afternoon to see the women.

Chapter Eighteen

Inverness was alive with people. Outside the Stag tavern, barrels were being rolled off a cart. The smell of stale beer wafted from the open cellar doors.

Head down, Nancy hurried past the clanging, cursing delivery men, then criss-crossed roads, through the market square, out to the fringes of the town. In a few short minutes she was standing at the gate of the women's cottage. A cloud of scent hung in the air, sweet and resinous, that seemed to emanate from the tree in the corner of the garden, in its spring plumage of small greenish flowers.

The gate creaked as it swung open and before she reached the end of the dark path, the door was unlatched.

Daughter peered out, milk-skinned, a smut on her nose, dressed in her ash-grey apron. A crooked smile spread across her broad face. 'We thought it'd be you. Back already.' She looked at the cat, skulking in the bushes. 'Come on, Greymalkin!'

Today the cottage felt almost homely. The dried plants hung more plentifully from the ceiling beams, and there was a nutty smell in the air. The table had been moved to one side, and the three women were sat on stools around the hearth. A pot sat on a trivet, lid clanking gently, while Greymalkin slunk around the legs of the stools. Nancy screwed up her eyes.

'I'll not be here for long,' she said curtly. 'Just to parley.' Her glare was lost on the women, who smiled in return. Mother had the toad on her lap, stroking his head, while Granny leaned two-handed on her stick. There was a stool pulled out beside them, as if they had been expecting her.

'Dandelion tea?' asked Mother.

'This might seem a little... *far-fetched.*' Nancy's forehead creased. 'My friend has been coming to see you, and I fear he has formed some fanciful notions.' She paused.

Mother raised an eyebrow. 'Your friend? The Scholar? Oh yes. We felt you here last night. My bones sensed you peepin' over the wall. Whatever he thinks, we cannot alter his perception.'

There was no possibility the women could have known she had been crouched there. Her face remained rigidly composed, but her imagination was raising its hackles, growling.

Mother tilted her head to one side. Her eyes seemed to pierce into Nancy, as if she knew the tumult in her mind. 'He's been poking the fire these last few months, a year mebbe, asking questions he shouldn't, peerin' at us, shoving his bony nose in where it ain't wanted. But the other night, he went further than ever before. Accusin' us of all sorts. Spittin' like a snake. We never knew he was goin' to be such trouble. He used to have such a happiness about him. Him and her.'

She gave a mirthless laugh. 'Everyone in the town knew him. Everyone! How he'd returned from studying in the big city.'

Nancy thought of Caleb, his eyes clouded with trouble. She leaned forward, speaking urgently. 'Tell me then, without riddles or stories – what happened to his wife? I was led to believe he'd married and was blissfully happy.'

Mother smiled sadly. 'He was.'

Daughter shook her head. 'They were like swifts flitting through the sky. Very diff'rent to how he is now. Lost.'

Nancy spoke carefully. 'But why, why did he lose himself? Was it because of his wife?'

There was a sputter of sparks from the fire. 'You really don't know much of Mrs Malles?' said Mother sharply. 'That's very interestin'.'

'We knew he'd hid his memories of her away. Too painful. But I'd have thought you of all folk might have found out about all of it by now,' said Daughter.

All of it. The offhand phrase seared into the air.

The eyes of the women were on her, their intensity causing Nancy to shift on her seat. She rubbed her head. This lack of sleep was causing her mind to buckle.

Since she had learned that Caleb had had a wife, Nancy had tried to picture what she might have looked like. Yet it was near-impossible. Caleb was so single-minded, so pensive. Surely his wife would have been equally solemn. Yet Isobel had told her of dancing and parties. Although she had no belief in spirits, it had felt as if she were trying to grasp at a spectre.

She cleared her throat. 'What was her name?'

Daughter's eyes came alive. 'She was called Cassandra.' Cassandra. Caleb had mentioned a Cassandra, that rainy day on the rock. The girl who had not been allowed to continue her education and had married. Caleb had been describing his own wife.

Mother continued. 'When she first came up this way, kindness shone from her face like mornin' sun through the window.' She turned to the other women. 'Remember? That first day we saw her?'

Granny clapped her hands. 'It was in the time of the sixth moon. She and he sat up on top of that fast little cart, bowling through town on the way to the big house. Mrs Malles had lost her bonnet somewhere on the road, so her fair hair was blowing like marsh grass in summer. Skinny as a spindle, she was.'

'Mmmmhmmm,' said Mother. 'They were laughin' so hard together, as if they were the only ones on Earth. Oh, such love.' She looked hard at Nancy. The thought of Caleb so light and free of cares was strange. Mother continued. 'Some town folk here said it was unseemly to be that happy when his father had only just passed, but that was pious nonsense. Everyone was happy to see that mean ol' man gone off to the Land of Spirits.'

'Do you remember,' said Daughter, 'that pile of rotten furniture that came out the big house? They threw it all out, piled high those brown tapestries that smelled of his pa's camphor poultices and burned 'em up on Midsummer eve. They hung silk embroideries on the wall what looked like a peep into a dream.'

Granny clapped her hands. 'She started to come by the stall regular; one of the few bold enough to talk to us prop'ly, she was, and knew enough of herbs that she might ask us to look her out some borage in the hedgerow. We would root out what she needed. Then she'd come by here, over to see us at the cottage, sit on that stool you are on now.'

Mother whispered, 'She knew of the stars too.'

Nancy looked up sharply. 'The stars? What do you mean?'

Mother went on. 'Like you. She had all kinds of books. One told her when the moon would be full, which stars might be seen in the sky. She showed us once. Made us laugh, so it did. As if you need a book. Your eyes should be up in the skies, not down on some paper!'

'She was interested in astronomy too?'

'Of course, child,' Mother said. 'She showed us her maps of the sky.'

Nancy could scarcely believe what she was hearing. Caleb's wife had been versed in the stars. Was this why Caleb had persuaded her to join him in study at Blackthistle? It was obvious that he knew next to nothing about astronomy, yet he was consumed by the idea of it. Perhaps this explained why.

Reluctant to betray her feelings to the women, she nodded encouragingly as Granny continued.

'That girl's mind was sharp like a whet-stoned knife. Always learnin', always searchin'. So when she asked us to teach her to scry, we knew she'd be a quick learner. Daughter taught her how to peep, did you not, my sweet herb?'

'Aye, she was quick as a hare. Took to scrying straight up. Got the knack almost straight away. She could peep in a puddle and still see what was comin' clear as day. She used it good too.'

Granny stroked her chin. 'She'd send baskets of flour and rabbits just as families were on the edge of starving. Furs the day before a new bairn came into the world. She knew when a boat would be pulling into harbour, and make sure she was down on the docks, to meet the captain and be sure he had his men spend their money in the tavern that needed it the most. She could feel right and did right.'

Mother held up her hand. 'She would have made an admirable conjurer for sure. But then she didn't need to ever turn her hand to that, did she? Didn't ever need to make somethin' from nothin'. Never went without, never had to sweat for a livin'.'

Nancy felt a pinch of pity for Caleb. Life with Cassandra sounded so sweet. 'How long ago did she disappear?'

'Must have been... eight summers ago? Maybe nine?'

Nancy reeled away from the revelations. It was confusing that someone so extraordinary should have left no trace at Blackthistle, that her doting husband had not a portrait on the wall, that the walls of the house were bare-stoned.

'But she were a good lady,' said Daughter. 'Her and him both. That old, cold house came alive, didn't it? Must have been three, four happy years they had. Five Christmases of parties in the hall.' Her face softened, and she grasped Nancy's pale fingers in her coarse tanned hand. 'And of course, that dear little boy.'

Boy. Nancy's head jerked alert. 'There was a boy?' Her voice trailed away. Of course. The little red ball Caleb had taken so shortly from her. Here was the 'all of it'.

Daughter's fingers stroked Nancy's, yet she did not pull away from the overfamiliar gesture.

Granny spoke softly: 'There was a child.' Her face creased. 'Oliver.' She sighed.

Daughter let go of Nancy's hand. 'Little Oliver. His ma would bring him to the market, buy him a cake and lift him up so he might look in the barrels of eels. Came by here with him and he'd run around the garden, climb that big tree. Thought the world of him she did. And his papa did too. He was a little cherub.' Her face darkened.

'What happened to them?' Nancy put her fingers to her temples. She could not imagine the pain of losing a wife and son.

'Huh!' said Mother, 'He went with her. Y'see, after Oliver was born, Mrs Malles started to be less *alive*. Bit by bit that twinkle in her eyes started to soften, fade away. Her smile wasn't so wide. As Oliver grew bigger, she seemed to shrink away. She had *la tristesse* that sometimes comes after a child. And that sadness had her in its grip.

'The poor girl came less and less to see us, until she was never here, and even stopped her trips to town. The parties stopped, an' there were no more bonfires. No-one went in that house any more, not even most of the household. Just that McLoone woman and one maid. They said that Cassandra was terribly ill. We missed her visits, then when we did finally see her, she looked skin and bone and skittish as a pigeon.'

'She came back to see us that last time before she disappeared, though, didn't she?' Daughter said. 'Came through that door, and she looked like she'd been living on cobwebs and dust. Her eyes were queer, all black and shiny like buttons, and she stared at us as if we was about to make off with her purse, was all furtive like. She whispered as if there were spirits on her shoulder. She was talkin' nonsense about the stars, about how she might get taken up into 'em, fly up into 'em, right up there into the heavens, and find somewhere safe and happy. She had that book, flipping the pages, as if the secrets of the world were hidden in there somewhere. We tried to talk, we was that worried about her, but soon as she'd come, she left. Stole something special from us too.' She pursed her lips and looked at Mother and Granny.

'Yes,' said Granny, 'the sun had gone, she was turning to ice. She spoke only to ask if we had any of what she needed. And when we refused, she waited until our backs were turned and took it anyway.' She sighed.

'What did she take?'

Granny snarled, 'That what wasn't hers to have,' in so ferocious a tone that Nancy shrank back.

'We tried to speak to her, to give her hope, but, no.' Mother shrugged. 'Nothing. And then we didn't see her again, or little Oliver. No-one did. The Scholar was on his own in that big house, and there were no questions allowed to be asked. No mention of her, of him.'

Daughter whispered. 'Maybe she did get taken up into the stars. No-one knows. Even we. S'just black when I try to peep.'

Although she was seated, Nancy put a hand out to the table to steady herself. The room spiralled. Not only had Caleb lost his beloved sweetheart and child, but they had disappeared in the most horrible of circumstances. Circumstances that were wreathed in cloud. She stood up, dazed, her breaths heavy.

She whispered. 'And Caleb? He's been trying to find out what happened to—?' She had difficulty forming the names. 'Cassandra and Oliver?'

The pieces of the puzzle were falling into place. 'He thought that you had something to do with their disappearance?'

Daughter's eyes were unblinking. 'That he did,' she spoke gently. 'Chary, he was. Knew she'd been round here, knew that we was cunning folk. He never liked her talking to us – she told us as much herself. Took his time reckoning though. He didn't come round to see us just then, not for a while. He took his time, so he did.

'You remember, Granny? Two summers, maybe three, after Oliver and Cassandra disappeared? There was that day when we spotted him walking out over the fields. Followed him, we did.'

Granny nodded. 'Oh, we did. Followed him along that muddy road, through the trees, watched him all the way to the village, to Forres.' She looked at Nancy. 'That's where we had met the Thane, Macbeth, all those hundreds of years ago, see? The Scholar had worked it all out. Where everything had happened all them years before.

'Such a mind, that one. He went back again and again, walking for miles, reading from his book. We'd hear him, always with the voices, the speeches, puzzling where every last thing took place. Very clever boy he was. Very clever. Still, even he took his time making sense of it all.' She rubbed her chin, wisped in hair.

Mother held the toad up in front of her face and stroked his head. 'He kindled those embers though. Blew gentle on 'em. Learned more. Two summers became four, then the flames caught. Five summers down, he'd come and look hard at us in the market. He'd stand there, staring, yet never talking. But he thought he knew something. His eyes burned brighter and harder and those flames started to burn thicker, faster. Then, as he convinced himself that us teaching her how to scry was to blame for her leavin' the world, he started to lose himself in that fire.'

Granny wheezed. 'He stepped right into it. No care for its heat. He knew, child. He *thought* he knew something. He'd look at us as he passed us in the street, look right into us. Deep. That stare.'

Daughter's eyes grew wide. 'Then last winter there were notes pushed under our door. Mother read 'em.'

'I did. He started most mannerly, asking to make an appointment. As if we were society ladies!' The women smiled. 'But we didn't want him in here, with his bony nose stickin' in our business. So we stayed silent.' She put her finger to her lips. 'Ignored him.'

Daughter sighed. 'Didn't stop, though, eh? The notes, they carried on. He be such a clever one, but it even took him a while to work out. To be sure of what he knew. But he got there. And now he is certain, there's no locking that box back up.'

Granny shook her head. 'Your ears heard him!' Her voice became deliberate, losing its crackle and taking on a more sonorous tone. 'He knows who we are.' The three women grinned, showing teeth streaked with brown stains.

'But we can't help him, see? He's in so much pain. Deaf to any reason. Thinks that somewhere inside us, he might find his son, his wife. Like we had eated 'em up. That us teaching her scrying was to blame for her leavin'.'

'But where did she go? She can't just have disappeared?'

Daughter shrugged. 'We can't be sure, my dear. No-one can. We tried peepin', scryin', but can see nothin'. But there's no havin' her back. Of that we are sure. We've told him, yet he's asked us over and over how to get her home till we closed our ears. Didn't listen no more.'

Nancy pinched her nose. The fire's heat was stifling, and this was all too much. The more the women spoke, the more their words rang true. The story about Caleb's wife and child made sense of some of the mysteries of Blackthistle. Surely there was not a chance on earth that these women's claims to magical powers held any water? Or that Caleb's suppositions had any root in reality? Yet the women's eyes shone with what appeared to be conviction. It was clear that they believed themselves to wield some kind of supernatural abilities. Suddenly, she craved the security of her books, her charts.

'I need to go back,' she said hoarsely. 'To Blackthistle.'

'Of course, child. That is as it should be. You have much to think about.' Mother stood up and took down a jar of dried flowers, spooned some into a square of paper and twisted it shut. 'You must be exhausted. Take a pinch of these in a tea when you need. It'll calm you.'

Granny stood and reached out, and her tiny, worn hands encircled Nancy's pale, unlined fingers. 'We can help, I think. Come back here in two nights. Sunday. An hour before sundown. The world is waking, and the round belly of summer grows. We're past Beltane, you know, and now the Wild Hunt is abroad. Odin is riding. We can smell Midsummer. It's a time for weaving magic, for stars, for peeping.'

She brought Nancy's hands close to her sparrow chest, her heart pulsing through the thin, mottled skin. 'I see the darkness on the horizon. I can hear the distant thunder. There is great peril for you approaching. For the Scholar too, perhaps even more. The time is coming swift on swift. It feels now as it did when Cassandra left us. That low wolf growl gets louder each day.

'We need you to fulfil our promise to Hecate. I feel in every bone that this is what we were brought back for this time around. It's important you believe us. So we must show you beyond doubt, we can prove that we are who we says we are. Show you what we showed Cassandra. So you can help him. Maybe more.' There was urgency in the woman's voice. Nancy nodded dazedly.

'Good! Now go. Rest while you can,' said the old woman. She turned and took the lid off the pot on the fire, sending steam and a smell of cloves into the dark cottage. Still numbed, Nancy turned and left. The door closed behind her with a thud.

Chapter Nineteen

The swifts had returned to Blackthistle. Seen through the breakfast room window, they arced across the sky, silhouetted against the sun. Yet even those darting angels could not ease Nancy's feeling of dread. The grey flagstones of Blackthistle House might have been cool to the touch, but the air in the house was stifling. Outside, above the lawn, a shimmer hovered. May had barely raised its dozy head, but when she had stepped outside to smell the garden this morning, the heat felt like midsummer, and hummed with faint menace and the constant hiss of names – Cassandra. Oliver. Again and again she wondered where they might have gone. The black despair that might have driven Cassandra to the brink of desperation. What the women might have told her that pushed her to that edge, and how Caleb's despair rattled at the door of their cottage.

Still she reasoned, desperately, maybe the women were merely skilled herbalists but used those skills in the most exploitative way, selling overpriced trinkets and potions. Perhaps they had been making a fine shilling, fleecing Caleb.

Yet that logic was coming undone. Those visions that had taken on three dimensions, the women's tales that came alive as vividly as any oil painting. The picture on the back of the cottage. And the names snaked back. Cassandra. Oliver. Cassandra.

She was certain that she had heard Caleb's sigh trailing through the corridor in the early hours. However, on opening her door, there was no sign. If she saw him, should she speak of Cassandra, of Oliver, of the women? An involuntary shiver ran down her spine as she remembered his raging anger that night outside the cottage. His hands might be fine and slender, but he was strong. She imagined them closing around her neck. It was so very hot. Perhaps she was starting to lose reason.

That evening, the study at least was a little cooler. She took down the model of the solar system from the shelf and slotted it together, placed it on the table, then wound it up. It purred into action, the little planets whirling round and round. Each orbited neatly on its track around the sun, little moons wheeling about like fireflies. Watching them pirouette, as ever, helped her focus her thoughts.

The tiny Earth spun blithely round the Sun. Her world had been tilted on its axis, away from the comforting predictability of arithmetic and towards the chaos of magic.

The rigidly reassuring embrace of science was being wantonly torn away by these women – these *witches*. She still blanched at the word. Cunning folk, conjurer, root-worker, wise woman slipped through her thoughts unhindered. But *witches*? *Witches* ratcheted and grated and, when she attempted to say it aloud, it caught in her throat like dried spittle. Yet witches is what they called themselves, and they claimed to hold the secrets of magic. *Magic*.

Her finger trailed down the stack of books on her desk. Copernicus buried in a pauper's grave, his model of heliocentrism seen by the Church as a vindictive affront. Galileo, the astronomer forced onto his knees by the Spanish Inquisition, and made to renounce his discoveries. More books, more names.

Perhaps it was merely the nature of what was described as 'magic', or more precisely, *who* practised it, that excluded it from study. Much of the knowledge was, after all, peculiar to women. And surely she, above all, knew of the extra obstacles that must be tackled before a female voice might be acknowledged.

The witches had told her how they would grow and prepare herbs for healing, ensure frightened mothers might birth their children and remain alive, and prepare the terrified and the sick for death. In the cities these fundamental tasks had been scrubbed of their earthiness and mystery and assigned to male doctors and funeral assistants, but in the wilds they were still the domain of crones and harridans. Yet Nancy was sure that the women had as fine a command of cures as the physicians of London – Isobel seemed convinced that half of Inverness went to them for remedies – and almost certainly a gentler bedside manner. They certainly knew something of the machinations of the solar system too, perhaps much more than she had ascertained.

Hidden from the pompous spotlight of academia, this vast knowledge that belonged to women across the country, across the world, was banished to the shadows with the bats, rats and cats, and dismissed and stigmatised as 'magic'. If this was magic, then surely every astronomer, every philosopher, every chemist was a warlock. Surely she too, was a witch.

'Witch.' She spoke the word aloud, surprised that it came a little more smoothly to her lips.

The model of the planets slowed to a stop. Nancy put a finger on the little ivory Venus. It was ice-cool to the touch.

Her eyes were starting to droop, so she rolled up her charts. Outside, a warm zephyr wheezed through the trees. It sounded like the oldest woman's keening laugh. She sighed, stood and rubbed away the condensation on the window. Peering out of the rattling casement she looked for the stars, her constants, but a thick fog shrouded the Earth. Head down, she took the candle and went to her room.

Tomorrow, she had promised to stargaze with the women. She knew that she must find out more, reason with the women – the witches – to attempt to untangle science, fate and magic. She thought once more of Daughter's hands, shining darkly with blood, then tilted back her head and closed her eyes.

Chapter Twenty

The late Sunday morning heat was heavy as velvet. Nancy woke groggily. In a few short hours she was due to keep her appointment at the cottage in Inverness.

She rubbed at her eyes, willing her mind to sharpen. The women had promised stargazing and peeping and had spoken of a Wild Hunt. The machinations of scrying were fascinating, and its revelations compelling. But most of all Nancy thrilled at the prospect of watching the heavens alongside the three sisters – it felt strangely electrifying.

She rose from her bed and pulled back the curtain, letting sunlight flood the room. Opening the window did not bring any cooling draught, but it felt a useful thing to do. On the sill was her little red leather-bound copy of *Macbeth*. She picked it up, sat in the high-backed chair next to the window and started to flick through the pages.

'Double, double toil and trouble;
Fire burn, and cauldron bubble.'

It was a struggle to picture the crones in a dripping, airless cavern, hissing these words at Macbeth, presenting their seductively lethal predictions like a silver plate of poisoned marchpane. Their lines were sparse, harsh, almost comically hysteric. She pored over each spiky utterance, searching for clues, the nuance that might lend some credence to the trio's claims. Yet she found little to support their fantastical story.

A quiet knock at the door. Isobel entered, carrying a jug of water and bowl, and put the wash set on the dressing table.

'Thank you for your help. I think the blue dress today.' The girl helped her pull on the light cotton frock, sprigged with tiny stars.

'I'll take an early luncheon in here.' Nancy splashed cold water on her face and down the back of her neck. Peering into her looking glass her eyes looked tired, the pupils wide.

She sat on the chair by the window and tried to read a little, but took in nothing. Isobel brought luncheon, or 'nacket' as she called it – some ham, and a thick slice of bread. Nancy's stomach grumbled. She had not realised how hungry she was. She told the girl that she had an appointment later that day, and that she might not be expected to return early that night. Isobel looked at her suspiciously.

'Please be sure to tell Mrs McLoone that she shouldn't wait up for me, as I may be home late. I have my key. I am meeting friends, and they will drive me home if needed.'

Isobel eyed her suspiciously. 'Friends? Where you goin', ma'am?'

'To Inverness,' Nancy replied lightly.

The girl did not say a word, but shook her head as she left the room.

The stiflingly hot afternoon passed slowly. Nancy leaned on the window, watching a hawk circle over the back of the house, holding her breath as it dived into the field, sending up a plume of dust. Perhaps it held a baby rabbit, a shrew in its talons. Some tiny morsel of fluff and flesh, ripped apart in an instant.

She packed a small carpet bag with a black velvet cloak lined with emerald satin, her leather rum bottle and a comb, then walked down the corridor to her study.

The door was slightly ajar, and the room smelled faintly of sun-warmed spices. On the shelf, the tiny planets of her orrery were moving slowly, the whirr and tick of the movement shone through glittering motes of dust.

Someone had recently been here. Caleb. She hurried to her desk. Two books lay askew and her papers were not stacked in quite as orderly a fashion as she had left them. She could imagine Caleb's long fingers tracing over her notes, his eyes frantically scanning her neat writing. Nothing seemed to have been taken, but she felt a prickle of fear. What had he been looking for? What did he want from her? She breathed a sigh of relief that her treatise was locked safely in the trunk that sat in the corner of the room.

The clock struck four. She groaned. There was no time to tarry, so she did not have the luxury of dwelling on what might have happened here. It was important she was prepared for tonight; telescope, pens, ink and paper and almanac all fitted neatly into the carpet bag. Nancy took a deep breath. Outside, the trees shimmered and bent in the heat haze.

*

Even though it was late afternoon, pale Inverness blistered in the intense sun. Two weeks had passed, but the bridge's parapets were still studded with May Day's large, ribbon-tied bunches of branches. Their leaves were brown, the colours sun-leached. Nancy put down her bag and paused, looking across the river, wondering for what Caleb might have been searching. Even if she had caught him rifling through her things, she was not sure what she might have said. On her return from town she must steel herself and talk plainly and seriously with him.

The heat was oppressive, and she'd never seen the streets of the town so quiet. A stray murmur floated out of an open window, the odd bang of pots and pans. A shout echoed from around a corner, but as she turned into that street, there was nothing but dust on the pavement.

The market square lay empty, silent bar the echo of Nancy's metal-soled boots on the cobbles. A shadow, smaller than a child, darted between buildings, but Nancy turned too late to identify its owner.

She was thankful to find herself standing outside the cottage, its uneven stones and turf roof bathed in sunlight and the sound of humming and singing coming from within. The door opened before she could knock. Mother, sleeves rolled up, spoon in hand, was wearing more gaudy clothes than usual: a purple dress embroidered in gold, a red velvet scarf tied high around her knotted hair.

She laughed throatily. 'At last! Where y'at, *ma chérie?*' She clapped Nancy hard on the back as she entered the cottage.

The low-beamed room rustled with activity. Greymalkin was on the table, slinking against a handful of stringy mushrooms, some yellow, bell-shaped flowers and thick, white roots. Next to the mound of ingredients stood an opened bottle of whisky. Daughter hummed tunelessly as she chopped a pile of fresh herbs, while Granny stood over the bubbling pot, sprinkling the fungi into the gelatinous mixture and muttering. Her tattered dress was sleeveless, her spindly arms nut-brown and etched with deep wrinkles. She looked up at Nancy.

'Child! It is good to see you.' She walked over to Nancy and pinched her cheek. 'The stars are waiting for us.'

'I am very much looking forward to our stargazing,' said Nancy, patting her bag. 'I have my books and equipment.'

'And what of the Scholar?'

'I think that Caleb – Mr Malles – has been looking through my work. My room has been disturbed. I don't know what he might be looking for, but his interest seems tied in some way to the stars.'

'Huh. I wonder,' said Mother. 'It's not good, mark my words. The dark clouds are gathering apace. I feel something dreadful is almost upon us. Tonight, however, things might become more clear. We must know what he's searching for. Discover why you're here, and why we've been called once more – what we must do this time around. We will run wild with the wolves, make powerful magic if we need to. We must fulfil Hecate's wishes, as we have done before – as we will do long after.'

Mother opened a little bag and turned its contents out into her palm – a pinch of black seeds. The others smiled as she threw them into the pot. Daughter levered the pot from the fire with a stick and placed it on a stool between the women.

'Black spirits and white, red spirits and grey,
Mingle, mingle, mingle, you that mingle may.
Titty, Tiffin, keep it stiff in.
Firedrake, Puckey, make it lucky.
Liard, Robin, you must bob in.
Round, around, around, about, about,
All ill come running in, all good keep out.'

Their tuneless voices clashed like rough rocks. A wind came through the window, flicking the curtain wide open, and whirling around the three women's bobbing heads. It ruffled their hair, and they threw back their heads and shrieked with laughter. Nancy found herself giggling manically too. A sudden calm descended, and the shrieks subsided into gentle chuckling, the women standing close, arms wrapped around each other, heads bowed towards the centre of the circle. They were murmuring, stroking each other's hair for almost a minute before breaking the ring. Nancy held her breath, not wanting to break the moment. Then they pulled apart.

Daughter took the pot, spooned the mixture into a glass jar and screwed in a silver stopper.

'We are done. It is ready.' She gripped Nancy's hand. 'Sister, this is strong, strong magic. Not for everyone. Only us that know it can use it. S'important. It can break a weak mind, take you somewhere there's no coming back from. Only them's that ready can use it. Be warned.'

'She is right, Child of the Moon,' said Granny. 'Our salve is sacred and not for all. It can be dangerous.' She picked up her staff and a lamp. 'Come! It is time to leave.'

Mother clipped her belt around her waist, picked up the bottle and slipped it into one of her deep pockets. She secreted her toad somewhere in the folds of her cloak. 'I'm ready. Daughter? Come on, *chérie.*'

Daughter took down her copper bowl from the wall. 'I is ready.' She took Nancy's hand and pulled her to the door. 'Steel your soles. We have a walk in front of us.'

Chapter Twenty-One

It was the kind of evening that should have seen old men sitting on stools outside their front doors, spitting in the dust and arguing good-naturedly, children throwing pots of water at each other, and neighbours shouting greetings. Instead the town remained still and empty, as if holding its breath.

The hard road turned to soft track. They were in the country, walking away from the low sun, the green hills blushing pinkish-purple and the fading, golden light gilding the trees.

They made a curious procession: Granny, hobbling in surprisingly sprightly fashion, occasionally grubbing in the dirt with her stick; Mother swaying gently from side to side, the bags hanging from her belt chinking; and Daughter, singing softly, a tune last heard by Nancy as she rocked on her wooden horse in her nursery. Greymalkin the cat skulked behind them.

Nancy sidled next to Daughter. 'Does Granny have a place in mind to stargaze? I've found some truly exceptional spots.'

'Of course. She knows where she goes! We go where we are drawn, where we always go.'

Half-hidden in the bushes, a signpost read 'Culloden'. The place that but a couple of decades ago swallowed a generation of boys, lost in the mud and the blood. Isobel had told her that swords and bones still surfaced every winter in that sodden field. Even now she fancied the cloying scent of decaying flesh rose from the weeds.

Her pace quickened. Now she was alongside Mother and Granny. Daughter caught up as soon as her breath would allow. The trees grew a little thicker, their leaves forming a canopy above the narrow path, creating a hollow way. An owl flapped slowly overhead, white and ghostly, shrieking as it flew into the dying sun.

In the centre of the spinney was a clearing. Somewhere nearby, a burn burbled. Nancy could make out what looked like a perfectly circular arrangement of stones. As they drew closer, she could see that the stones were placed in some kind of order – large ones forming a circle, smaller rocks filling in the wheel. A waist-deep channel led through the rocks to a round chamber in the centre, open to the elements. The sun was melting like a glob of wax into the horizon and the air felt charged, febrile.

'What is this place?' she whispered to Daughter.

'We call it the Ring,' she said, 'been here years, thousands prob'ly, maybe more. We got places like 'em where I come from too, though not as big as this. Mother had something akin to it near where she was born she reckons. Granny says she remembers her folk building them in her north countries as well.'

'That I do,' said Granny. 'Special places these are. Always have been. Come up here at midsummer and the sun shines straight down here.' She pointed with her stick. 'And into here.' Her stick indicated the channel. 'Onto the back wall, lighting it bright. Same at midwinter.'

Nancy wrinkled her brow. She knew that ancient people had possessed a rudimentary knowledge of the movements of the sun, but to see it realised in physical stone form was impressive and a little humbling.

The oldest woman turned to Nancy. 'Your books and writings reveal nothing new, my dear. This moon, these stars have been above us since the Earth was hot.'

Nancy gripped the telescope in her pocket.

Granny chuckled. 'Show me your talisman.' Nancy fur-rowed her brow. How did the woman know what she held? But something about Granny's manner reassured her.

'Here.' She placed the instrument into the woman's liver-spotted hands. The woman turned it over a few times, then held it to her eye. Stars had started to pop into the rapidly darkening sky.

'I like this toy. I like this *telling*-scope.' She turned and scanned the sky then squealed hoarsely. 'The moon, I can see every part of him shine. Look at him.'

The old woman held her position for a full minute, the only sounds the whispering firs and the wheezing of her chest. Slowly, she exhaled with a sigh, and brought the telescope down from her rheumy eye. Nancy saw her cheeks glisten-ing with tears. The old woman sighed, 'Máni – my god of the moon. Never have I seen him so beautiful. You are very lucky to have this magic, my child. Take care of it,' said the old woman gently, handing back the instrument.

The air shifted with the gentle swell of a breeze. The women shot each other expectant looks. Something was afoot.

Mother took the glass jar from her pocket and held it above her head. From somewhere deep inside her rose a low hum. Granny and Daughter joined her, both holding the same rumbling note. Granny stamped her staff on the floor rhyth-mically.

Mother intoned, 'See us from the furrows rise, from root to branch in darkened skies.'

The others held the hum.

Daughter came forward, holding her bowl high. 'I take your threads, to spin and weave, warp and weft your destiny. Bring me bones that I might cast fresh entrails plucked from first-born calf.'

Granny spoke with a voice as brittle as winter ice: 'In these fields of mud and gore, we were three and now are four, standing small in giants' stones, foxes' fires to warm our bones.'

None of the women were now humming, but the deep rumbling grew louder. Mother uncorked the jar. 'Henbane plucked from blood-soaked moor, mandrake powder, hellebore; Boil'd up with sap of yew, fill'd high with ergot roux.'

The strange noise stopped.

She dipped her fingers into the clotted mixture, her eyes never leaving Nancy's, spread the paste onto her face and neck, then passed it to Granny. Granny and Daughter did the same, licking their gummy fingers. Daughter held out the jar to Nancy.

'The salve. Now, it is time to fly.'

Nancy screwed up her eyes. 'Fly? Surely we are here to stargaze.' She pointed up at the dark sky.

Daughter giggled. 'S'right. We'll be gazing. More too. We'll be with them. In them. Y'll see. You need to see. To believe. S'why we're come.'

It was impossible, of course. Yet Nancy felt compelled to do as the women were doing. There was something between them, a bond, a kinship she'd never before experienced. And an impossible-to-resist, dangling promise of being with the stars – *in* the stars.

The glittering eyes of the women were upon her, steady, encouraging. She had swigged from mugs of negus to warm her through cold nights and sipped raspberry brandy from delicate glass flutes at tiresome parties, but she suspected this concoction might bring more than merely a sore head in the morning. Reckless behaviour made her feel uncomfortable, and this felt foolhardy beyond all comprehension, but she suspected that, if she wanted to learn what might be happening, she ought to follow the women's example. Swallowing, she gripped the jar hard, plunged her fingers into the waxy substance and rubbed it onto her temples and down the outside of her throat. The rest of the salve she tucked safely into her pocket.

The tar-like slime burned a little. It smelled of sweet resin and green spring leaves, with a trace of something rotten and earthy. A warmth surged across her skin, a tingle through her veins, and she giggled.

They sat on the circular arrangement of rocks.

What are we doing here? Nancy thought. She heard the words echo into the still night air, although she was sure she had not spoken them.

'This place is bone-and-dust old,' said Granny. 'Can you not feel? The spirits are rising from the moors, they are gathering from the harrows, from the barrows, from the yew and the dew.'

As she spoke, Nancy heard a chorus of sighs – the trees perhaps, rustling and creaking in unison. She fingered the telescope in her pocket.

'When we will be starting our stargazing? I have my notebook.'

Mother laughed. 'Soon enough.'

The sound from the woods seemed to grow more insistent. Nancy fancied she could hear leaves growing, blossom popping open, the hum of sap rising. Then a melody, thin and reedy, drifted across the fields. Nancy recognised it as the tune the women had been singing earlier in the evening. This time, she joined in their performance. Her confidence swelled.

They sang louder, repeating the refrain:

'Round, around, around, about, about,

All ill come running in, all good keep out.'

They were intoning harmonies now, counter-melodies snaking between each other, over and under. Granny beat her stick on the floor, the earth seeming to shake with every strike. Boom, boom, boom. Never a strong singer, tonight Nancy knew the melody she needed to sing, found every note confident and true.

The women stood, and joined hands to form a circle, leaving a space for her. Nancy stepped between Daughter and Mother. Her hands slipped into theirs with a crackle like summer lightning. This was odd, most odd, but the smiles on the faces of the others reassured her. The women held her gaze, wide-eyed and expectant.

As one, they threw back their heads. The sky was now alive with stars. How dazzling they looked tonight, like the sparks that flew from a blacksmith's anvil, frozen in time. The women's pupils were wide and black, smiles stretched across their faces.

These women were so free. Their feet threw up clouds of dust as they danced, tattered cloaks splayed out behind them like bat wings, screaming into the still night air. Nancy might turn on her heel and flee into the night, or dance in this circle forever.

Mother and Granny dropped hands, and Mother led the snake of women around the stones, weaving between each rock, touching each lightly as she went past. Nancy was sure she saw flames remaining after each stroke of the stone. Granny was at the back of the line, stamping her stick and shouting,

'On, on! Faster, faster!'

The song continued, although they had all stopped singing. Nancy could hear Daughter's laugh in the line behind her. She could feel every sound in the forest, each footstep ringing like bells. They moved more swiftly. As their steps grew quicker, the stones started to glow green. Nancy looked down at her own feet and noticed that they were now hovering a few inches above the grass. How queer! Yet it felt as if the earth were still hard beneath her feet. Soon their toes were level with the tops of the stones, and then they were at the highest branches of the trees. Mother squeezed her hand.

Higher they rose, strung out like a washing line. In the distance, under a pall of smoke, was Inverness. There was the sea, glittering and infinite. Below, the fields. It was colder up here. Nancy's skin goose-pimpled. *She should have been scared,* she thought to herself, *but who could be scared when the heavens were set to envelop them?* They swept across the fields, brushing the tree tops, circling around a croft, then low over a field of sheep, sending them scattering; then up, up again over Inverness.

The town looked so tiny from above, its streets laid out like a child's toy set, the huge church by the glittering river small enough to fit in her hand. They swooped over the roof-tops, through the plumes of smoke coming from the chimney stacks.

Around and over Inverness a few times, then Mother turned, nodded and pulled them in a different direction, out to sea, then suddenly up vertically. Nancy could see the dark outlines of the distant mountains against the serpentine skies. They moved faster now, so high that the curve of the Earth was visible, so beautiful Nancy thought she might burst.

Higher still, into the blackness, moving so fast the wind burned her cheeks and she gripped Mother and Daughter's hands more tightly. Now they were beyond, almost into the cosmos. Beyond the grip of Earth. The wind should have been roaring in her ears, but instead it was quiet. She could hear Daughter breathless behind her, Mother chuckling in front, Granny behind, shouting, 'Onwards!'

Since Nancy was tiny, she had dreamed of what it might be like to soar among the stars, and now here she was. In that pitch-velvet stillness. In that other-worldly light and silence, soaring among those points of brilliance, racing towards the moon, up and over. For one moment she felt a pang of long-ing for her parents to be here, with her, but in an instant the thought was gone, extinguished by another explosion of wonder.

The women made a slow, arcing turn; up, round, into the upper arches of the skies. It seemed they had peaked, passed their destination. They hurtled, back through the night, steer-ing closer to Earth, closer, closer, and then she was not in the heavens, but coming up through the damp, sodden mud, up through the sod, until they were lying on the wet grass on their backs, looking up at the stars, cloaks damp from dew or sweat – Nancy couldn't tell.

Daughter lay beside her, still holding her hand tightly, mouth open, rapt. Beyond her was the outline of Granny, stick aloft, as if conducting an invisible orchestra. She turned her head. There was Mother, laughing quietly to herself. Nancy blinked. Mother turned her head,

'Where y'at, child?'

'I don't... I don't know. Up there. I saw—' She took her hand from Mother's and jabbed at the sky.

'*Incroyable*, huh?' said Mother, 'Take your time, *chérie*, no hurry.'

The four women lay staring at the stars, breathing heavily. Nancy wiped the sweat from her brow. The trees were still moving in a most disconcerting manner, their leaves forming pictures and their branches bending in an unnatural fashion.

'What happened?'

Daughter squeezed her hand. 'Thank you,' she whispered, a little dazed-looking. 'We've never been so far, never known enough, but you... your clever mind...' She shook her head and whistled. 'Such a voyage.'

Nancy felt in no way responsible for the journey they'd just taken but hadn't the strength to argue. Just now, she needed to rest a little. It wasn't clear whether they'd left the ground, or if they'd been lying here the whole time. Her cloak felt wet through, as if she'd been in this place for hours, yet the other women had experienced the same visions as her – impossible. She rubbed her head. It felt a long time since her life had been in any way rational, she realised, and she missed normality. The supernatural was exhausting.

However, her mind was steering back slowly to somewhere approaching its usual state.

The trees resembled trees, the women's features had settled into their conventional alignments. The sky was losing its pitch, glowing jade orange over the mountains. They must have been here all night.

One by one, the women struggled into sitting positions, Daughter giving Granny a helping hand. Their faces were wreathed in tired smiles.

Granny sighed, 'We had quite the wander. Nancy, thank you for your navigation. Ah, your eyes. She – Cassandra – her face was as full of wonder as yours.'

Cassandra had been on the same voyage. A little more light shone on the mystery. Cassandra. Caleb! Her study. 'I need to get back to Blackthistle.' She rose slowly from the cairn. The trio's faces swam in front of her, as if part of her mind still lay in the skies. Dazed, she left the women without bidding them farewell. She heard them singing gently as she walked away.

Ordinarily, she would have been thrilled that she had stayed awake long enough to greet the rising sun. However, today her mind felt as if it had been run through a mangle, squeezed dry and her body wrung into exhaustion. Yet her feet kept plodding, one in front of the other, because at that moment walking seemed like the only constructive thing she might do.

She shaded her eyes with her hand, staring into the depths of the yellow, pale blue sky. The sun could not be far below the horizon. Her face felt hot. She needed to focus on getting back to Inverness, to Blackthistle, to find out what Caleb had been searching for. And what he might do next.

Chapter Twenty-Two

Later, she could barely recall that walk back to the big house. Her vision had not yet stabilised, and she ached with fatigue, half her mind still flying somewhere beyond Orion's belt. By the time she reached Blackthistle, the sun was beating down on her head, her grimy skirts brushing along the gravel drive. She had no wish to be seen in this state, so slipped around the back of the house and down the steps to the basement, where she suspected a kitchen door would be open. Perhaps she might reach her rooms unobserved.

She took off her shoes and tiptoed across the flagstones of the empty kitchens, the stones cooling her feet. Up the winding stair to the entrance hall.

Already, the angry-looking sun was rising on the dial of the long-cased clock. She glanced up at the large window just beyond the turn of the steps. Silhouetted against it was Caleb.

'Good morning, Miss Lockaby.' There was a quiver in his voice. His boots echoed on each step as he walked towards her and stood uncomfortably close. A grey crease ran beneath each of his eyes and his breath smelled like the sharp tang that drifted from the doors of morning taverns.

He glanced at her muddy skirts and stockinged feet. 'An early-morning walk? Stargazing perhaps?'

'Yes, it was such a clear night. Warm too. I got a little carried away.' Her laugh sounded forced. She took her telescope from her pocket and gave what she hoped looked like an apologetic smile.

Caleb moved closer, his nose wrinkling. The salve's resinous, earthy scent still snaked around her. The skin on her neck where she had rubbed it throbbed, and the jar in her pocket seemed to burn coldly against her thigh. Fear prickled in her stomach.

'We must speak. Now. The study, perhaps?'

His tone suggested she had little choice, and she was so tired, too exhausted to argue. 'Of course,' she muttered, and walked up the stair.

Sun beat through the windows of the study. It was already stiflingly warm. Caleb stared out of the window. His figure looked thinner than Nancy remembered. She thought of the day before, his fingers searching through her papers that still lay on the desk. Yet she left any accusations. Now she wanted to hear what he had to say.

He had gathered himself somewhat, and spoke more evenly. 'Since I was very young I have always been fascinated by our fortune, how our lives might be mapped out from our birth. Have you read of the Fates?'

She shook her head. 'I'm afraid my knowledge of classics is rather sparse. I know only those names taken for constellations.'

He continued to gaze at the landscape outside. 'The Fates, the Moirae... three Greek goddesses whose nimble fingers twisted and knitted the thread of each human story into knots.' He turned and traced an arc into the air.

'Klotho, Lakhesis, Atropos,' he explained, 'Weavers of destiny. They appeared at all mortals' births, to spin the thread of their life.'

Her filament had led to Scotland, where it had intertwined with other strands: Caleb, Nancy, Cassandra, the women.

'But there's more.' He tapped his finger on the table. 'I know this seems absurd, but it's not just the Fates, Nancy. These women are constants. These three, these women, are dotted through history, across time. Have you read of the Norns?'

Nancy shook her head. Caleb continued.

'They were a trio too, from the northernmost parts of Europe; women from the ancient sagas who used yarn to weave their people's futures. Those threads again. And the French have three goddesses – Matres, they are called – while if you get them drunk enough, the Irish in the town will tell you stories of a trio of warrior women that formed the Morrigan. Three, three, three. Then in *Macbeth*, the three weird sisters. Three.'

The witches. Nancy felt a dull thud of dread in her chest. She thought of what Daughter had told her, how Hecate had called on the women time and time again. How, confusingly, time seemed to stretch and bend around their stories. These trios of women... were they all Daughter, Mother, Granny?

She laughed thinly. 'Weird sisters? I'm sure I don't know anything of which you speak.'

Rubbing the locket around his neck, he moved closer still. His eyes shone. The stream of words continued, to Nancy's ears, more jumbled. 'There is more, more, Nancy. These names – the Fates, the Norns, the Matres; those trios that appear over and again, written and sung about, worshipped and dreaded – they're all wayward, they're all weird, Nancy.' His voice rose in pitch, 'All of them witches. I pray that my withered soul is delivered and that you stay safe, for I know those hags are not mortal. And for the love of God, you must never see them or speak of them again!' He spat out the words.

Nancy looked at him sharply. 'I think, Mr Malles, that I am capable of choosing my own company.'

'Those witches are dangerous,' Caleb hissed.

Nancy drew herself as high as she could in her exhausted state. 'The women have a very persuasive manner and a mastery of plants, that is all. Is there something amiss with having an understanding of a subject? My mind is equally full of such knowledge, although my realm is not the soil and the seed, but the stars and the planets, and I have the means and education to present my knowledge in an acceptable form.

'It seems to me,' she continued, now more animated, 'that if you have the barest ability to reason your theories in writing, if you cloak them as alchemy, physic or philosophy, if you have enough money to have them published, and – most importantly – you wear breeches and have a swagger in your stride, then your knowledge becomes solemn fact. Acceptable. If you wear skirts, your thoughts are dismissed as fantasy, hysteria, or even... evil magic.'

For a moment, the trace of a smile played around Caleb's lips. Then his face hardened. 'I think we both know that these women have more than a persuasive manner and a mastery of plants, Nancy.'

He was right. Of course Mother, Daughter and Granny were a little more than root-workers or wise women, healers or soothsayers. They were capable of feats that could not yet be explained by mathematicians and physics. The *yet* was important, she reasoned, for the time when it could be explained would come. Perhaps not in her lifetime, but it would come.

However, she knew that to admit that now would be foolish and perhaps dangerous. 'Mr Malles. I think you may be sickening for something.' Her voice was low and precise.

'I am perfectly well, Miss Lockaby, as well you know. I have always been perfectly well. We are both aware of the horrors of which these women are capable. A warning – if you wish to keep your position at Blackthistle, if you would like to preserve any reputation you have as a woman of natural philosophy and astronomy, then you will not see those women again. It might be grossly unfair, but my words hold more water than yours ever will, and I can – and I *will* – ruin you, Miss Lockaby.' His voice hissed.

Nancy put out a hand to steady herself. She was near-delirious through lack of sleep, but managed to muster an imperious tone. 'Again, I will see who I please, Mr Malles.'

He fixed her with a stare. 'I fear you will come to regret your choice, Miss Lockaby.' Caleb stalked out of the room, closing the door behind him. Nancy heard his heavy breaths outside for a few moments before his footsteps echoed down the stone floor of the corridor. She picked up a bottle of ink and flung it at the closed door. Its contents splattered against the stripped wood and pooled on the floor.

The little jar of salve still seared icily in her pocket. Although her hands were shaking so hard, they could barely hold a key, Nancy opened the trunk in the corner of the room, threw the salve on top of her treatise, and locked the lid. Then she tottered down the corridor, into her room and collapsed on the bed.

Chapter Twenty-Three

Sleeping in the daytime was not anathema for Nancy. Her family had often taken naps during the afternoon to make up for long nights at the Observatory. However, this tiredness was different – heavy and total. She had no dreams, just blackness, as if every vision had been wrung from her mind the night before. She slumbered through the sticky heat for a few hours. When she awoke, she felt no more refreshed than when she had crawled on top of her bed. Her head ached and, as she sat up, her stomach churned. Isobel had brought in her lunch.

Nancy whispered, 'Isobel, I feel terrible.'

The girl looked concerned.

'Oh ma'am. You do look queer. So pale.'

She held her hand to Nancy's head. It felt cool, but made Nancy wince in pain. 'You're running hot. You must get back into bed. I'll fetch Mrs McLoone.'

Although Nancy felt terrible, she knew she had little time. 'Isobel. I must get up, I simply must.'

The girl cocked her head to one side.

'Not yet, ma'am. You have to sleep.'

Nancy reached out and squeezed her hand limply.

'I can't. I must get up.'

'You'll feel better if you get a little more rest, ma'am.'

Nancy fell back on the bed and immediately slept, yet her mind would not still. She was climbing up the hill towards the Observatory with her parents, pointing out constellations as she went, their admiring laughter floating into the night. Now she was in the garden at Crooms watching the edges of the pile of treatises curl and brown and burst into flames. Then in a carriage, rolling and bumping to Scotland. Finally, among the stars, swooping and leaping with the women.

Distorted equations about the Fold looped endlessly through her mind. Snippets of *Macbeth* snaked between the numbers, fusing with the mathematics. Her mother's neatly rendered sketches of holes and gates, the universe folded in on itself, cracks in its creases. The Fold must be one of these cracks; a hole that led who knew where. The women, their faces dancing and dipping in front of her, lit and licked by flickering flames, half in darkness, could they really be witches? She moaned gently in her half-sleep, then started the slow swim to the surface where dreams end and the real world begins.

Her thoughts became a little more lucid. Caleb and his wild claims about the women. Then, ringing in her ears as she woke, his words: 'I can and I *will* ruin you.'

Though she still felt wrung-out, there was no time. Swinging herself out of bed, she felt cool cotton brush against her arms. Her nightgown. Isobel must have undressed her while she was asleep. She crossed the room and peered into the looking glass. Her lines were etched more deeply, dark shadows smudged beneath her green eyes, her skin grey and dusty. A splash of cold water went some way to jolting her out of the fug, but still her mind moved sluggishly.

Her time at Blackthistle had been a blur. Caleb, the bluff, straight-backed stranger on horseback, lip curled with a trace of contempt, had seemingly mellowed into a keen pupil, humble enough to allow a woman to teach him the mechanics of the cosmos, and with a mind rooted in letters that was equally open to the wonder of numbers.

That she might be as entranced by the magic spun from words had come as something of a surprise. Caleb had opened the door to places spun into being from naught but a pen and parchment. Where her starry universe was fixed into infinity and ready to explore, his worlds were coaxed into being from the minds of man. Somehow, those two worlds had meshed and intertwined.

Slowly, however the carapace of the respectable Shakespeare scholar had chipped away, fallen to reveal a twisted soul tortured by loss. And for him to threaten her so... She could not live under the same roof as someone who could speak to her in such cruel fashion.

She should never have come to Scotland. The invitation had come at a point when her academic life in London was slowing to a standstill. It had felt like a fresh chance, a way to gain respect in a world that was rigged against her and all women who wished to learn, discover, break new ground. Yet all she had found here was obsession, despair and madness. Whether that was Caleb's or her own, who knew. It felt as if she were teetering on the brink of losing her mind.

She must get back to Crooms. To Cora. To the Observatory. To bow her head and sharpen her pen once more and find service as one of Maskliss' computers. The transit was but twelve days away. She would view it and, she hoped, the Fold from here, although, at this moment, she found it difficult to muster enthusiasm even for that. Then she would return to Greenwich. She shook her head. Tomorrow she would write to Cora and request a carriage be sent.

She must go to her study and start to organise her things.

It was time to go home.

It was time to admit defeat.

Chapter Twenty-Four

The corridor smelled faintly of burned hair, as if something had passed through, leaving singe marks in the air. As she approached the study she noticed the door was ajar. Entering the room, she stifled a cry. The place was in disarray. Sheets of paper were scattered across the floor. Books were splayed on the table, pages ripped from them and screwed into balls. Her precious Halley's leather cover was ripped in two. The large telescope had been upended, its tripod legs helpless, like an old man who'd fallen in the street. She gently brought it upright. The lens Mr Dolland had patiently milled and ground by hand over weeks was now disfigured by a scar-like crack. Tears pricked her eyes. Surely Caleb would not have done this. He was an academic, had respect for books, for instruments, for knowledge. Above all, he knew that to her this was more than cold apparatus, this was her means to peer into the heavens. In wrecking them, he was wrecking both her memories of the past and the possibilities of the future. Yet it could only have been him.

She cast an anxious glance at the trunk in the corner. The lid was shut, but the lock hung open, broken. Fearfully, she opened it. The salve was gone. Her treatise was gone. Her notes gone. Her knees gave way and she sank to the floor.

Caleb had always wanted something more from her. His quiver as she first spoke of the Fold. His eyes that shone a little too brightly, the neat flow of questions that led her into revealing more than she might have wished. It was becoming more and more obvious that the man who had sat so eagerly learning at her side had always had but one thing he wanted from her.

To find out more about the Fold. And, for that information, he was prepared to ruin her reputation. To ruin her.

What a fool she had been.

From deep inside her, a fury began to build. How did he know about the Fold? How long had he known about it? She thought of the gift of the book, given just at the right time. The meeting on the rock, planned perhaps, where he gave her sips of rum in order to lull her into telling him about her theories. Her fists balled. She must find him. She must look in those places she had never been allowed to enter. His rooms.

She walked down the hall slowly, deliriously, ghost-like, one hand trailing on the wall for support, her footsteps near-silent. Caleb's study lay on the left. She was suddenly tremulous. Perhaps she had lost her mind.

A quick glance up and down the corridor. Empty. She put her ear to the door. Silence. For one moment she paused – breaking into a man's room was not the action of a sane woman. She suspected that her fever still lingered. However, there was little time left to debate the rationality of her course.

With some effort, she turned the handle with a solid click. It was unlocked. Slowly, slowly she opened it. A thrill ran up her spine, sharpening her senses. The room was empty. Perhaps she ought to go elsewhere to look for Caleb. But curiosity compelled her. Here she might find more.

Her feet made no noise as she tiptoed across the room. The walls were lined floor to ceiling with bookshelves and there was a worn carpet on the floor. Beams of sun stabbed through a thick, red curtain, its pile moth-nibbled. The place smelled of Caleb. It felt claustrophobic and, like the Octagon Room at the Observatory, intensely masculine. Her breaths were shallow, her movements silent, yet she could feel her pulse throb in her ears. She looked at the books on the shelves. Shake-speare, yes, but more: *Petit Albert, The Clavicule of Solomon, On Agrippa, Malleus Maleficarum.* Titles that promised sinis-ter contents. There on his desk were papers. Scribbles mostly, about *Macbeth.* An envelope addressed to her, here at Black-thistle, the writing unfamiliar. There was no return address on the back, no indication of who might have sent it. Curious, she peered inside, but it was empty.

She was distracted by a ticking sound. She tilted her head. Yes, a low whirring. The envelope must wait. The noises came from behind a red curtain. Pulling it aside, she saw a door set into the panelling. Another room. A room that held who knew what.

There was nothing for it. Slowly, she turned the handle.

Chapter Twenty-Five

Her teeth bit into her bottom lip. In contrast to the dark, oppressive study, this room was huge, light and airy and burst with colours. Red leather sofas were piled with jade velvet cushions, tapestries hung in rainbow hues, vermillion carpets soft underfoot. It felt like a cocoon spun from rainbows. The place was filled with glittering motes of dust, sparkling in the sun that flooded through an enormous, single-paned window. It was unmistakably a room furnished by a woman. Cassandra.

The ticking sound came from something on a tall, skinny-legged table. She walked closer to see an orrery spinning. Its clockwork motor was humming. Larger than hers, it was fashioned entirely from gold and silver, the planets glistering in the morning light as they rotated around their sun, their moons tiny sparkling precious jewels; diamonds, emeralds. The filigree arms were curved and intricately laced, with only a hair's breadth of clearance as they swung on their orbits around the centre. Despite her fear, she sighed at the crafts-manship. It showed no sign of slowing, so she reluctantly reached out a finger and stopped the movement. She picked it up and held it to the light. On the curve of the cylindrical base was an inscription:

I am constant as the northern star,
Of whose true-fixed and resting quality
There is no fellow in the firmament.
To C from C

To C from C. She wondered who might have been the recipient. Did Cassandra buy it for Caleb, or Caleb for Cassandra?

Nancy could have sat with the orrery for hours, watching its movements, but she knew she should move fast. Regretfully, she tore herself away.

The longest wall of the room was entirely shelved. She recognised the paraphernalia of the alchemist: bottles stained with brown residue, a little burner, glass tubes and funnels. Books and a large globe sat in one corner. The walls were covered in astronomical charts, maps, handwritten lists, tables, diagrams of lunar phases, kept in place with brass pins. Some of the handwriting was in a mysterious, florid script, a script annotated and criss-crossed in Caleb's spidery hand.

Here was pinned a physiology diagram; there a picture of a spotted toadstool or a scribbled theory of how to combine metals into gold. Between them were glittering gossamer trails, so delicate she could barely tell if they were cotton or spider web, linking country capital to half-moon, tide time to areas of the brain, newspaper clipping to a sketch of a snail-shell-like Fibonacci curve. Nancy's eyes grew wide, her fingers tracing the golden strings. It felt like she'd opened a door and stepped into a mind that never stopped, moving ever forward like the hands of the gilded clock atop the Greenwich Hospital. A mind that knew as much of geography, of alchemy as astronomy and herbalism.

In the centre of the room sat a rough desk piled high with clutter. She walked to it. A flat piece of onyx, so shiny she could see the whole room reflected in it. Bowls. A polished glass ball, gleaming in the sun, held on silver claws. These were used for scrying, that she knew. They must have been Cassandra's. The tools for peeping, taught to her by the witches. Yet they were free from dust, recently polished. Here, then, was where Caleb spent his days.

Nearby stood a series of Musschenbroek's Leyden jars; water-filled containers that could store electromagnetic charge, and an electrical machine, like those used for demonstrations on the stages of London. This must be the source of the flickering, pulsing glow she'd seen through the window. Caleb, desperately experimenting, trying all that he could to find his wife. Scrabbling with her equipment, attempting to recreate what she had done.

The stone flagstones were marked with what looked like scorch marks. She walked over to them and rubbed them with her foot, watching them come away. On the floor by the window were three scratches worn into the flagstones. Just like the scratches in the Observatory, worn over the years by the brass-capped legs of the huge telescopes.

Still moving as quietly as was possible, eyes wide, she flicked through a shelf of books. The tracts here seemed older and frailer than in the other study. There were Shakespeare volumes that looked over a century old. Others were more disconcerting. *The Discoverie of Witchcraft, The Codex Gigas, The Munich Manual.* Witchcraft. She pulled down a little book bound in tan leather and opened it. Its pages were handwritten, sprinkled with diagrams of flowers, dragons perched atop worlds and women bathing.

Her gaze flicked up to another shelf, and her eyes widened. *Roemer, Newton, Flamsteed, Galileo, Copernicus.* It could have been her own or her mother's collection. She opened a copy of Halley's *A Synopsis of the Astronomy of Comets.* It was annotated in that florid script, scattered with questions that she too had asked.

Her heart started to race and she moved quickly to the table. On it lay some papers and books. Urgently, she began to leaf through the sheets and manuscripts. Many were covered in Caleb's beetle-trail scrawl. Most of the text was indecipherable, but she could make out the odd word. She searched through them for any form of clue, but could find little that made sense.

Then, a bundle of small books. In the front of the first was an inscription in the same ornate hand. *The Diary of Cassandra Malles.*

Chapter Twenty-Six

The yellowing leaves were written entirely in the same looped hand that littered the Halley. Nancy flicked desperately through the mostly banal – although endearingly chirpy – entries about housekeeping and parties. But a word leapt boldly from one page. 'Stars'.

> *23rd March 1752*
> *Sing tara-tara! C and I have been married a whole*
> *month. To have found someone so suited seems as a*
> *dream. Not only is he most handsome, but his heart is*
> *generous and steadfast. Never before have I felt someone*
> *listening – with intent – to me and treating me as an in-*
> *tellectual equal. C is even encouraging my interest in the*
> *stars and has set up a little observatory room in the attic*
> *at Durham House. Familiar Spitalfields is below, but my*
> *eyes are fixed on the skies.*

Fixed on the skies. The evidence was incontrovertible. Cassandra had been an astronomer too. Nancy's hands trembled with such force, she could barely steady the page enough to read. She looked out of the window at the sun sinking towards the distant hills. There was no shred of doubt. Caleb had lied. He had brought her here under false pretences.

A glance over her shoulder. Caleb might return at any moment. More entries about appointments and lunches, interspersed with astronomical notes. Although it was clear that the majority of her work lay in books elsewhere, it was obvious even from these tiny fragments that Cassandra was a most diligent researcher her entries tracking the rise and fall of stars and the orbits of planets across the firmament over Edinburgh. Another entry caught her eye.

> *13th April 1753*
> *A most invigorating conversation with C this evening. I had thought my theories a little far-fetched, and that I see astronomy in the most unlikely places. Yet, after our visit last night to a performance of* A Midsummer Night's Dream, *it seems that he might be minded to agree with my notion that Shakespeare was as obsessed with the stars as I. Tonight we were quite caught up in taking down his copies of* Macbeth, Julius Caesar *and* King Lear *and finding the shooting stars, the constellations shifting and moving across the pages. Shakespeare writes of meteors being 'exhaled from the sun'; a description that delighted both C's romantic literary mind and tickled my scientific brain. Oh, surely no two people have been better suited in love. If only C might find a little more time for me away from his books.*

A twinge of guilt. These private notes were not meant for Nancy's eyes. Yet she felt as if she must continue. These diaries surely held the key to the mysteries of Blackthistle and Caleb. She turned the pages, scanning them as quickly as she could.

> *29th April 1753*
> *Who would have thought that birthdays as a married woman would be such fun? In the morning, C presented me with the most astonishing five-foot telescope, with a huge lens crafted by Mr Dollond himself! It must have cost C's father a small fortune.*
> *   This afternoon, we took a carriage to Vauxhall Pleasure Gardens. What colour, and the crowds were thicker*

than ever! Excitingly, I bumped into Mr J.B. with whom
I conversed a little about my interest in astronomy. He
has taken my card, and I his, and he says I am to send
me some of my work. Disappointingly, C seems to have
no interest in these affairs. I'm not sure he even heard me
when I told him my news. Perhaps I bore him with my
endless star chatter and should be more circumspect in the
future.

A five-foot telescope with a lens crafted by Mr Dollond.
Caleb was most generous. The grooves on the floor, surely
they revealed where it had stood. Nancy looked around the
room. There was no sign of it here now.

15th June 1753
Another letter, at last from Mr J.B.. He is most enthu-
siastic about my work. I am near-delirious with excite-
ment. He has asked if I would like to correspond with
his niece, Mrs E.L., a woman apparently most accom-
plished in astronomy, and who, he tells me, is keen to
encourage my learning. I have written to her this very
evening.

J.B. E.L. J.B. Nancy swallowed and checked the date. Her
mother would have been 35, working alongside her uncle,
James Bradley – J.B. – at the Observatory.
    E.L. Elizabeth Lockaby.
    The room whirled and for a moment she rested her head on
the table, then continued reading.

9th July 1753
Mrs E.L. has replied! I feel as if I am embarking on a
new voyage. She has suggested that, as two women in a
world of men, we are duty-bound to share our discoveries,
and that, if she might be so bold, she will extend a hand
of support to me in my endeavours. Diary, I feel that this

*might be a friendship to treasure. C still takes little interest
in my mathematical endeavours, as he is so busy with his
Shakespeare thesis.*

She flicked through the diary. The next month's sparse entries
told of the death of Caleb's father, and the couple's relocation
to Inverness.

22nd August 1753
*I have done my best to make Blackthistle our home and
I have busied myself making it more comfortable. Inverness may not have the grand parties, huge libraries and
social whirligig of London, but it has beauty and Scotland now seems at peace after the troubles. Caleb assures
me that he is at peace with the death of his father and
we both feel happy here. I continue my research, and
have set up a study of my own. This place, it seems,
suits us. My only regret is that I did not get to meet
Mrs E.L. in person, and will not for a while, as we are
obliged to stay in Inverness for the foreseeable future
and have no plans to return to London even for a short
holiday.*

Nancy turned the pages of the diary faster, searching for more
mentions of Elizabeth. On to the next volume, and the next.
Here and there she found hints, ghostly traces of who she pre-
sumed to be her mother, reminders of letters Cassandra was
to write and pleasure at receiving another missive from E.L.
From the tiny mentions Nancy seized upon, it was apparent
that the women had formed a trusting and respectful bond,
yet there was nothing substantial in the diaries about the correspondence until she reached 1756.

12th May 1756
My perseverance and persistence has been rewarded.
E.L. has finally shared her 'goose-chase' theory that she

kept from me for so long. And it is quite the proposition.
She tells me of an account from a Monsieur del Sol of
France that she uncovered of the last transit, describing
a chasm in the sky that seemed to open briefly before
Venus's pass in front of the sun. She calls it 'the Fold'.
I am intrigued! She sent me some bare notes, but has
apparently written an entire thesis on the phenomenon,
which I cannot wait to read. She plans to have me a
copy printed that she will send under separate cover.
I am not to tell anyone of her work; even J.B. frowns
upon her notions and so she works in secret.

Nancy felt tears prick at the corners of her eyes. She could
barely credit what she was reading. Cassandra and her
mother had been friends. Confidantes. Research partners
even. Her shoulders shivered involuntarily. Caleb must have
read these diaries. He must have known who her mother
was. Exactly who she was. But why had he brought her
here? There was no time even to think. She looked around
nervously, barely able to breathe, yet not able to stop turning the pages.

29th May 1756
The more I read of E.L.'s notes, the more convinced I am
that her theory is correct. Her work is so advanced. She
pulls together so many threads, and weaves them into an
extraordinary hypothesis. My competence is far, far below
hers, yet I intend to do my level best to comprehend her
work. I must know more, and have written asking her
to send a copy of the entirety of her research by return.
I have kept my word, however, and told no-one of her
theories. Not even C.

Nancy stopped reading and took a deep breath. Soon the
diary would reach June 1756 – 25th June. That hot, still,
phlox-scented night in London when her parents' carriage

had rattled away from Crooms, never to return. She reached the page, but the date passed with an unremarkable entry about a day spent in the company of some of Caleb's work colleagues. Nancy bit her lip. For Cassandra, it had, of course, been a day like any other. However, she kept reading, pages turning faster and faster.

> *13th July 1756*
> *Mr J.B. has written to tell me the most awful news.*
> *E.L. is gone. Dead. A carriage crash of all things. Oh,*
> *my dear E.L. All day I have shed tears for a woman*
> *I never met, and fear they will not stop. She had a hus-*
> *band. A daughter! My heart aches. At supper, C asked*
> *why my head drooped and I made some excuse about*
> *being exhausted as I cannot confide even in him. Only*
> *you, dear Diary, only you. Yet tonight I have deter-*
> *mined that I will continue E.L.'s work, although I may*
> *never get to read her thesis. I know so little of it, my*
> *mind is so weak in comparison alongside her extraordi-*
> *nary brain. But, for her if nothing else, I must find out*
> *more. After all, I will be here for the transits, to prove*
> *her theories, and she will not.*

A sharp stab of grief pierced Nancy's heart. How she missed her mother. And so, evidently, had Cassandra. If only she had known at her mother's death of the existence of this brilliant woman. She had a suspicion that under different circumstances, she and Caleb's wife might have been fast friends.

In the diaries that followed, there were scraps of mathematical notes, descriptions of late nights toiling over charts and calculations. Cassandra described her happiness at the move to Inverness and the pleasure taken in decorating Blackthistle. There was even a mention of 'dour old McLoone'. Then another entry.

8th September 1757
Joy of joys! I believe I may, at last, be with child. The
women from the market's herbs have succeeded where all
else has failed. Magic? Medicine? I care not. All that I
know is that C and I are blissfully happy.

Outside, the sun was sinking over the distant hills. She leafed
faster. Cassandra's pregnancy was detailed over the next
months. Then:

15th April 1758
He is here. Little Oliver Malles has arrived. I am exhausted
beyond all knowing, and can barely raise a hand to write,
yet feel I must record that today C and I have been blessed
with the most beautiful, spirited child. Welcome Oliver.

Then, an uncharacteristic gap in dates.

2nd May 1758
I am sorry to have neglected you, my dear Diary. Oliver
is my world, yet that world is, at this moment, very small.
I have barely ventured beyond my bedchamber. I have
been so enfeebled I have barely been able to look at any-
thing aside from my dear little boy. Soon I will feel more
alive, I know it. Spring is now here, after all.

More entries told of night feeds, of sore breasts and days spent
with drooping eyes and flagging brain. They were at their
old rate, yet the handwriting was smaller, the letters closer
together. Soon they told of Oliver eating a little porridge, of
his first steps, and his first word.

30th May 1759
A delight to leaven my melancholy. Tonight Oliver and
I were outside in the fields, gazing aimlessly at the stars
I have so neglected these thirteen months gone. From

nowhere, my darling boy pointed at the sky, then uttered
his first word – 'moon'. Oh Diary, for one moment I
believed I smiled. C is, of course, equally delighted.

Yet this happiness seemed short-lived. Another entry more
than a year later read:

24th September 1760
Full Moon again, and I am tired, so tired, yet cannot
sleep. The darkness has settled once more, and I feel lost
under its fug. It has been over a year since it first held
me tight in its grip. My dearest boy has brought me
such joy, yet that joy is cloaked in inescapable melan-
choly. I fear it grows within me, growls more savagely
with each day that passes. Today I spoke once more to
the women at the market, and have determined to visit
them at their cottage in order that they might better help
me. C is not overjoyed at the prospect, but says I must
do as I wish and that the women did, after all, help
bring Oliver to us.

Nancy's eyes widened.

30th September 1760
Such a day. A visit to the women in Inverness. Their
names are so curious: Daughter, Mother, Granny. We
talked of herbs and apothecary and they gave me some
remedies for my melancholy. We spoke of birth and death,
and of seeing. Diary, dear Diary, something extraordi-
nary happened. I do believe that the women transported
me, they took me with them into the past. They showed
me their lives! Lives that had been led hundreds, if not
thousands, of years ago. They said it was a form of what
they call scrying. C does not know, and neither shall I
tell him of the events of my call or any future visits. I
fear he would think I was losing my mind.

15th October 1760
Diary, I can scarcely sit without thinking of my next visit
to the cottage. I now make an excuse to call on the wom-
en most days. They have suggested I might want to learn
how to scry. Perhaps I am craving the herbs they give
me, but I think more it is the women's company. I am
still in dark turmoil, yet my mind is alive with thoughts,
teeming with ideas.

That poor woman. The melancholia had her in its grip. There
had been a woman, Mrs Penny Featherstone, who had held
the floor at a Bluestocking meeting, telling of the dreadful
sadness that had come upon her after the birth of her second
child. The voices that had nagged at her, whispering of her
failures, her horrible appearance and how her husband must
be ashamed of her. Her despair had driven her to consider
jumping from the highest window of her house. A woman
blessed with a fine mind and the sharpest faculties, lost in a
bleak fog. Unused to discussions of the heart or temperament,
the room had fallen silent, awkward, until Mrs Montague had
taken Mrs Featherstone's arm and led her away. Nancy took a
breath. Then back to the diary, turning the pages faster, faster.

21st October 1760
I have restarted my work to expand E.L.'s theories, an
undertaking sorely neglected for the past year. Yet I am
frustrated. There are too many unknowns, holes in the
sparse notes she sent me. If only I might have seen the
whole thesis. If only!

3rd November 1760
Another night, and more despair. I have tried to loosen
its grip, but the hold the melancholy has on me is too
strong to shake. Today I visited the women once more,
and they introduced me to scrying. I watched Daughter

*fill her bowl from the stream, then she showed me how
to look – but not look – at the reflection on the water's
surface. Diary, I was able almost immediately to see. I
saw straight where I wanted to: back to when E.L. was
still alive, into her study, looking over her shoulder as she
wrote about the Fold!*

Nancy could not stop reading. Surely Cassandra's mind was
faltering. She could not, surely, see or scry as the women
claimed to do. Yet...

7th November 1760
*I have seen. I see. I look into my little gold bowl and
peer over her shoulder as she writes. And I write here
with her. I feel as if I have some purpose in life beyond
Oliver and Blackthistle. When I work, my load is light-
ened. As soon as my pen is in its pot, however, my tears
flow.*

Here, tucked into the pages of the diary were some yellowing scraps of paper bearing Cassandra's handwriting. In
her almost childish writing, was a near-facsimile of Nancy's
mother's work. A mosaic of genius: the diagrams, the numbers, the holes, the tunnels, the loops. Only one vital element
was missing – the coordinates where the Fold might appear.
The coordinates that she had scribbled outside the observatory, on that hot, sticky night of the transit eight years earlier.
Nancy's hand trembled. How on earth had this woman, with
no training, no hand to guide her, come almost frustratingly
near the same momentous conclusions as she and her mother
if not by seeing, but by peeping? She read on.

25th February 1761
*I rise at midnight to look at the skies and the stars. Again,
no sign of that flow and ebb in the northern quadrant*

that I know must come at the transit. C knows not of the exact nature of my work, but still maintains that I am chasing shadows, that my mind is softening, that I am losing myself to the skies. He despairs of my sadness, yet cannot help. He finds solace in his Shakespeare. Oliver is dreamy, but, of course, he cannot understand. The women see a little. Yet I have not told even them of the Fold; they could not possibly comprehend.

2nd May 1761
The most extraordinary thing. Oh Diary, Last night the women took me into the skies. They know of my love for astronomy, and told me I might see more with them. Truly I believe we flew among the stars. I am so tired I barely know where my world ends and the cosmos begins, yet I know that tonight my feet left terra firma and I was in the void that lies between here and heaven! We flew! A salve. There was a salve. The salve drove our flight.

The writing was small now, tight and knotted.

6th May 1761
I am hollowed-out, exhausted. Lost. I think only of escape and that flow of stars, of my calculations, my theories. How I long to share them with C. Yet that is impossible! I have a fanciful notion that the stars beckon me towards them, that they will welcome me among them... that perhaps I might fly as I did with Mother, Granny and Daughter into the heavens and join their dance. My nights and days blur into one. Yet my thoughts are aligning. I scry and I peep. I look forward and see only a whirl of stars, a rip in a dark sky from which pours light. The Fold. That tear in the skies. Perhaps I might find succour there in the ebb and flow of the stars. Perhaps I might find peace. I am beginning to wonder if that is my destiny. To take a journey into the Fold.

The ebb and flow of stars. Nancy looked upwards and breathed out slowly. There were so few who knew of that space in the cosmos that ebbed and flowed, danced and spiralled. Oh Cassandra. She thought of the slow pirouette of lights and breathed harder. The writing had become a little more disjointed and difficult to make out.

> *20th May 1761*
> *C is fretful, I believe he thinks I am bewitched! If only he might join me in my studies, but he scorns anything outside the realm of sonnets and speeches, plays and poems. If only I might tell him of what lies beyond, perhaps I could convince him. My books, my studies yield more and more, yet I am constantly tired, constantly in the gloom. Oliver remains steadfast. I think of the Fold. The transit. The salve. The salve that might fuel my journey into its safety... Oliver and I.*

The salve! Was that the piece of the puzzle that had been missing, that Caleb had been searching for, imploring the witches to tell him? Nancy thought back to the night at the stone cairn, remembering the flight through the heavens. The flight that she was not sure had been imagined. The women had told her that Cassandra had taken the same journey before her. Nancy clapped a hand to her mouth. That poor woman. Her mind had become untethered. No wonder she had grasped at straws. The writing was now scrawled, etched deeply into the pages.

> *23rd May 1761*
> *I have done the most dreadful thing. I am but a common thief. Yet I feel no remorse, for I need that thing above everything else. While speaking to the women, I stole their salve and now I have it in my possession.*

It seemed as if she truly believed that she might fly up into the Fold and there, find some salvation, some peace. It seemed an extraordinary leap, and yet. Nancy had seen that sight, had witnessed that phenomenon. It was true. There could be nothing closer to how heaven might appear. And if Cassandra had seen it, peeped it, scried it? Oh Cassandra.

> *29th May 1761*
> *I feel my feet leave the Earth nightly. Oliver will be by*
> *my side. Always with me.*

There were few entries afterwards. Nancy bit her lip in the knowledge of what was coming. The last merely read:

> *4th June 1761*
> *I am lost. I do not know if I even wish to be found. I*
> *pray the heavens may take me. I am sure of the date and*
> *time. Oliver and I will be in place. And I have the key. I*
> *am ready.*

Nancy's hands trembled as she read the final lines. Cassandra seemed desolate, destroyed. This must be the last entry she had made in her diary. 4th June 1761. Two days before the last transit of Venus.

Nancy felt as if she were in a hurricane. Her ears roared, her eyes were wide. Caleb knew that his wife had been obsessed with the Fold. Caleb had already known of the Fold when he brought her here.

Slowly the thoughts started to align as neatly as those tiny planets on her orrery, but the precise nature of their configuration remained just beyond comprehension.

Caleb wanted his wife and child by his side once more and thought their disappearance had something to do with the Fold. Although she was certain that he would not have been able to discern her mother's identity from the scant information in the diaries, Caleb had tracked her down. And, fool that she had been, she had been tempted into his home. Into the house where laughter had stilled and hope foundered.

The orrery on the shelf finally drew to a halt.

Chapter Twenty-Seven

Nancy wanted to put her head on the desk and sob. More strands tangled into this complex web, skein upon skein, knotted more and more tightly. Caleb's actions seemed like those of a madman, yet it seemed he was lost in heartbreak, desperate and wandering, just as she had once been.

But she knew she must be swift. She stood, ears pricked, ready for the sound of a footstep outside and walked back to the entrance. On the back of the door were pinned a tiny portrait and a cutting from a newspaper. A woman and a small boy gazed from the painting: the child cherubic and smiling; the woman with fair hair and a more serious expression. She moved closer to the picture, reached out and touched the woman's face. This then was Cassandra.

The cutting was yellowing and curled, thin as peeling silver birch. Its print was faded, as if worn bare by someone else's eyes. It was from the *Caledonian Mercury*. The date, grimly familiar.

> *Inverness, 8th June*
> *On Saturday last, Cassandra, the wife of Mr Caleb Malles, and his small boy Oliver disappear'd without trace. Mr Malles has offered a REWARD for any information that might lead to their recovery, be it ALIVE or DEAD. Mrs Malles has been of unsound minde for several months and it is feared she has taken both her life and that of her son. The pair were last seen departing Black-*

thistle House in the early hours of the sixth day of June.
All offers of information to the Parish Constable.

Nancy felt winded. Although she knew Cassandra and Oliver had vanished, to see their disappearance described in such bald terms was overwhelming, and the date. The date. It was grimly inevitable, and as she had suspected, they had indeed left at the last transit. The incandescent Cassandra. It was apparent that Caleb's wife had been as obsessed – more so perhaps – with the Fold as she, and, at her lowest ebb, had concluded that her only chance for redemption and peace lay beyond that glowing, shining rift in the sky.

Cassandra must have reached in despair for this black hole of worlds beyond the cosmos and magic. For one brief moment, Nancy wondered if perhaps she and Oliver might even have been able to reach it. After all, hadn't she thought herself to be among the stars last night with the witches? Perhaps Cassandra's departure had been foretold by Hecate centuries, perhaps millennia ago. Ridiculous. Cassandra had merely, tragically, been lost in her despair. She had taken her life.

Mother, Daughter and Granny had, unwittingly, shown Cassandra the final piece she believed she needed to complete her crazed puzzle. She had stolen their salve, thinking it might allow her to fly among the stars and into the Fold.

What fate had befallen the poor woman and her bright, unsuspecting son? The thought of their bodies lying pallid and bloated in a burn on the moor came unbidden. Uncovered in the cold, their bones turning to dust over eight long summers. It was nearly unbearable.

A final look around the room. The scribbled notes, burns on the floor and haphazard ephemera pinned to the walls suggested that Caleb had been secretly poring over his wife's work, working desperately towards finding Cassandra and Oliver. It felt a place of frantic investigation, a once-calm study ransacked by someone lost in grief, grasping at every chance to understand what had happened. Delirious for answers, reason, but, despite having a knowledge of the basics of mathematics, unable to take the dazzling leaps of logic and audacious loops and connections needed to develop the theories necessary to understand the Fold.

He had striven to make sense of his wife's disappearance, retracing her calculations, trying theories of his own, and attempting to learn how to scry, yet he didn't have the vital parts of the puzzle he thought he needed – the coordinates and the salve. His grief must have been a burden almost too heavy to bear. The melancholic insanity that had gripped Cassandra seemingly had its fingers tight around Caleb too.

He had needed someone who had followed the same path as Cassandra, someone who had studied, who was open to something beyond. Someone like her. Someone whose papers told of the exact location one might see the Fold. Whose papers had been stolen. Someone who – unwittingly – had even brought him the salve. Oh! What dreadful, desperate plan had Caleb for when that wrinkle in the skies appeared once more?

Nancy rubbed her face and picked up as many of Caleb and Cassandra's papers as she could carry. There was a soft creak in the room next door.

Still in shock, she ducked out of the door and into Caleb's study. A wide-eyed face greeted her. 'Oh, ma'am. What are you doin?'

'Isobel! You gave me a shock!' Nancy exclaimed.

'I heard a noise. What were you doing? Nobody 'cept Mr Malles is allowed in there.'

'I… I'm not really sure, Isobel.' The thought of Isobel nosing around the room set her nerves jangling.

'Tell me, what do you know of Mrs Malles's and Oliver's disappearance?'

The girl looked at her with fear in her eyes. 'Barely nothin', ma'am. I liked the bairn, Oliver. He was a sweet thing. But I was still a wee girl when they went. I can hardly remember it. Their going missing wasn't talked about in town much, not with the witches there, with their big ears a' flappin'.'

'Do you really think the women had something to do with it?'

'They say that Mrs Malles spent a terrible lot of time at their house. I do remember that she got awful thin, that she would pace up and down, up and down. We'd hear her at night, walkin' the corridors. One night I saw her out in the garden, with little Oliver, lookin' up at the stars, and she was spinnin' around like a top. Mr Malles was out there too, fair spare with worry, poor man. Ma said they put a hex on her.'

The girl gulped. 'I'm so sorry, ma'am. I should have said more about Mrs Malles and wee Oliver before. When we walked. I just… They was never spoken of in the house afterwards. Mr Malles even sent that big telescope of hers back down to London. Like he couldn't bear lookin' at it.'

'There's no need to apologise, Isobel. You are a loyal girl.' There was a creak outside, and Nancy glanced towards the door, 'Come, let's go to my room.'

'No need to fret, ma'am. No-one will come upon us. Mr Malles is gone.'

'Gone? What do you mean, *gone*? Where?'

'To London, ma'am. He's gone to London.'

Nancy looked at her sharply. 'London? Why?'

The girl shrugged her shoulders. 'Dinnae ken. He left in an awful hurry earlier. By coach.' She looked at the floor.

'I see.' If Caleb had left in such haste, he must have firm plans. Nancy's mind was roiling. She was sure he must have taken her notes and the salve with him, and judging by the swiftness of his exit, he wanted, for some reason, to get to London in time for the transit.

'Do you know where in the city he was going?'

'To Durham House, I believe, after all these years! Who knows what he wants there.'

Nancy thought of the five-foot telescope that had been sent back to Spitalfields. It would be more than big enough to see the Fold. She grimaced.

'I might have an idea. He said nothing of his intentions to you then?'

Isobel shook her head. 'No. Perhaps he might have spoken to Mrs McLoone.'

She held little hope that the housekeeper might know what Caleb was doing. He was secretive at the best of times, and on the manic evidence of the study, had started to lose a grip on his senses. She needed to speak to the witches about what she had found, and she needed to be quick. The transit was only twelve days away.

Chapter Twenty-Eight

The women had looked apprehensive as she walked into the cottage. They were sitting around the rough table, four cups of chicory coffee steaming in front of them.

Nancy started to babble. 'Caleb's gone. He's taken the salve I had in my trunk. And I think he wants to use it to find Cassandra. I looked round his study, her rooms. She knew my mother. He… he believes that she took Oliver up into a great rift in the sky.' Her voice faltered and she took a deep breath. 'It sounds ridiculous. But I assure you–'

Granny nodded. 'Nay. Not ridiculous. This explains much. Now sit and tell us everything, slowly.'

'It's just so preposterous!'

'Daughter has felt something,' muttered Granny. 'Something has stirred. Something's on the rise. Come, child, tell us.'

Nancy sat on the stool. She rested her chin in her hands and closed her eyes. 'I don't know what I believe any more. You wouldn't understand.'

Mother raised one eyebrow. 'We wouldn't?'

Nancy swallowed. 'I'm sorry. You are right.' She sat back on the stool, feeling its hard, wooden seat under her skirts, and explained.

She told the women of the great whirl in the sky, the phenomenon predicted in her mother's books that she had witnessed eight years before. How she had seen this swirl open. She told them of the corridors that her mother believed ran from the Fold. The holes that led behind the stars, snaking behind the frame that held whole galaxies in place. And how somewhere behind that fabric were other worlds, other universes even.

The women nodded their heads. 'Tell us more,' said Daughter shortly.

'It appears every eight years. By my calculations, this one is due at exactly the same time as the transit. Do you know about the transit?'

The women shook their heads.

'A transit occurs when a planet passes directly between the sun and another planet. The first becomes visible as a shadow against the sun.' The women's faces remained blank. Nancy picked up a silver-lidded jar that sat on the table. 'Imagine this to be Earth,' she picked up a little golden bowl, 'and this is the sun.' She placed them a foot apart on the table.

'Now, say this stone,' she picked up a white pebble, 'is Venus.' She placed it between the others. 'See? You would be able to see its shadow from here,' she pointed at the jar, 'as it passes in front of here.' She indicated the bowl. The women nodded.

'The pass happens twice in eight years, then there is a gap of 121 years. Then the passes happen again, then another gap of 105 years. And so it goes, over and over. A black spot passes in front of the sun – it's really very exciting.' She started to talk faster, 'It happened in the year Macbeth and his wife died. And it's going to happen again this year.'

The women stared at her.

'What other years? When did it happen?' Mother's voice was low and urgent.

'Let me think. Eight years ago, of course, 1761. Before that in 1639, when it was first observed by Crabtree and Horrocks. 1631 was when Kepler predicted it would appear. But before that too. Way back into time. Let me think... 1518 and 1526. 1396 was the last one not part of a pair. Then 1275 and 1283. Before that, 1153.' She wrinkled her forehead.

The women's mouths were open. 'And further back?' said Mother.

Nancy closed her eyes and concentrated. 'Before that it occurred in 1032 and 1040. Then, in 910, 797 and 789 and... 554 and 546.' She exhaled.

'Oh, Child of the Moon,' Granny breathed, 'These times. That is when we have been called back. These years are when Hecate has called us.'

For a brief second, it was as if Nancy's heart stood still.

Mother's voice was urgent. 'In 1639, we were with a giant army, defending this country on the banks of the Tweed, willing them on, flying above and swooping on their enemies. That day we saved many lives, as Hecate bid.'

'As Hecate bid,' repeated Granny and Daughter.

Mother continued. 'In 554 we whispered to that good man Columba to set up his monastery. In 797 we were here when the horned invaders from the north thundered into the little towns. How many women, many children, we helped to safety. It seems we are brought back at the times of your transits... your *Folds*.'

Granny coughed. 'My child. Perhaps this transit, it resembles Beltane, or Samhain on Earth. At those times the edges between our world and others get thin – full of holes. Like an old sieve. It becomes easy to work magic, to peep through those gaps into other places. My bones tell me this transit helps unlatch those cracks in the heavens. That we might see into other worlds, that they may pour into ours. That the Fold might indeed even open to one who is ready, waiting. Dangerous times.'

Nancy shook her head. 'No, that cannot be possible. It's preposterous.'

Granny continued, with a sharp look. 'Yet I can see how Cassandra might have thought it, can you not? That she knew exactly when it would open once more. How that girl was ready to greet it when it appeared. All she thought needed was that one thing we had.'

Nancy shook her head. 'The salve?'

Granny nodded. 'It was that which she stole from us – the flying ointment. Maybe she thought she could fly up into the Fold. I don't know. We'd used it with her too, y'see.'

Nancy's head pounded and she leaned on the table. 'Caleb has the salve he stole from me. He also has the coordinates of the Fold. They're in my notes. So he knows exactly where he has to look. And now he's gone to London. Is he trying to outrun us? He knows that I suspect him. What can he be doing?'

Granny shook her head. 'Think, child. You went into the rooms. Did you find anything there that might help us? What has the Scholar already found?'

Nancy spoke slowly: 'The place felt almost like a science laboratory. But more *esoteric*. As if he were experimenting with something beyond natural philosophy. Something more,' she paused, '*alchemic*.'

Mother shook her head. 'Tsk, tsk. That will never work. It's this man's way of studyin' magic: forcing it, trying to pin it down like it was a wiggling rat. All numbers and directions and rules. Take three ounces of iron, and one of copper. Hold the flame here for five minutes exactly. Boil this mixture for five and thirty seconds. And abracadabra, here is your gold!' She snorted. 'No-one will make gold like that. No-one! All these philosophers, boiling and measuring and watching their clocks. No gold is gonna come from that.'

'If you be wanting to make gold, you need to feel your way to it,' said Daughter. 'Feel that magic comin' up through you and out of your fingers. You need to curtsey to the stars, bow to the sun. You need to know how to call on the Old Ones, the words that bring them to your shoulder. To grow the crops as the moon grows fat. Not just throw some pieces of metal in a pot and hold a flame to them.'

Granny coughed. 'Y'see, you can't learn magic from a book, girl. You have to grow it inside you. And you need more than one to let it grow further. You cannot work magic alone. Power comes from two, from three, from more. From the crone to the mother to the maiden. Together we are strong.'

Nancy's academic heart stilled. 'I suppose my work is man's magic too?' she asked, a little coldly.

Mother smiled wryly. 'You're an interesting one.' She tilted her head sideways. 'You, your mother, perhaps... there's something beyond these numbers and rules. You feel something too. I don't think you would have found the Fold without that feeling.'

Her words made uncomfortable sense. Nancy remembered the first time she'd opened her mother's notebook. Of course, there were calculations – so many calculations – but the leaps and connections she had made seemed almost to come from a place beyond rationality. Perhaps there was a point at which science had to meet some sort of magic – or at the very least intuition – in order to make a giant bound. Maybe her beloved equations really did not hold all the answers alone.

'There have been times when the numbers seem to come from somewhere else, some power brewed deep inside me. I'm not sure. I'd like to think it was my mind and the hard work I've put in, but perhaps—' Nancy stopped.

'It ain't found in a bottle or a glass tube, that's for sure,' said Mother. 'It's from the earth, the mud, the seeds, the trees you sleep under, the cave in which you shelter.' She shook her head. 'It's in your courses, the blood that comes with the moon. The Scholar's magic is cold and hard. It might eventually work, but the rewards will turn to ashes in his mouth.'

Granny pursed her lips. 'I'm not so sure. This is powerful craft he is dabbling in. We must beware. He dances on the edge of your academic world and our elemental place. Perhaps he plans to fly up into the Fold, to find poor Cassandra and Oliver up there somewhere. But he's barging his way in rather than feeling. It is so dangerous. I feel as if Hecate has brought us back to stop this. If he opens it, he might bring down all kinds of horrors on our heads. Horrors we cannot even begin to comprehend. That the world cannot begin to comprehend. Hecate is rarely wrong. We must stop him. Come. We have little time before this transit. Twelve days you say?'

Nancy's face was grim. 'Twelve days.'

Mother and Granny looked up from the fire. 'You'll need to pack your things tonight, then,' Daughter said.

Benjamin Lockaby's methods of persuasion had been a source of endless amusement to the Lockaby family. 'The housekeeper has packed us a picnic,' he would say, apropos of nothing, at eight in the evening. 'So we must make use of it. I thought a midnight feast at the top of the hill? We might take our telescopes.' And so they would find themselves on a stargazing mission that lasted into the early hours. Not that Nancy or her mother minded such jaunts, but her mother did laugh wearily at the clumsiness of her husband's faits accomplis.

Daughter's unsubtle push was straight from Benjamin's playbook.

'So I am to trail after Mr Malles? Alone?' Nancy raised an eyebrow. The women were persuasive, of that there was no doubt, yet she knew that to follow Caleb to London would mean danger. To trust them blindly seemed a little foolish.

And surely, if she were to follow him, to attempt to dissuade him from his folly, then there was a risk that she would have no chance to view the Fold with the calm appraisal it required.

There was so much to document, so many theories to finally prove, and yet she was being asked to forgo her only chance of viewing her great discovery.

The women glanced at each other. Daughter got to her feet and pulled down her bowl from the shelf. She filled it with water from a brass jug that stood on the table.

'Let's see.'

As she peered into the shiny bowl, her pupils enlarged into onyx pools. She gripped Nancy's hand firmly. Nancy gasped. She could see what Daughter could see, looking into the still water – glimpses of people, windows, landscapes. As they coalesced, there were familiar faces. Her mother and father.

They were in the drawing room at Crooms. Her mother laughed as she and Papa looked over a map. Her mother pointed at the sky through the window. Then the Octagon Room in the observatory, with Uncle James clapping Papa on the back. The door opened. She spotted herself, running to her parents, begging to be allowed to look through the big telescope. Then Mama writing in her little emerald book, smiling to herself as she puzzled over what must be the Fold.

Nancy gasped. Something awful. Her parents, their faces white, eyes staring, blood seeping onto the dark, dry ground on which they lay. Her mother's emerald-green dress spotted with dark patches, her limbs bent awkwardly, her blue eyes open, yet clouded. Daughter's anvil fist held firm to Nancy's wriggling hand. The scene darkened. Now Nancy could see the sky, spangled with stars; stars that were moving, round and round, like a waterwheel. It felt as if she were in the heavens, the whirl filling her entire field of vision. Then, inevitably, the centre split, and beams of light shot out. She was so close she imagined she could hear the light, as one might hear a bolt of lightning sear through the air.

She felt Daughter's grip tighten, heard an intake of breath. There was a feeling of rising dread, of a force pushing relentlessly against the bulging skin of the sky, desperate to get out. Cold terror gripped her. Much as she wanted to get closer, to peer in, she dared not, for fear of what horrors she was now certain lay behind. She shook at Daughter's grip. Now she could hear something animal-like growling and howling and screaming inside the fissure. She knew, beyond all doubt, that behind the opening a dreadful, wild, power strained at the leash, talons scrabbling and clawing, trying to get through. She could bear it no more. She shook her hand as hard as she could manage, and was free. In an instant she was back in the kitchen. Three pairs of eyes were focused on her, wide in fear.

Granny whispered shakily, 'You, child. It's got to be you. You can feel what's right. This is why we are back this time. This is why Hecate wanted us here – to help you. This old crone knows it.'

Nancy knew the woman was right. She knew that she must go to London, to try and stay Caleb's hand. Even if, perhaps, it meant putting aside her ambitions to document the phenomenon, to prove her hypotheses. The power, the beast behind the Fold, must be stopped.

She nodded. 'I can see. It feels as if Caleb has become monstrous with grief, that the Fold has behind it the most dreadful danger. See?' She held out a trembling hand. 'I am frit beyond belief. Yet I know I must go after him. I knew from the moment the maid told me he had left for London.' As she spoke, the depth of that conviction struck her. She had no choice. It seemed there was terrible danger abroad, and helping was now her duty, whatever the consequences.

Daughter gave her arm two quick squeezes. Her eyes were serious. 'Try not to fret. Try not to falter. If you want to pull him back from whatever dark place he's headed to, and to keep us all safe, you'll need to have strong roots. Feel them deep in the earth, holding you fast.'

Although she barely wanted to admit it, Nancy felt almost as if some kind of fate was leading her. A filament there from birth. Gripping that thread as tightly between her fingers as she could manage, she watched it stretch into the distance, leading her towards London.

'Then it is decided,' said Granny. 'You will follow the Scholar.' She tapped her head. 'Think hard – for what reason must he be in London? That will help you find him.'

Nancy spoke slowly. 'I'm not sure, but perhaps he believes he needs Cassandra's telescope to see the Fold. He could have used mine, but it's broken now. Maybe he feels he should use her telescope. So he will be going to Spitalfields.'

Mother nodded. 'I do not know about such matters, but this sounds possible. You will go on ahead. We will stay here and prepare.'

Nancy looked at Daughter. 'How should I stop Caleb? I don't know what I'm meant to do.'

Daughter gripped her hand. 'He can't be allowed to try and fly into the Fold. Look to the stars, look inside your noggin'. Use that clever mind of yours and you will find where you must be.' She looked darkly at Nancy. 'You must stop him in whatever way you can.' Nancy felt a wrench deep inside her.

Mother nodded. 'Your magic will come. It'll rise from deep inside, where it's always slept. Trust this power.'

Nancy put her hand on her stomach, but she felt no power, just a growing sense of unease.

'I don't know what I need to do.'

A glance passed between the women, and Daughter squeezed her hand again. 'Now, that I can't scry, that's for sure. You saw the bowl. You felt that power, that lightning bolt in your hand. What will be, will be. You will know what you must do. This is about more than you two souls. This is about,' she waved her hands around her head, '*all* of this. All you can see and more. It felt as if that Fold has the power to destroy us all in its deadly fury. So you must be quick. Get there before this transit begins.'

'She's right,' said Granny. 'The Fold is opening, and I feel the Scholar will do all he can to keep you at bay. I'm sure he suspects you'll follow.' She shook her head. 'And there is much at stake. It rests heavily on your shoulders. But you're a good 'un. Clever as a crow. Your hand will be steady, your heart true, your head clear.'

The enormity of the task ahead, and the thought of tackling it alone, made Nancy feel a little faint. She shook away Daughter's touch, steadying herself on the table. 'Will I see you again?'

'When we are needed, we will come,' Daughter said calmly, resting a hand on Nancy's arm. 'Don't fear. Call for us.'

'We must be together here for a while,' said Granny. 'If the Scholar attempts to enter the Fold, we will need all our power, and only as a three can we create the most powerful magic.'

'The highest magic asks much of us,' said Mother. 'All three of us must give up a little of our bodies, our blood and our souls. But together we are strong, like streams running into a waterfall.'

The three embraced her before she left. Daughter's hug crushed her with reassurance, while Mother held her shoulders, telling her what a strong spirit she had. Granny was bird-like in her arms; Nancy felt each vertebrae knuckled under her hands. The oldest woman whispered in her ear, '*Lykke til*. Good luck.'

Stepping into the front garden as the sun started to dip towards the horizon, a cloud of scent enveloped her. Violets.

Chapter Twenty-Nine

Tick-tock, tick-tock. Nancy could hear the big clock in the hall as she sat, her breakfast untouched on the table in front of her, staring out of the window of the dining room. It seemed to mock her with every swing of its pendulum. Eleven days were barely enough time to get to London, let alone find Caleb in the city. Her packed trunk sat in the hall.

Last night, Mrs McLoone had been stood in the shadowy hall waiting for her return. Her long face was lit only by the candle she held. 'Ma'am', she had whispered, 'Isobel told me you were looking for Mr Malles. He's gone to London, as you know. Oh ma'am. I'm fair worried.'

More words than she had spoken in all Nancy's time at Blackthistle. The woman looked exhausted. Nancy put a hand on her arm. 'You must be. Mrs McLoone,' McLoone's arm trembled under her touch, 'I— I am going to follow him. To London.'

The woman's mouth fell open. 'Ma'am!'

'I know about Mrs Malles, about Oliver. How devastated he was... still is. I think he's misguided, that he has lost himself in grief, but I must follow him. I must help him. Tell me, why do you think he is going to London?'

McLoone shook her head. 'Half-crazed, he looked. As if his mind was elsewhere. He was gabbling about that telescope. That he needed it, that it was the right thing.' She closed her eyes. 'What was it he said. I must get it right. "I must see it as she did, my eye to the same glass..." Something like that, I think.'

Nancy could sense the woman's concern. 'Thank you, Mrs McLoone. That is a huge help. You've been a loyal friend to Mr Malles. I know you must have been a rock after Mrs Malles and Oliver disappeared.'

'Fair lost in grief he was.' Mrs McLoone's eyes had misted over. 'A fine woman. And the bairn was a little lamb. When she disappeared, first thing the master did was send away that telescope that stood at her study window, straight back down to London. Couldn't bear the sight of it, he said. He shut off that study of hers. Closed it up and banned us all from going in there. And there was to be no talk of her, or little Oliver.' She pulled away from Nancy's touch and wiped away a tear. 'We were all hushed. Not a word was to be said. I know he started going back into the room a few years after. Would see those strange lights, hear the scrape of something ungodly.' She touched the crucifix that hung around her neck. 'We'd hear him sobbing sometimes and he started to get very thin. Had that haunted look about him. You know. You saw it too. I felt as if I could not do a thing. Couldn't speak plainly to him about it for fear of his anger. Because I needed this position, ma'am. There are many starving and I couldn't be one of them.'

It appeared that the ice had melted. Now she had started talking, there seemed to be no stopping her. Nancy bit her lip, 'Does no-one know what happened to them? Were there no clues?'

'To begin with, nothing. It was as if they had just stepped off this world. Mr Malles was going fair spare with worry for days. Every day, he'd rise before the sun, go out walking the fields, calling for them. It was heartbreaking to hear him, ma'am. For months he did it, then one day he stopped. Just stopped, and never mentioned them again. A year after they went missing, a fisherman found a necklace, ma'am, on the stones near Alturlie Point. It was her locket with the wee picture of Oliver. They each had one. The master wears his still. He wouldn't look at the one they found. It was no good. I still have it, hidden away for when he might be ready. I know he's not sound of mind, ma'am. But please. He was a good man. He is a good man.'

The poor woman looked as if she were about to burst into tears. Nancy patted her arm. 'You went far and beyond that which one might expect of a housekeeper. Mr Malles was lucky to have you.'

The woman nodded mutely.

'Now, for Mr Malles's sake, I must find a way to get to London. I don't have much time, so something fast. I will be lucky to find a carriage willing to go such a distance at this short notice.'

'If I might, ma'am, I have a friend who works on the post-chaise. I will find something for you.'

Now, in the morning light, Nancy spotted McLoone's hair-pin figure walking speedily up the drive. The housekeeper was almost breathless as she came through the front door, a few strands of hair out of place, but with a near-triumphant look on her face. 'I have one, ma'am! It is coming in an hour!'

Nancy went to fling her arms around the woman, but, at the last minute held back and patted her bony arm instead.

'I will, of course, be travelling alone.'

The woman put her hand to her mouth. 'I thought perhaps Isobel might—'

'No. It will be safer for everyone if I am without a companion. I can look after myself. I have packed simple dresses that require no assistance.'

'But, ma'am. I wasn't thinking about dresses. A solitary woman…'

Nancy spoke kindly. 'A driver can be charged with my safety. And as far as scandal is concerned, I care no more.

The idle prating of those with nothing better to do holds no fear for me. What might they say, after all?'

Mrs McLoone stared long at her. 'That I would not know, ma'am,' she said eventually.

★

Taking her leave of Blackthistle had been more affecting than Nancy had imagined. The heat was fiercer than ever, so she'd chosen her lemon poplin dress with orange trim, which afforded some degree of relief. Mrs McLoone and Isobel had stood side by side on the drive as she made her way down the steps.

Her big trunk was already loaded on to the top of the carriage, and the wrecked telescope would be sent to Greenwich by ship. Nancy was sure that she would not return to Blackthistle in the immediate future. She felt a little deflated – if this turned out to be a fool's errand then her return might be viewed as a defeat. She imagined Maskliss and the men at the Observatory laughing into their sleeves at the sight of her limping home. But that image of the Fold that Daughter had shown her, hungry and fierce, and battling to open and unleash who knew what on the Earth, made her determined. Her return to the capital had purpose – to stop Caleb making a terrible mistake.

Isobel was melodramatic. 'Ma'am, Mrs McLoone tells me that you must go, for Mr Malles. I wish you all the luck.' She moved forward and made an awkward curtsey. 'You have changed me. I will miss you, our studyin', our days. I'll even miss that tangle o' hair.' Nancy had given her a sharp look, but with no reprimand. This was, after all, a goodbye.

'Thank you, Isobel. I will miss you too. You have been a rock, and I am indebted to you for your help. You must come and visit me in London. I will send for you when I am settled.'

The words caught a little in her throat. *Settled.* She could barely promise herself she would survive the next few days or weeks, let alone return to any kind of normality. She bit her lip, 'And thank you, Mrs McLoone. I appreciate everything you've done.'

McLoone met her eye and nodded. 'Right you are, ma'am. I'm sorry to say goodbye.' She moved forward and whispered, 'Good luck. Please, help him. God speed.' She pressed something into Nancy's hand. A locket. Cassandra's locket. Nancy nodded and turned away, then climbed into the carriage.

The pair waved until the cart turned the corner towards Inverness.

Chapter Thirty

If anything, this coach journey was even more uncomfortable than the trip up to Scotland had been. The black walls of the carriage were hot to the touch, and even with the curtains drawn back there was little fresh air. Nancy felt the midday sun beating hard on the roof. Although the driver had been directed to use the turnpikes, and they had been picking up fresh horses and driving through the night, Nancy knew that she had very little time. The driver had harrumphed when she asked when they might be in London. 'With luck, on the fifth day of June.'

Nancy had given him her most imperious gaze and explained that that wasn't possible; that she must be there by the afternoon of the third day at the very latest, and he should drive as fast as he could. An extra couple of pounds had greased the deal. Yet she was painfully aware that they would be very lucky to reach the capital before Venus made her trek across the sun.

However, they had made fairly good time thus far and, four days into the journey, were already in England, tracking across a flat, heather-speckled moor. She glanced out of the window. A pair of shiny pheasants stared back at her, fat and handsome.

She sent a silent thanks to McLoone for ensuring she was the only passenger. Not only was she far more comfortable, but could also spread out her map charts and books on the seats.

Astronomers from across the globe would be feeling the same anticipation. Although they, of course, were more concerned with measurements and timings than the fearful power that lay behind the Fold. Nancy felt a flutter of sadness. How wonderful it would be to feel again the same optimism at the thought of having a front-row seat at one of the modern age's most spectacular astronomical shows. To be smoking a piece of glass in order to protect her eyes when looking at the sun, ready to view and measure and note and confer, and to calculate the new, and chart the uncharted.

Charles Green would be in his little portable tented observatory in Tahiti, hopping from foot to foot in anticipation of the transit, although she half-suspected that if there were pretty girls in the vicinity, he'd probably be distracted. Back in London, Dr Maskliss would be carefully calibrating his astronomical sector and sharpening his quill, ready to track every degree, every second of the transit.

Even the King, in his powdered wig, with his coterie of nodding acolytes, would be praying there would be no cloud. The highest man in the land might be luxuriating in his brand-new observatory in Richmond Park, yet, at fifteen after seven, he would stand in the same stance as the lowest, gazing skywards, awestruck at the universe's neat symmetry.

She peered again and again at the tiny figures and diagrams in front of her, trying to glean something – anything – fresh. Her eyes were raw from trying to make sense of them, but their significance remained frustratingly out of reach.

There was time now to read the notes she'd found in the secret room. Maps of the land around Inverness, marked with straight red lines, intersecting and criss-crossing, and of London covered similarly. So Cassandra had also been looking to London. There were charts too, a thick wad of them, detailing phases of the moon and yes, the transit. Some were printed, some drawn over much later in Caleb's spindly hand. She continued flicking through the notes. The writing was near-illegible.

What secrets had Cassandra uncovered? She looked out of the window. Above the moor, the air bent and shimmered.

Nancy now had only a week to get to London. She glanced at a map, finding the road along which they raced, traced the path they must take and whispered, 'Faster, faster!'

Chapter Thirty-One

Mr Warbon shook his head. 'Even if I drove the horses 'til their hooves bled, I can't be sure—'

'But I must be in London before the third. In four days. I must!' Nancy had thumped the table so hard their plates had rattled. The other customers of the Golden Fleece looked over their shoulders. The people of York were, evidently, unused to a woman with determination.

The driver looked at her and shook his head. 'Never have I known a passenger to be in such a hurry.' He narrowed his eyes. 'What d'ya want to be there so quick for, ma'am?'

Perhaps she should explain that her future, perhaps even more, depended on her getting there on time. She looked at his ruddy face and glassy eyes and decided against it.

'That is my business, Mr Warbon. But I will pay you double if we make good time.'

He had taken her by the arm and hurried her to the carriage, bread roll still in his beefy hands.

As they rumbled through the uneven streets, she thought of her own sprawling city. Her place was high above it, atop the observatory that stood on the hill at Greenwich, at dusk, waiting for the sun to set. She missed the Wren spires colouring orange at dusk, the hulking white Hawksmoors like vast ships, the gilded top of the Monument in the far distance, glinting in the final rays of the sun.

Caleb was a day-and-a-half ahead of her, so would not yet have reached Spitalfields. He must stick out on the streets of

the city like a crow among doves, his black shirt and breeches
sombre next to the extravagant colours of the preening dan-
dies that flocked between the coffee shops and pleasure
gardens; his wild curls free like a farmworker's rather than
bound tight under a fussy wig.

★

Another three days in the jolt and rumble of the coach.
Three more days of fret and finger-drumming and glances
at her watch and poring over charts, maps of London and
books. Three nights at grubby, noisy inns, changing horses,
barely sleeping, her bed jammed against the door for fear of
unwanted visitors.

They had rolled through towns, cities, yet Nancy had barely
glanced out of the window. Ignoring the coarse bantering of
the farmworkers as they pushed fat pigs around the market
in Leeds and the jostling theatre of the characters gathered
outside the inns of Sheffield, she'd chosen instead to read
Cassandra's notes over and over again, scouring her complex webs of intersecting lines, maps and orbit paths. She was
painfully aware she had only one more day.

Today was Friday.

The transit was tomorrow.

They were due into London this evening, Warbon had
promised, yet she still had no idea what she needed to do.

The afternoon was darkening. A few spots of rain splashed
onto the roof. Some blessed relief from the relentless heat.
Soon the deluge was hard on the windows, running in thick
rivulets that blurred the clouds and bent the horizon. Its beat
echoed on the roof above her like massed drums, while the
leaden sky rumbled threateningly. She lit a lamp and leafed
through her papers. Outside, a flash of lightning illuminated

the wheatfields. It was stark, bone-white, and something in its nature reminded her of that dreadful light that she had seen flickering in the window of the secret room.

Another lightning crash, close enough that she heard it sear and rip through the air, followed almost immediately by a loud crack of thunder. The carriage shook. Outside, the sky loomed charcoal-black. A pen pot and her lamp went clattering to the floor as the vehicle lurched heavily again and came to a halt. There was another noise beyond the rain and the thunder. The shout of the driver.

She pulled up the hood of her cloak and opened the door. The road was dark and slick with rain. Another flash of lightning, and for a moment Mr Warbon's whiskery outline was silhouetted against the white. He lifted his lamp, and she could see his face, dripping with rain, and fearful. His black oilskin was heavy with water and his wig and hat sat off kilter.

'Ma'am, this is no place for you. This storm… I've never seen one rise so fast and with such ferocity.'

'Mr Warbon, I must be in London. We cannot delay now.'

'Oh no, ma'am. We can go no further in this weather. We are stuck firm and will not make the next inn. We must wait here tonight and get some help first thing tomorrow. I'll tether the horses and sleep beneath the carriage.' The wind buffeted the words away.

Nancy remained tight-lipped. She could feel warm rain coursing down her back. With each heartbeat a second passed. *Tick. Tock.* It was looking increasingly unlikely that they would make it to London in time. The stars were, of course, hidden behind the thick cloud, which disorientated her.

There was nothing more she could do out here. Best to wait in the carriage. Taking a deep breath, she ran her hand through the sodden mess of her hair.

She needed to get to Caleb in time. The transit would start at fifteen after seven the following evening, and it was clear the carriage would move no further tonight. She bit her thumbnail. They were frustratingly close. Perhaps twenty miles from London. Each lightning strike lit up the outlines of three huge trees on the hill that rose next to them. It was late. If at all possible, she must get some sleep. She would need every fragment of concentration tomorrow.

Chapter Thirty-Two

As the sun rose, Nancy's eyes snapped open. Today. Everything rested on today. She had had little rest. Several times the crash of thunder had sounded terrifyingly close, and when, in the early hours of the morning, the storm had calmed, what lay in the day ahead filled her with bitter dread. Her back ached from trying to sleep propped up on the seat, and she was already perspiring. Despite the storm, the heat was still oppressive.

The driver's thudding feet sounded above her head, and his grunts told her he was hauling himself into the seat. She stuck her head out of the window. 'Mr Warbon, might we be moving?'

The coach pulled like an impatient dog and they were sailing again. She stuck her head out of the window. The sky was blue and calm, the heat blistering once more, steam rising from the fields.

They passed through marshes, still cracked and brown despite the storm, long-legged wading birds pecking eagerly at the puddles among the patches of sun-bleached grass. A few small children waved as the coach passed them by, but Nancy felt unable to return their greetings. All she could think about was the time, the seconds passing.

The sun was nearly overhead. Midday.

Then, in the distance, she saw it. The city, warping and bubbling through the thick, hot air. Her city. It looked tiny, a pile of boxes beneath a thick, black fug, distant over the brown flats. She shouted up to Mr Warbon, 'I see it! Faster, please, faster!' With a grunt, he whipped the horses harder, urging the coach onwards.

Nancy stared at her watch. One o'clock, two o'clock. Faster, faster.

She took her orange leather bag and rifled through it. A purse, the papers, her telescope, paper and pen.

Now they were tearing through Hoxton Fields, then the houses rose around them, the roads metalled and clanged beneath their wheels. Mr Warbon was making good on his promise, leaning forwards, urging on the horses. There was no compromising their speed. Mothers pulled small children out of their path, glowering as the black-and-yellow coach thundered past like an angry wasp. Ordinarily, Nancy would have been mortified, but now she was like a blinkered horse, focused solely on reaching Spitalfields. It was fifteen minutes before four o'clock.

'Norton Folgate! We are nearly upon it!' Mr Warbon's voice was hoarse. The houses here rose grand and tall, the pavements alive with men in shiny black-buckled shoes and breeches more colourful than she had seen in months. Their faces were pinched and unsmiling. A sharp right turn. 'Spittle Square! Here, here.'

The house was more handsome than she had anticipated. Five-storeyed, blue-shuttered windows as tall as a man, and built from rich brown-and-red brick. Mr Warbon helped her down from the carriage, and she hurried up the steps. She pulled the bell cord three times.

A lugubrious man clothed head-to-foot in black opened the door and peered over his glasses. 'Can I help?'

She had expected Caleb to answer the door. Her dress suddenly felt very grimy. 'Is Mr Malles at home?' she stammered. 'Please?'

The man looked her up and down. 'No. He is gone.'

Gone. Where could he have gone to? She brushed some dust from her skirts. 'Would you be so kind as to tell me where he is, please.'

The man sniffed and paused. 'I'm not sure I should vouch-safe that kind of information.'

Nancy kept as much sweetness in her voice as she could muster. 'It's very important. He's not well. I am a friend.' Tears pricked her eyes. Surely she would not fall at the final hurdle, just for the sake of one awkward footman.

The man grimaced, paused, and then, to her relief, nodded. 'You are right. I am most concerned about him. He seemed agitated, uncommonly frantic. He arrived unannounced last night, after not visiting for all this time, and bid me make ready the telescope that's been hidden in the back room these eight years. This morning he had me order a Hackney carriage to Greenwich.'

The revelation hit her like a clap of thunder. Now she was sure where he must be. Where it might all end. Her beloved Observatory. The spot just outside the city with an unsur-passed view of the sky. The place where time began and ended, filled with those awkward, brilliant minds.

Yet the Observatory would be full of people, buzzing... Dr Maskliss. Not somewhere surely that Caleb's activities would remain unobserved. Her mind whirred. That night they had spent stargazing, she had told him of her favourite place in London from which to view the stars. The roof of the Observatory. The place from which a person might see the whole arc of the sky without interruption.

'Thank you. I will do my best to get to him in time.' She took her watch from her pocket. It was 4p.m. Three short hours and fifteen minutes until the transit. She stumbled down the steps and called up to the driver.

'Mr Warbon, what chance have we of getting to Greenwich by seven?'

Turning, he grimaced and shook his head. 'Very little, ma'am. We have to travel through the city and across the bridge. The streets are terrible busy and slow.'

Nancy balled her fists in frustration, hot worry humming in her ears. 'I must be there. It's really as desperate a matter as you could imagine.'

With a tilt of his head, the driver regarded her solemnly. 'I can see it's urgent, ma'am. I really can.' He pushed back his hat. 'Perhaps there's another way. If we could get you to the north side of the river... down to Blackwall, or Poplar... then we could get the ferry across to Greenwich. I'd come back over an' bring your trunk round the long way, through the city, y'see?'

Nancy's heart leapt. 'That is a capital idea, Warbon! We must try.'

She climbed back into the carriage, and heard his 'Yip, yip' to the horses. The coach lurched away. Through the greasy slums of Bow they raced. 'Yip, yip!' Past the red brick church tower with its mighty bell that sounded across half of the city. Now the green smell of the river was in her nostrils, that familiar, dank and putrid tang. She was nearly home. Here was the chapel built by the East India Company and the large white houses of those who had made their fortune from trade. She shivered – buildings stained with the blood of those bought and sold in the slave trade. She thought of Mother's people.

Then they were at the docks, thick with ships, their masts like a forest of trees.

From nowhere, Nancy recalled some lines from *Macbeth*: 'Macbeth shall never vanquish'd be until Great Birnam Wood to high Dunsinane Hill shall come against him.'

Nancy thought of the man who would be King of Scotland, lulled into contented certainty of taking the Crown by the witches' duplicitous prophecy. Like him, she trusted them, enough to chase after Caleb to London. For a moment, she wondered if her faith in their intentions might be misplaced, that they might be deceiving her as they had done the Thane. They were, after all, *witches*. Yet Hecate seemed to have clear plans, and the trio's deference and respect for the darkest of goddesses were evident. That ancient graveyard-dweller had been their saviour, transforming each from mortal to immortal. Nancy had seen the debt each woman owed to the goddess, and her bidding had seemed to drive the three of them, bind them together, guide them towards this climax.

Poplar Docks buzzed with activity: men painting ships, the scrape of saws and the tap of hammers floated across the Thames. Stevedores, lumpers, lightermen. Nancy, however, looked beyond the tangled triangles of rope and mast, sail and beam and over the river. In the distance she could just see the hill above Greenwich, the clump of trees at the top. She pulled out her telescope and put it to her eye, bumpily sweeping the skyline, finding the white buildings that followed the line of the hill. Just a little higher. She focused the lens, but the Observatory was obscured by trees.

The coach skidded to a halt. 'Here! This is it!' Warbon shouted urgently, 'Come, ma'am. There's a chance you might make Greenwich in time.' She jumped down from the carriage, pulling her bag after her and stood in front of the carriage.

'I'm going to run to the ferry, Warbon.'

'But, ma'am, this is no place for a lady. Look!' He gestured about him. 'Please, let me come with you.'

'I'll be faster alone, and I need you to look after my trunk.' She reached up and patted the heavy wooden box strapped to the roof of the coach. 'There are important things in there.

And look at me. You know I'm more than capable of looking after myself.'

The man smiled wryly and shook his head. 'I do believe you are right.'

Nancy ran off, as fast as she could, shouting over her shoulder. 'I cannot thank you enough, Mr Warbon. I'll see you at Crooms!'

He patted the coach roof and whispered, 'At Greenwich, then, ma'am.'

Chapter Thirty-Three

Viewed from the Observatory, the Thames was twisted and bending. In autumn, shrouded in mist, Nancy had fancied the river to be a huge snake, its head westwards in the city, biting, snarling and noisy, while the tail slithered out east, into the sea.

The quayside was loud with activity: weasel-eyed men jumped between the ferries that bobbed alongside the quayside. Women with baskets, swarthy dockworkers and entire ragged families sat patiently in each boat, waiting for their turn to leave. Faces turned and fingers pointed as Nancy passed, her orange-and-lemon dress dragging along the dockside, thick with dust and grime.

'Excuse me,' she tapped one of the men on his shoulder, 'I need to get to Greenwich.'

He snorted. 'Nothing to Greenwich, love. Deptford's the best I can do in the next hour.'

Nancy gritted her teeth. Frustratingly, Deptford was beyond Greenwich, further up the river towards London. It must be at least fifteen minutes' drive back to the observatory. Time was getting tighter and tighter. However, she fancied she could hear her mother's voice in her head, urging her on: 'Forward, Nancy, forward. Keep moving!'

She nodded. 'Deptford must suffice.' She jumped onto the man's boat and found a space on a bench between a small boy with a cage on his knee holding a black cat that snarled at her and a fat priest, damp with perspiration, who smelled of gin and tobacco. He flashed her a tombstone smile, but she stared ahead.

The boat pulled away, and soon it was bobbing on the muddy waters of the Thames. The ferryman rowed with sinewy ease, his oars sliding expertly between the waves. Soon they were passing Greenwich, where the scrubbed white buildings of the Royal Hospital lined the side of the river. Their familiar porticos and domed towers – both topped with golden arrows that today were pointing north – were quite the grandest buildings she had seen in months, and, even in her dishevelled, frantic state, she swelled with pride at the elegance of her neighbourhood. When she was tiny, she would weave in and out of the hospital's towering columns and bowl her hoop along its pathways, but she had never seen it from the river. It looked almost like a grand ship, about to set sail. But the building held one last promise. She held her breath.

There. That view. For a few seconds, the entire, symmetrical arrangement swung into perfect alignment, as precise as the moon's orbit. She could see up the wide, rod-straight avenue that lay between the two main buildings that passed through the immaculate lawns, out beyond the formal gardens and up the hill beyond. She followed its straight line up into the sky. And there it was. Just to the right of the path at the very top of the hill. The sight she'd missed. That familiar, square building, all red-and-white bricks, domes and telescopes. The Observatory.

But there was no stopping here; they rowed swiftly on to muddy, flat Deptford where a set of green-mossed wooden steps led down from the dock. The ferryman jumped onto a small jetty at the bottom and secured the boat. He gave her his hand as she negotiated climbing from the rocking boat onto the platform.

'Thank you.' She indicated Greenwich, to the east, 'I need to get to the Observatory very urgently. Do you think I'll find a carriage?'

His forehead creased. 'I doubt it. Maybe. You might have to wait though. Two hours? Three perhaps.'

Nancy shook her head in frustration. 'I cannot. I must be in Greenwich as soon as possible. I'll walk.'

The man looked at her. 'You mustn't do that. This place is far too dangerous for a woman on her own.'

She shook her head. 'I have no choice.'

The docks clattered with the shouts of boatbuilders and the frenzied buzz of their saws cut through the fug of smoky, thick tar. Here were ships in all states of repair; some little more than a hull, others merely awaiting their final gilding. Each was aswarm with men heaving planks into place, varnishing, painting, making every vessel ready to glide down the river and into the wide world. Nancy had made a habit of lingering on the docks, dreaming of the final destinations of some of the finer boats, but today, she snaked through them, eyes focused beyond the chaos, barely noticing the rats scurrying around her skirts. Her thoughts were solely on getting to the Observatory.

She made her way through the yard, past the elegant brown-brick victualling buildings trimmed in white, and through the gates into Deptford. The din of the main road was disorientating at the best of times, but after months in the quiet of the Highlands, she felt as buffeted as a dandelion seed in a gale. It was like stepping into one of Mr Hogarth's paintings. Hawkers shouted in her face, grubby milkmaids sang loudly and out of tune, and barefooted children wove through the crowds.

At the side of the pavement a beggar waved his bloodied, bandaged stumps in a vain attempt to extract a few pennies from passers-by, his rotting limbs sending a revolting miasma into the air, although the smell was indistinguishable from the stink of the streets. Nancy's skirts brushed against the cobbles into the rotting vegetables and dirt, but she barely noticed. Her eyes darted up and down the street, but the ferryman had been right. There were no Hackneys to be had here.

She bit her lip in frustration. Time was running short. If she chose to wait for a carriage, she might be here for hours. Her mind whirred. It would take her about an hour to get to the observatory on foot. Wagering did not sit easily with her and there was too much at stake. She would have to walk.

These streets were not unfamiliar. Her father had often brought her down to the dockyard to watch the boats being built. Suspicious eyes looked her up and down, and she pulled her bag tight against her chest with every bump and barge.

Years of peering at the stars had fomented her keen sense of direction, and she had no doubts as to her route, but as she turned off the main thoroughfare and into the quieter backstreets, Nancy felt a prickle of worry. In the oppressively hot stillness, every noise threatened danger; a cutpurse or worse.

The city that less than an hour ago had felt so familiar was now hostile and alien. At this moment, she would have been happy to exchange the Thames for the River Ness. This underbelly of London suddenly felt merciless and cut-throat. She thought of the fan-clutching ladies that fluttered from salon to salon, scented kerchiefs jammed to their noses as they ignored the derelicts and lost souls groaning in the gutters while they rode fortified from brigands in their sedans and Hackneys. How often had she shut the blinds rather than look out on the squalor?

She pulled her hood over her head and kept her gaze down-wards. The cobbles were green and slippery, and the brackish fug of Deptford Creek lingered in the late-afternoon air. She could feel her heart beat faster and her breaths becoming heavier. In haste, her ankle twisted, and she stumbled. She didn't dare pull out her watch lest it got snatched but could feel time ticking away.

The tide was retreating, leaving flats of mud forested with the skeletons of abandoned hulks and smelling sharply of effluent and dead fish. A rickety wooden bridge crossed the creek next to the water mill, and she stumbled over it, gripping its railing tightly as her feet slid on its mossy planks.

Beams glinted in the yellow water pooled in the sludge. She turned and realised the sun was lower in the sky than she had imagined. Soon, Venus's silhouette would be tracking its way across its glare, opening the lock on the Fold, leaving the world as vulnerable as a mewling baby.

Caleb might even be atop the Observatory by now. She shivered at the thought of what he could be preparing.

As she reached the other side of the waterway, she broke into as much of a run as she could muster. Now her hood was thrown back, her bag banging on her thighs. She was aware that her muddied skirts and flushed face must make for an outlandish sight, but ignored the stares of the group of children standing slack-jawed on the corner and ran determinedly.

The buildings became more and more familiar. Queen Elizabeth College on her right, the Mitre Tavern on her left. The Saturday-evening sounds of shouting and singing filled the air, the smell of beer drifting across the street. Those sounds would float up the hill, through the window of Crooms. She was so close. Much as she wanted to run to the house, to smell the roses that tangled around its front door, to see Cora and bury her nose back in her own soft bed, she could not let herself be distracted.

Instead she took a left-hand turn and then entered the park through a gate. The guard nodded. She'd always had a pass, but was so well-known to the park-keepers that she'd never had to produce it.

And there was the Observatory. The sun was low behind the rows of elms that lined the terraces, its light filtering through their leaves and dappling the path in front of her. Somewhere over to the right was her favourite part of the park – the little spring that trickled from ancient rocks, battered cups placed ready for a hot day. Cora called it 'the Motherstone', and whispered that devil-worshippers had danced there for thousands of years.

Sweat trickled down her back. It was still hot, and her dress felt heavier and her lacing tighter than ever, as she ran as fast as she could. She had never moved at this pace for this long, and the hill was steeper than she remembered.

Her lungs roared with pain, but now she pushed faster up the slope. Her feet knew every incline, every furrow in the ground, her eyes every tree. The path curved up round to the right, and she looked up and shaded her eyes with one hand. Above her on the hill to the right stood the Observatory, its white edges gold in the evening sun. She peered at the roof, trying to ascertain if anyone was upon it. A few more steps and she'd be at the top of the hill. She slowed, suddenly fearful of what might await. Her breath came in huge, painful gasps, every fibre of her aflame with effort and hair sodden with sweat. She wiped her brow with her sleeve, but the dampness remained. Her skin felt slick and her clothing saturated.

She took out her watch. Six-thirty.

There was a side door in the observatory wall. She slipped through it, then looked at the red bricks of the building. The rose hedge was still there. Squeezing behind it, she found the green-painted door – unlocked, as ever – and the back staircase that led to the roof. She crept up the stone steps, familiar under her feet. As she reached the heavy door at the top, she paused. Behind it lay her secret, special place, on the roof of the world.

She knew what – *who* – would be there. She swallowed and turned the handle.

There, stood a figure, thin as a birch twig, clad in black. Caleb.

It was as if her feet were no longer touching the ground, as if she were gliding above the pavement towards him. As she approached, he raised one eyebrow, as if she was expected. 'Nancy. So you've decided to join me.'

Chapter Thirty-Four

Caleb's voice flowed like quicksilver. 'I should have known you'd follow me. That you'd track me down. I tried to get away, thought you were sure to stay in Scotland, with the wide, dark, wild skies. "Men at some time are masters of their fates: The fault, dear Nancy, is not in our stars, But in ourselves..."'

Nancy's feet touched earth again. Caleb stood beside a large telescope. His eyes gleamed with a raging fervour, while his cheekbones were sharp on his face, as if he had not eaten for weeks. He ran a hand through his hair and looked her up and down.

'Caleb, what on earth are you doing?'

He looked at her and laughed. 'I think you know exactly what I intend to do. And I would rather you had let me do it alone. But you chased me. You are here.'

Caleb took the salve from his pocket and held it up to the light, his eyes gleaming, 'The time is almost upon us.' Nancy felt fury rise in her at the thought of the salve being stolen from her locked trunk. She spoke through gritted teeth. 'This is foolish. You must stop.'

He put his finger to his lips and looked up at the sun, a wild grin on his face. 'We have little time left, but we're both ready for this, are we not? Can you feel the air? How heavy it is, how ripe? It feels as if the Earth has been waiting for this moment too.' He made an expansive gesture, indicating behind Nancy.

The atmosphere felt unbearably oppressive. Nancy was reluctant to turn away, but she followed his pointing finger and turned to look out at the view across the city. *Her* view. She leaned on the white balustrade. There was the river, wider and more pearlescent than she remembered. On its banks the white boxes of the hospital appeared to wobble in the heat. The Hawksmoors, the Wren spires poked up into the sky like jabbing fingers, and there, round and white and familiar as her own face was the dome of St Paul's Cathedral.

Surely it was her imagination, but the city seemed to warp skywards as she inhaled. The trees just below the ridge of the hill quivered, as if they were about to pull up their roots and move towards the Observatory.

Above them, the sun throbbed gently in the sky, bubbling a little at its edges, ready for its appointment with Venus. That planet might feel as she did; taut with anticipation and steeling itself for what was to come. On the horizon, a bank of dark cloud was starting to build. She didn't know if it was rage or fear that made her quiver so.

Behind her, a presence. She felt Caleb's breath on her neck. She didn't turn, and spoke as calmly as she could.

'It feels as if there's another storm brewing. But I don't think you really care for my thoughts.'

She turned to Caleb, the city wide behind her, the sun starting to sink towards the horizon. In the distance, a haze had formed.

'I've read everything, Caleb: your notes. Cassandra's papers. How did you find me, Caleb? How did you know about my interest in the Fold?'

Caleb smiled. 'Now, that, that really was down to fate, Nancy. For five years I wheeled in grief, bewildered. When I discovered her diary, everything started to make sense.'

'But you had no idea who Cassandra was writing to. You didn't know who E.L. was. How did you find out it was my mother?'

'It was here, Nancy. In the rooms beneath our feet. I was desperate, flailing around, trying to find answers. I knew of Cassandra's obsession with the Fold, and determined to find out more. Of course, as you know, I am no astronomer. So I sought out someone who might help me make sense of everything. The Astronomer Royal. Dr Maskliss.'

Nancy clasped her hand to her mouth. 'Maskliss? But he doesn't even believe in the Fold.'

'No, he doesn't. But he didn't have to. I came to visit, giving the name of Mr Scholes rather than my own. He had no suspicion I was a student of literature rather than mathematics. A little light flattery, a judiciously chosen gift of a fine bottle of rum – everyone vouchsafes a little more than they would like after rum – and then *such* revelations.'

Maskliss! Nancy shook her head.

'Oh, he scoffed and shook his head, but buried in the ridicule he told me all I had come to find, and more. That he had heard Elizabeth Lockaby talk of this ridiculous thing she named *the Fold*. E.L. Elizabeth Lockaby. He told me that she studied under James Bradley – J.B. Suddenly everything made sense.'

Nancy's eyes burned with loathing.

'And, of course, there was more. Elizabeth had a child, Nancy, who had continued her work. I could scarcely believe it. I felt for you so. Maskliss was so dismissive of you. Called you, "the human calculation machine", as if you were a piece of equipment. Then laughed as he told me about your theories. Theories that my darling Cassandra had sweated and toiled over too. Theories that only those with the most beautiful of minds could both imagine and have the wit and cleverness to document and shape. When he laughed at you, at your mother, he laughed at everything I held close to my heart. I knew you could not be happy in this place, and that Blackthistle would provide the sanctuary you needed. I easily managed to ascertain from him your whereabouts. That you were to be found at Crooms, in Greenwich.'

Nancy choked. 'So you tracked me down like a dog searching for a rabbit, then lured me to Blackthistle?'

He rubbed his forehead and stared at her. 'Perhaps I did not tell you the whole truth. But would you have believed me if I had told you? Would you not have run like that rabbit into its burrow?

Nancy could not damp down the fury rising inside her, 'But it was more than that! You needed the coordinates too! And you stole them from me!'

Caleb had the decency to look a little shame-faced. 'Of course, I suspected that, of all the souls in the world, you would have the piece of the puzzle I needed. Although, by God, I had to try hard – gifts, rum, flattery – you were that reluctant to let it slip from your fingers.'

'That didn't give you the right to take my work from a locked chest.' Nancy's voice had descended into a growl. 'Or to steal what else was in there.'

Caleb looked at the jar in his hand then back at Nancy. 'You had taken exactly the same path Cassandra had trodden before you. You had met the witches too. You really were exactly who I needed.

'You see, I wanted someone who might understand. Someone who could help me fathom what was happening. Someone with logic and reason, but whose mind might be unlocked, who was willing to look beyond the university library and out, into the stars. Someone who would help me detangle myself from the threads of fate, yet might come to believe in magic. Someone like Cassandra.'

This was the first time she'd heard him say his wife's name.

Caleb looked at her intently. 'I believe your mind has been unlocked, Nancy.'

Nancy thought of the woman who had first arrived at Blackthistle. Her rational reasoning, her brusque dismissal of anything not provable by calculation or hypothesis. Her rigorous analysis and utter conviction that the truth would only be found between the angles of sextants and the tick of watches. Now, as she felt the dying sun on her back, and the dread that roared louder with every second that passed, she shuddered at that woman's naivety.

For why else was she here if she didn't believe that magic might exist in this world? Had she not seen those women wield it? Had she not dived into far-off lands, seen her face in a painting hundreds of years old, travelled around the skies in a single night? Could she now finally allow herself to admit that these women were more than herbalists, wise women, root-workers?

Caleb was right – her mind had been unlocked. They *were* witches. Yet she would not give him that pleasure. Caleb had justified his deception, his lies, in such a selfish manner. He had put his longing for answers and justice above all.

'How can you defend such despicable actions? Perhaps if you had approached me in a straightforward manner—'

His nostrils flared. 'And run the risk of you taking fright and cutting me off completely? I couldn't risk that.' His eyes were wide. 'Cassandra, she—' Caleb's expression suggested he might be teetering on the brink of losing himself.

She reached out and touched his arm. 'Caleb, you must understand that Cassandra is not up there.' She tried to speak more gently. 'No-one really knows where your wife, your child might be, but I'm sure it's not in the Fold. I do know, however, that you would be a fool to try to prise open whatever lies above us. You have no idea of the danger and power that might lie behind it.'

Caleb moved closer and whispered,

'I am in blood
Stepp'd in so far that, should I wade no more,
Returning were as tedious as go o'er.'

His eyes glowed intensely.

'I know already of its power. It consumed Cassandra. And my Oliver.' His voice broke a little. 'But it will not consume me. And it will give them both back. Even if I must force it.'

He stepped towards her. Now they were only inches apart. Beads of sweat glistened on his forehead.

'Cassandra was cleverer than any of us knew. And she was sweet once too, full of light and colour and love.' He half-closed his eyes. 'But then the bleakness descended; the darkness that comes upon women after a child. She was lost, the waters closed over her head. She was only searching for the way out, a path back from her darkness towards the light.

'The witches, they were the ones who put ideas in her head. Who gave her whatever she needed in order to take that path. They taught her to scry, and she used that magic to look over your mother's shoulder and see her dreadful theories in full. They took her flying and showed her the salve.'

He pinched the top of his nose. 'All her thoughts were about that theoretical place where the stars wheel. When she thought that she might open it, it became an obsession. By then she was no longer Cassandra. She was lost to me, turned into a witch. They were the ones who sent her into that deathly abyss. And she took my boy with her! My dear, dear boy!'

Nancy's heart clenched. Caleb had been driven to the brink of insanity by grief. He imagined Cassandra and Oliver were in the Fold, and that they might still come back to him. She thought of the raw hurt she still felt at her parents' passing.

The darkness from which only Mr Bradley and Cora had been able to pull her. Yet that grief was something she must endure. It was the price she paid to be human and to feel, to love. The thought of putting countless others in peril, of lying, deceiving, merely to assuage her suffering, was unthinkable.

His voice faltered. 'She was already lost to me, her head was in the stars long before her mortal form followed. But my darling Oliver...' His face crumpled as he pulled the silver locket he always wore from its chain and opened it, thrusting it into Nancy's vision with shaking hands. Inside was a picture of a little boy with black curls and violet eyes. 'My little boy, lost beyond the firmament. Taken from me by those damn crones!'

Nancy's throat was dry. Here, laid bare, was the pain that drove Caleb, leading him to this horrible gamble. He must have guessed that by attempting to interfere with the Fold he would be endangering himself, perhaps many more people. Yet still he pursued this most ghastly of quixotic quests. Before her stood a desperate man who wanted his precious wife and son returned at any cost.

Through the folds of her dress she felt the watch in her pocket, the seconds ticking. They could only have minutes before the transit started and the Fold started to open.

'What are you going to do?'

'I'm going up there to find them. You showed me how. You made it apparent to me that I might use these precious hours when the Fold opens. This is my last chance to open that crack in the universe and get Cassie and Oliver back.'

Somewhere far below, the bell of St Alfege rang. It was a quarter-past-seven. The transit was about to begin.

Chapter Thirty-Five

Humility was part of the appeal of astronomy for Nancy. Galaxies, the heavens, stretched for hundreds of thousands of miles above their heads, and on the other side of the planet, moved elegantly and precisely in vast sweeps, while diligent astronomers below quietly watched and observed. If there was ever a discipline that shrank the self, stargazing was surely it. To feel that insignificance was soul-crushing to some, whereas others felt their religious convictions shatter into a million pieces as they realised the scale of the universe. She had seen clerics refuse to even handle a telescope.

Yet Nancy took the contrary point of view. Her heart soared at the thought of the thousands, millions of stars, suns and planets hanging silently in the skies beyond the vision of the men and women with their eyeglasses. What secrets they might hold, what civilisations might have already risen and fallen across those infinite miles. To think that Caleb might consider he could have some influence on those stars. Why, even the King himself would shake his head at the arrogance.

Now, as the transit was almost upon them, she felt sickness rise in her stomach and her legs buckle. It was as if she could feel the world tremble beneath her feet, panic-stricken at what might lie ahead.

'No. This cannot be, Caleb.' She turned and looked towards the sun. A gauzy cloud had settled in front of it, filtering its brightest light. There was no need for the smoked glass in her bag. She would watch the transit bare-eyed. She fancied that already she could see Venus nibbling at the edges of the fiery circle, commencing her six-hour journey. This was real magic. She could not tear her gaze away, yet she must try to reach Caleb.

Her voice rose. 'It's insanity! You cannot interfere with the cosmos. The women… Hecate told them it was perilous.'

The two of them stood side by side, both peering at the sun. He spoke agitatedly, 'Hecate?' He shook his head. 'Those *women* are but pure evil.'

Reluctantly, she tore her gaze away from the sun and fixed him with a steely gaze.

'You deceived me. You always knew who I was.'

He turned to her, his eyes haunted with guilt. There was a tremble in his voice, 'Your work is spectacular.'

Behind him, she could see the sun, smoked in cloud, and in front of it, the tiniest, tiniest black dot. The transit. How she had longed to see it again. It felt as if her life were hung around the transits, and the Fold. The Fold! She should be studying, noting, proving her supposition to be fact. Yet here she was.

Caleb pointed towards the sky, away from the sun, towards the north. Her spine tingled and she followed the line of his finger. In the distance, the sky wrinkled, as if it were frowning. She looked harder. The light, daytime sky darkened around the spot, midnight-blue billowed out like paint in water. The stars shone as brightly as if they were watching them from the fields at Blackthistle. Then slowly, almost imperceptibly at first, they started to swirl.

'It is coming!'

He was right. This time, the Fold was bolder, huge, visible to the naked eye. Nancy's mouth hung open at the sight. The Fold. It was real, and this time so enormous surely, everyone would see it. She had been right. So very right. For a moment, her heart soared.

She spoke deliberately. 'If you truly love them then you'll stay here. Keep your memory of Oliver safe, that locket next to your heart.'

Caleb shook his head in disbelief. 'But their places are here, beside me. Surely you understand? I am willing to do whatever it takes to take me to them. Whatever the price. I love them with a love that shall not die.'

The pain in his voice echoed as if he were standing on the edge of the vastest abyss. He took the jar of salve and held it against the sun.

His eyes were now completely black, speckled with tiny silver points of light. He started to mutter words Nancy recognised from *Macbeth*.

'Stars, hide your fires;
Let not light see my black and deep desires.
The eye wink at the hand; yet let that be
Which the eye fears, when it is done, to see.'

Caleb's voice was louder now, almost shouting. He tilted his head back and closed his eyes, dipped his long fingers in the jar and rubbed the salve roughly onto his throat and face.

She looked up. The Fold's darkness had started to bleed more urgently across the evening sky. Below, she saw people in the park turn and point at the swirl of blackness and stars that appeared to melt across the heavens. Kitchen hands spilled out of the building, shading their eyes and watching the dark whirl. This was a hundred times bigger than the last time it had appeared. It was terrible. Her nails dug into her hands.

In the black darkness, among the swirl Nancy could see something else. A crack, neat, as if cut by a surgeon's knife, spilling traces of cold light into the darkness. It throbbed as if it were keen to come undone.

It was time. Nancy swallowed. Hot resentment rose from her stomach into her throat, condensing into cold anger. Despite all his flattery Caleb had used her. She felt something pulse deep in her, from her stomach, up through her throat.

Throwing her arms wide, she looked to the threatening skies. Her voice spiralled from between her lips. She fancied she could see its trail, golden and sparkling like splintered gold. It rose upwards, reverberating against the leaden darkness that flooded the sky and seared across the city, shaking the church spires and down into the earth, causing the earth beneath her feet to rumble and quake.

'Daughter, Mother, Granny! Come to me, I beseech you!'

Chapter Thirty-Six

She leaned back on the balustrade, panting for breath, her chest and throat afire, and tore her eyes away from Caleb, away from the Fold. Clouds still shrouded the sun so she did not need the smoked viewer in her pocket. The tiny speck of Venus was determinedly making its crossing – the sight was elemental. Here were the fundaments of the universe, their interplay made clear, paths mapped in front of her eyes, with no need for charts or measurements. It was as if her textbooks had become corporeal.

Something else black flickered across the sun. Then something more. A cloud, perhaps. Swiftly, it grew, coming towards her. As it neared, she could make out individual dots, then wings; a huge mass of birds that seemed to stretch across the horizon. They blotted out the light, casting mottled shadows below, and now they were overhead. Nancy raised her face and spread her arms. She could feel the air in turmoil beneath their beating wings, the sound of the flapping like loose sails in a hurricane. Yet, unlike her first encounter with the crows, now she felt a calm strength.

She looked at Caleb. His face was contorted in rage. The birds began pulling at his hair, grasping his coat in their talons, pecking at his face, his eyes. He shook them loose. The birds started to squawk, bodies falling from the air in a tangle of black feathers, agonised caws echoing down the hillside. The smell of burned flesh and feather cauterised the air. The flock retreated high into the skies, leaving only three circling Caleb.

The crack was quivering harder now, with more light spilling through, and it seemed as if it were about to burst.

The three birds descended. They were huge, four times the size of a usual crow, glossy and with an oily rainbow sheen to their feathers – greens, purples and golds shining from the black. For a split second, their feet touched the ground, and, as they did, each bowed its head and tucked its wings close about its body. A shake, and a bend of the air, and three familiar figures emerged.

'You came!'

Relief surged through Nancy. There stood Daughter, Mother, Granny. Each wore black robes, made from a material that seemed so dark as to suck the light from around it. Their pupils were like dark craters and there was an ethereal glow about their faces, as if lit from the inside.

'You called and we came.' The glow faded, and the women were as flesh-bound as Nancy remembered.

Caleb screamed, 'You, Nancy, are one of them! Damn all you witches to hell!'

Nancy pointed towards Caleb. 'He would not listen to me! We must... How to stop him? To stop that? What's happening? It's so fierce, so huge!' She pointed up at the Fold.

The looked up. The Fold was bulging, as if something behind was pushing with all its strength. There was a terrible creaking, cracking sound, louder than any thunderclap Nancy had heard.

Wind swirled around them. It felt as if they were in the centre of a storm.

Granny shook her head and shouted above the din. 'This'll be why we were brought back this time. Looks like it's wilder, larger, more greedy than when you saw it, child. So dangerous.'

Daughter pointed. 'Look!'

Caleb's head was tilted back, his arms outstretched, barely aware of the world around him.

'He must not be allowed!' Nancy ran to Caleb, but the hurricane around him was too strong.

The three women clung to each other, buffeted by the gales. Nancy ran to join them, head down, hair streaming in the wind. She walked as if through water, agonising step by agonising step, each more effortful. After what seemed like minutes, she grabbed Daughter's hand. As Daughter pulled her close she felt a jolt of energy, as if she'd been filled with white heat. The four wrapped their arms around each other's shoulders, all faces turned towards Caleb. It seemed as if he were gathering his energy, working up power to take flight.

Nancy felt subsumed, as if she'd melted into the other women. Caleb was right. For now, she felt as if she were one of the witches. As Granny raised her staff, she felt its knobbled surface as if it were in her own hand. Their vision was her vision. Their thoughts coursed through her head. Their memories combined and crashed into her vision. They spoke together, urgently, rhythmically,

> 'Spirits from the moor and tor,
> Barrow's dead and harrow's gore,
> From underneath the yew and dew,
> Ghosts arise, walk swift and true.'

They repeated the rhyme over and over, building it into a droning incantation, layered in harmonies.

Caleb shook his head. 'Your parlour tricks will not work on me. See, it opens!' Nancy followed the streak of light. The crack had started to split. Light spilled brightly across the sky. It appeared close to them now, coming lower in the sky.

Nancy felt the witches pull her more tightly into their circle. Thoughts surged through them. 'He is too strong. We are lost. We are lost.'

'No.' Mother pulled them even closer and a flash of energy rippled through the women. Mother shouted, 'We are stronger! Draw deep, draw together!' She started to stamp her foot rhythmically, beating out the same pattern her drummers had set centuries, millennia before.

Caleb threw his head back further. The sky was now almost entirely dark, a Sargasso Sea of stars, whirling slowly in a spiral; at their centre, the crack of the Fold widening, opening. It seemed only a few hundred yards away now, and getting closer by the second.

Nancy closed her eyes. She could not contemplate the horror that was about to happen. The Fold was nearing, dreadful. The chant of the witches was in her ears, the rhythm insistent. The crack widened, light pouring out in broad beams against the black sky. It opened like a jaw, ready to swallow. Nancy shook her head. This, then, was how it would end. She took one last look at the sun, at Venus, and drank it all in.

The witches threw back their heads and screamed, their voices splitting, a choir of agony, their cries shaking the earth.

Through the wind and the shaking, on the other side of the roof, she saw two points of light, two lanterns. A figure, dressed in dark, flowing robes. The witches' embrace grew tighter, and they inhaled together, holding their breath inside their lungs lest it blew away the delicate sight.

Hecate.

She advanced slowly, as if moved by some titanic, unseen hand, her robes fluttering in the gale. The witches, fingers dug into Nancy's back, her shoulders, her arms.

'She came,' said Daughter. 'She is come.'

Hecate looked calmly at the agonised figure of Caleb.

The witches' chants grew louder, the fractured harmonics so harsh that Nancy worried her ears might bleed. Their robes billowed in the hurricane, eyes wide and focused on Caleb, sparks spitting from their fingers towards him.

'Double, double toil and trouble;
Fire burn, and cauldron bubble.'

The familiar phrase echoed around the crest of the hill. Every brick of the observatory below their feet shook at the roar, as if Jericho was about to fall.

Then, the witches screamed. With a fury and power beyond thunder and lightning, beyond the skies. It felt as if they were channelling all of the anger that might be summoned from their existences, remembering every slight, every slash of the whip, every dismissal, every punch and blow they had suffered. Caleb, knocked by the tumult, looked upwards, his hair streaming in the wind.

Nancy screamed, 'Caleb, stop!'

She glanced across at the shadowy figure of Hecate. Her finger was raised, pointing at Caleb. Nancy's nails dug into her hand, as against the tempest, she tore herself free from the women, put her head down and walked painfully, slowly towards him. The force of the wind blew back her hair, her clothes, but, inch by inch, she gained ground. Behind her, the witches' shrieks faded into the tumult.

Suddenly it felt quiet enough to speak, as if they were in a bubble, insulated from the babel. 'Caleb, please.'

He tore his gaze from the Fold and looked her in the eye. 'Nancy, this is my only chance to take back those who were torn from me.'

Tears coursed down her cheeks. 'They weren't torn, Caleb. Cassandra took Oliver and left this world, but not into the Fold. Mrs McLoone kept it from you, but—' She pulled the locket from the folds of her dress and held it up to him. 'They found Cassandra's locket on the beach. You will not find them beyond.'

Somewhere behind the blur of tears in his eyes she saw the faint spark of reason. 'I can't, Nancy. I must try.'

'You can.' She glanced at Hecate. She felt a power, a dark, cobwebbed ancient force that she knew instinctively originated from inside her. There was no spell, it was not magic. This was a power seeded by her parents, and born through years of late nights studying alone, years of defying snide remarks, years of following her own path.

And Nancy knew she might stop Caleb. She might not have magic in her veins, sparks did not trail from her fingertips, but she had reason, she had experience, and she felt that power rise inside her.

'Caleb, I have no more regard for my reputation. I know that around me I can see magic, and I care not that I shall be ridiculed for saying so. I have seen crows that are women. I have flown among the stars and see? There is Hecate herself! Six months ago, I would have laughed at such a thought. Who knows, I might be going insane. Yet I am willing to wager my reputation on trying to stop you. Because when I look up, I see something fearsome. Look at it!' She jabbed a finger upwards. 'I know that the world is not strong enough to bear such power. Why would you want to put what we have here in peril, just so your agony might be assuaged? I know that at heart, you're a good man, Caleb. I know you are driven and drowned by your agonies. But don't let yourself be consumed by them. Let them rest.'

She stepped back, tears running down her cheeks.

Caleb shook his head. 'I'm sorry, Nancy.' He looked up once more. For a moment, it seemed as if his feet left the floor, as if he were starting to drift upwards.

The world shuddered. Then a stream of lightning flashed through the sky, louder than anything she'd heard in her life. For a brief moment Caleb was bathed in white light, more pained, more vulnerable than ever. He looked down at Nancy, his eyes full of frustration, fear. Then they softened and he relaxed his body, as if in acceptance, and fell down onto the stone tiles.

Slowly at first, the whirling stars and the darkness started to leach from the sky, to fade back into where the crack had been.

Granny made a quiet moan. 'It is done.'

In a breath, the rift started to seal itself, sputtering a little, as if reluctant to close, but then shut tightly. The wind and noise dropped, and the world became silent.

On the ground next to Caleb lay his locket, the chain broken. His eyes were open to the sky, a smile across his lips. He looked finally at peace. Her cheeks shining with tears, Nancy picked up the necklace and put it on his still chest, then took Cassandra's locket and placed it next to his. Then she crumpled on the ground, a heap of dirty cotton linen, heavy flesh and saltwater. She sobbed hard, her heart heaving out of control, her lungs wracked with pain.

Through her tears she looked to the sun, Venus still doggedly tracking across its face, then the cloud slowly obscured her view. Hidden or in sight, Venus would continue her voyage. But Caleb's tortured journey was complete.

A clap of thunder. Real thunder, as if the world was reasserting its authority, and then the rain started to fall. Slowly at first, then a torrent, washing the heat from the air. A clean wet scent rose from the slaked earth below. She brought herself to her feet.

The witches gathered, holding Nancy tightly, forming a tight, unbreakable circle, and stood in the deluge, their robes soaked and sticking to their skin, faces running with tears and raindrops.

Chapter Thirty-Seven

Thirteen months later

Nancy stood in the dark, looking across a lit stage from behind a thick red curtain. In one hand she held a sheaf of papers, in the other, a pen. She felt a tug of nerves in the pit of her stomach. The air was warm, and a hubbub of voices bubbled up from an excited crowd. She peeped out. There was Mr Peter Dollond, holding court, while in the seats in the back were a few of her Bluestocking friends. And there, in the front row, sat an imperious King George in ivory silks. She closed her eyes and thought back over the previous thirteen months.

She hadn't visited the Observatory since that dreadful day. Cora told her of the seared grass and scorch marks on the roof that had been pored over by those in the Observatory brave enough to consider what might have happened. The rain would have washed them away by now, but Nancy had no wish to be reminded of the events of the previous June. Even the thought of looking out at that view from the hill made her feel heavy-hearted. Every dome, every spire, that wide horizon, was etched into her memory, forever connected to that night.

The witches had left soon after the transit.

'We cannot stay any longer,' said Mother, stroking her hair. 'I feel for you, child. To see the Scholar like that, it was cruel. But it had to be. You will feel vulnerable in this moment. That sadness will remain perhaps forever. But Hecate's bidding has been done – the world keeps spinning, and we must all return to where we are meant to be.'

'We must go,' Granny said. 'My heart aches for my people and I miss my little wooden house on the side of the mountain.'

'We will be together again. I'm certain,' Daughter had reassured her. 'Might not be in your lifetime, right enough, but Hecate will call.' She had gripped Nancy's hand. 'And we'll never be too far. Keep one eye open for the crows.'

'I will bow to every crow I see.' Nancy shook her head, suddenly aware of how weary she was. Every bone of her sang in agony, and she could barely keep her eyelids from drooping. 'It has been an extraordinary time. What of Caleb?'

'Shhhh.' Granny put a finger to her lips.

It had been hard to walk away from them, back down the hill to what now felt like a solitary, small life at Crooms.

Cora had opened the door, her face immediately creasing in panic. Nancy's hair was clogged with sweat, her skirts brown with grime. The maid had caught her as she staggered over the threshold and had near-carried her to her bath.

Her voice was high-pitched with fear. 'Oh, ma'am. What's happened to you? We had no idea you'd come back. You were at… at the centre of all that? That thing in the skies? Let's get you clean.'

As Cora washed away the grime, Nancy, through sobs, recounted the entire story. Cora's eyes grew wide, and Nancy worried that her head might come loose, she was shaking it so hard.

'I can scarcely believe it. Magic! Hecate! Witches! But you was always such a stickler for facts.'

The household had taken every newspaper for the next two weeks until Nancy told Cora firmly to stop. They had been full of stories of the Fold. Only they called it 'The Chasm in the

Sky'. The *Evening Post* suggested that: 'Most of the country had put down their evening cups, ploughs had stilled, and the streets were full of people gazing at this most dreadful sight.'

The Archbishop of Durham had preached a sermon the next morning suggesting that it was a portent, and that the people of England should expect a new saviour to be walking among them 'within twenty years', and that 'anyone who witnessed the Chasm will have had their faith in God confirmed, for surely, this was his hand'.

Dr Maskliss had come, banging on the door, demanding to speak to her, soliciting her help. But Nancy had pulled her pillow over her head and ignored his cries. Later, she had politely sent word up the hill that she required the return of her father's equipment.

Over the next month, stories flooded in from across Europe of the rift that had hovered so threateningly above the continent. Germans called it the *Wirbel im Himmel* while the French named it the *Porte Céleste*. Nancy had, in the little store near the docks, caught a unwanted glimpse of the notorious engraving by Mr William Austin that portrayed church figures and scientists fleeing in terror as a jaw-like hole hung over their heads, and bawdy songs about the Chasm floated from every tavern window.

For a few weeks, the pain of that night, of Caleb's death, was needle-sharp. Each morning there had been a blissful few seconds of sunlight and fresh sheets, and a new day before the memories and despair swept the sunny thoughts away like wooden houses in a flood. She had taken to spending her waking hours in darkness, awakening in the crepuscular late afternoon.

But slowly, like waves wearing the sharpness of a flint to a round pebble, the intensity of that evening faded, the loss a dull ache rather than a stab.

A month after that dreadful night, a crate had arrived. It was full of books. Cassandra and Caleb's books. A note sitting on top of them from Mrs McLoone explained that she knew of no better custodian.

The books now sat on the shelves of the library where, when the sun streamed through the windows, they looked just as any other tomes, no different from her Flamsteeds and Halleys. Yet by candlelight they flickered with possibilities and a trace of menace. One day Nancy was sure that she would immerse herself in them, that they might bring her closer to Cassandra and Caleb, that their philosophies, enchantments and alchemy would fuse with her knowledge of established science and she would make sense of what had happened. But for now, she would leave them unread.

She had not seen Granny, Mother or Daughter since that fateful day. Yet there were enough traces of them to bring a faint smile to her lips. The sea glass deposited on Crooms' sundial, presumably by a passing crow. A rough corn dolly that was left on the front step. And, one magical night, a clear sighting of the dancing, wavering northern lights, bobbing as if someone far, far north of her was shining a lantern onto the sky.

Eventually Nancy felt able to take newspapers and journals once more. Scientists had struggled to make sense of what, indisputably, northern Europe had seen. In Switzerland, Mr Lambert suggested it was a large comet, whereas Mr Lexell was convinced it was the tumult that had resulted after a planet had exploded. Dr Maskliss had spoken to the *Gazetteer and New Daily Advertiser* and declared it was, 'Some kind of rift, a *Fold*, if you will', which infuriated Nancy so much she ripped up the paper and used it as kindling.

It was as it lay in the grate, blowing into ashes that there was a knock at the door. Cora came racing up the stair. Nancy had taken the girl on as a second housemaid, and already she sported the highest hair in Greenwich, 'Ma'am, it's a man. Mr Ferguson. James Ferguson. He says that it's of the utmost importance he speaks to you.'

★

Nancy looked at her watch. The hubbub in the crowd died down. A hand on her shoulder. She turned.

'Good luck, my dear,' said Mr Ferguson.

On his first visit to Crooms, he had explained to Nancy about the guilt he'd felt since the night of the first transit. All those years ago. 'You were but a slip of a girl,' he said sadly. 'A girl who was transported by her conviction. A girl who I believed.' He told Nancy of his shame that he had not stepped in to defend her, to ask her more, to stop Maskliss' derision.

He told Nancy how their encounter, the night of the first transit in Maskliss' office, continued to burn quietly in his mind. How, years later, when he had seen a copy of *On an Anomaly* tossed onto a table in the Observatory, he had asked Maskliss for it, shamefacedly explaining that he'd had to tell him he wanted something to laugh at on the journey home. He told Nancy of his fascination with her work, how he had recalculated and checked her calculations, her mother's equations, and that they had added up. How he had tried to contact her in Scotland but had heard nothing back. Nancy remembered the empty envelope in Caleb's study.

On the night of the transit, he had been ready. There, like her, with telescope and the coordinates. He had gasped as the Fold ripped open the sky but he had taken measurements, charted, observed as calmly as he could. And how, as the Fold closed, he could not stop thinking of her and how, finally, her theories had been proven.

The crowd had stilled. She smiled at Mr Ferguson and looked down at the papers in her hands. They were freshly printed, smelling of ink. On the cover, in Caslon typeface, the title: *An Account of the Fold: A Study of Astronomy and the Exclusion of the Female Sex in a Letter by Nancy Lockaby, Cassandra Malles and James Ferguson.* He had insisted his name be last on the paper. She squeezed the publications tightly as she heard her introduction.

'And, so tonight we present a very special lecture. The Royal Society has made the most notable exception in its history. We welcome, for the first time, a woman to give a talk. Miss Lockaby will tonight explain her newest discovery and fascinating hypotheses, as she tells us of the Fold, and what she describes as her theories of space tunnels.'

Nancy turned and whispered to Mr Ferguson. 'You know, seeing the Fold up there, in the sky, hanging above us, wasn't that the most magical experience?'

He laughed. 'Magical? That's not the word I'd use for it, Miss Lockaby. As you know, we explained it all with mathematics.'

Nancy wrinkled her nose and smiled, and for a moment, it appeared to Mr Ferguson as if her eyes swam with stars.

Blinking, Nancy walked into the bright lights of the stage and took her place at the lectern.

Historical note

While many of the figures and events in the book are real, the character of Dr Maskliss is a combination of two Astronomers Royal; Nevil Maskelyne and Nathaniel Bliss.

Many, many thanks to Lily at Hodder, for her never-ending patience and encouragement, Gale Winskill for her sensitive editing, my agent Juliet Pickering at Blake Friedmann for her continued support and advice and Thorne Ryan for her enthusiasm and huge contributions. Thanks also to Will Speed, Katy Blott and Emily Goulding at Hodder for their work on the book.

Thanks also to Arthur, Dusty (sorry your contribution didn't make the final cut), Dad and Jeff for their love, to Sarra for her sympathetic ear, The Hare and Hoofe and Ye Nuns, and to Loulou for tea and sanity saving crafts.

A grateful hat-tip to The Science Museum's Science City 1550-1800 exhibition, and the Greenwich and Herstmonceux Observatories.